SIMP
SONI
STAS

VOL. 5

SIMP
SONI
STAS
VOL. 5

Tales from New Literary Project

SIMP SONI STAS
VOL. 5

EDITED BY JOSEPH DI PRISCO

RARE BIRD
LOS ANGELES, CALIF.

RARE BIRD

Set in Minion
Printed in the United States

Proceeds from book sales go toward supporting the work of
the nonprofit New Literary Project, newliteraryproject.org

10 9 8 7 6 5 4 3 2 1

Library of Congress Cataloging-in-Publication Data available upon request

Dedicated to
Simpson Fellows,
Iris Starn Fellows,
Bonnie Bonetti-Bell Fellows,
Jack Hazard Fellows
Past, Present, & Future

WHAT WE DO

Arts
Education
Lifts Up Everyone

Free
Creative Writing
Workshops for
Teenage Writers

Joyce Carol
Oates Prize:
National Recognition
for
Mid-Career Authors

NEW LITERARY PROJECT

WRITE YOUR HEART OUT

Teaching
Opportunities for
Cal & Saint Mary's
Grad Students

Fellowships
for
Creative Writers
who Teach
High School

Annual Anthology:
Simpsonistas

FOLLOW US FOR MORE

CONTENTS

PERMISSIONS

PEOPLE, PLACES, & THINGS
A MISCELLANY

The University of California, Berkeley, English Department. english.berkeley.edu/

Department Chairs, 2015–2023:
Prof. Genaro Padilla, Prof. Steven Justice, Prof. Ian Duncan, Prof. Eric Falci
The University of California, Berkeley. berkeley.edu/

Simpson Project Writing Workshops, Spring 2022—

Cal Prep. The Aspire Richmond California College Preparatory Academy is a public charter and early college secondary school, cofounded by University of California, Berkeley, and Aspire Public Schools. Tatiana Lim-Breitbart, Principal.

Contra Costa County Juvenile Hall, Martinez, California; Mt. McKinley High School, Contra Costa County Office of Education. Brian Murtagh, Principal.

Girls Inc. of Alameda County; Julayne Virgil, CEO; Gabi Reyes-Acosta, Jazmin Noble, Aja Holland, Carina Silva. girlsinc-alameda.org/

Northgate High School, Mount Diablo Unified School District; David Wood, faculty; northgatehighschool.org/

Iris Starn Writing Workshops, Spring 2023

Emery High School, Emeryville, California; Molly Montgomery, Teacher & Workshop Coordinator.

Simpson Fellows: Workshop Leaders 2017–2023
University of California, Berkeley, English Department—
To be known as Bonnie Bonetti-Bell Fellows, starting in 2024, generously sustained by James Bell.

Prof. Fiona McFarlane, Director

Uttara Chintamani Chaudhuri

Frank Cruz

Katherine Ding

Delarys Ramos Estrada

Lise Gaston

John James

Naima Karczmar

Mehak Faisal Khan

andy david king

Ryan Lackey

Jessica Laser

Ismail Muhammad

Laura Ritland

Alex Ullman

Noah Warren

Rosetta Young

Iris Starn Fellows: Workshop Leaders, 2023
Saint Mary's College of California, MFA Creative Writing Program
Generously sustained by the Starn Family
Prof. Chris Feliciano Arnold, Director
https://www.stmarys-ca.edu/graduate-professional-studies/mfa-creative-writing

Camila Elizabet Aguirre Aguilar

Carly Blackwell

Jack Hazard Fellows
Creative Writers Teaching High School
Summer Writing Fellowship
Generously sustained by System Property Development Company
Prof. Ian Maloney, St. Francis College, Brooklyn; Director

2023 Jack Hazard Fellows

William Archila
STEAM Virtual Academy
Los Angeles, CA

Victoria María Castells
Miami Arts Charter School
Miami, FL

Leticia Del Toro
Campolindo High School
Moraga, CA

Elizabeth DiNuzzo
The Albany Academies
Albany, NY

11

t'ai freedom ford
Benjamin Banneker Academy
Brooklyn, NY

Emily Y. Harnett
The Haverford School
Haverford, PA

Jeff Kass
Pioneer High School
Ann Arbor, MI

Ariana D. Kelly
Boston University Academy
Boston, MA

Kate McQuade
Phillips Academy
Andover, MA

Tyson Morgan
Crystal Springs Uplands School
Hillsborough, CA

Shareen K. Murayama
Henry J. Kaiser High School
Honolulu, HI

Sahar Mustafah
Homewood-Flossmoor High School
Flossmoor, IL

Ky-Phong Tran
Long Beach Renaissance High School for the Arts
Long Beach, CA

Vernon Clifford Wilson
Horace Mann School
Bronx, NY

2022 Jack Hazard Fellows (California)

Kevin Allardice
Albany High School, Albany

Julie T. Anderson
The College Preparatory School, Oakland

Armando Batista
Pacific Ridge School, Carlsbad

Adam O. Davis
The Bishop's School, La Jolla

Sheila Madary
Saint Mary's High School, Stockton

Molly Montgomery
Emery High School, Emeryville

Mehnaz Sahibzada
New Roads School, Santa Monica

Andy Spear
Head-Royce School, Oakland

Tori Sciacca
Richmond High School, Richmond

Simpsonista Award

Honoring extraordinary people who give voice to storytellers across the generations.
Michael Krasny, 2020
Public radio host, author, professor
Julayne Virgil, 2021
CEO of Girls Inc. Alameda County; not-for-profit visionary leader

Joyce Carol Oates Prize
2017–2023

Awarded annually, $50,000, not for a book, but to a distinguished mid-career author of fiction, that is, one who has emerged and is still emerging.

2023 Finalists

Rabih Alameddine

Clare Beams

James Hannaham

David Means

Manuel Muñoz (Prize Recipient)

Longlist & Most Recent Book of Fiction

Rabih Alameddine, *The Wrong End of the Telescope* (Grove Atlantic)

Kali Fajardo-Anstine, *Woman of Light* (One World)

Elif Batuman, *EITHER/OR* (Penguin Press)

Louis Bayard, *Jackie & Me* (Algonquin)

13

Clare Beams, *The Illness Lesson* (Doubleday)

Megan Mayhew Bergman, *How Strange A Season* (Scribner)

Francesca Lia Block, *House of Hearts* (Rare Bird)

Maud Casey, *City of Incurable Women* (Bellevue)

Myriam J. A. Chancy, *What Storm, What Thunder* (Tin House)

Lan Samantha Chang, *The Family Chao* (Norton)

Angie Cruz, *How Not to Drown in a Glass of Water* (Flatiron)

Alice Elliott Dark, *Fellowship Point* (Scribner)

Stacey D'Erasmo, *The Complicities* (Algonquin)

Hernan Diaz, *Trust* (Riverhead)

Jonathan Evison, *Small World: A Novel* (Dutton)

Kim Fu, *Lesser Known Monsters of the 21st Century* (Tin House)

Francisco Goldman, *Monkey Boy* (Grove Atlantic)

Mohsin Hamid, *The Last White Man* (Riverhead)

James Hannaham, *Didn't Nobody Give a Shit What Happened to Carlotta* (Little, Brown)

Annie Hartnett, *Unlikely Animals* (Ballantine)

Vanessa Hua, *Forbidden City* (Ballantine)

Lily King, *Five Tuesdays in Winter* (Grove Atlantic)

Lucy Ives, *Life Is Everywhere* (Graywolf)

Adam Langer, *Cyclorama: A Novel* (Bloomsbury)

Zachary Lazar, *The Apartment on Calle Uruguay* (Catapult)

David Means, *Two Nurses, Smoking* (FSG)

Manuel Muñoz, *The Consequences* (Graywolf)

Celeste Ng, *Our Missing Hearts* (Penguin Press)

Margaret Wilkerson Sexton, *On the Rooftop* (Ecco)

Gary Shteyngart, *Our Country Friends* (Random House)

Namwali Serpell, *The Furrows* (Hogarth)

Lynn Steger Strong, *Flight* (Mariner)

2022 Finalists

Christopher Beha

Percival Everett

Lauren Groff (Prize Recipient)

Katie Kitamura

Jason Mott

2021 Finalists

Danielle Evans (Prize Recipient)

Jenny Offill

Darin Strauss

Lysley Tenorio

2020 Finalists

Chris Bachelder

Maria Dahvana Headley

Rebecca Makkai

Daniel Mason (Prize Recipient)

Peter Orner

Dexter Palmer

Kevin Wilson

2019 Finalists

Rachel Kushner

Laila Lalami (Prize Recipient)

Valeria Luiselli

Sigrid Nunez

Anne Raeff

Amor Towles

2018 Finalists

Ben Fountain

Samantha Hunt

Karan Mahajan

Anthony Marra (Prize Recipient)

Martin Pousson

2019 Finalists

T. Geronimo Johnson (Prize Recipient)

Valeria Luiselli

Lori Ostlund

Dana Spiotta

Joyce Carol Prize Longlisted Authors' Publishers: 2017–2023
(with number of their authors listed)

270 Longlisted Authors

50 Publishers

35 Finalists

7 Prize Winners (6 houses)

Algonquin (10)

Back Bay (1)

Ballantine (2)

Bellevue Literary (4)

Bloomsbury (6)

Catapult (4)

Celadon (1)

Coffee House (1)

Counterpoint (11)

Custom House (1)

Delphinium (1)

Dial (2)

Doubleday (5)

Dutton (3)

Dzanc (1)

Ecco (18)

Elixir (1)

Flatiron (2)

FSG (14)

Grand Central (1)

Graywolf (9) **(2023 Prize Recipient)**

Grove Atlantic (7)

Harper Collins/William Morrow (3) **(2017 Prize Recipient)**

Henry Holt (1)

Hogarth (4) **(2018 Prize Recipient)**

Houghton Mifflin (4)

Knopf (11)

Little, Brown (15) **(2020 Prize Recipient)**

Mariner (2)

MCD (7)

Melville House (1)

Nan A. Talese (1)

New York Review of Books (1)

Norton (8)

One World (1)

Pantheon (2) **(2019 Prize Recipient)**

Penguin (16)

Picador (2)

Putnam (6)

Random House (7)

Rare Bird (3)

Riverhead (26) **(2021 and 2022 Prize Recipients)**

Scribner (3)

Simon & Schuster (5)

Soft Skull (1)

Soho (4)

St Martin (4)

Tim Duggan (1)

Tin House (4)

Viking (6)

Jurors (in rotation) for the Joyce Carol Oates Prize 2017-2023:

Heidi Benson

Anne Cain

Laura Cogan

Professor Mark Danner

Joseph Di Prisco

Professor Joshua Gang

Jane Hu

Professor Donna Jones

Regan McMahon

Professor Geoffrey O'Brien

Professor Katherine Snyder

David Wood

Professor Dora Zhang

Judges for the Joyce Carol Oates Prize:

New Literary Project Board of Directors

Board of Directors

Joseph Di Prisco, Chair, Author, & Educator

Diane Del Signore, Executive Director

Shanti Ariker, Senior Vice President, General Counsel, Zendesk, Inc.

James Bell, Founder & Chairman, Bell Investment Advisors; Community Leader

Uttara Chintamani Chaudhuri, PhD Candidate, UC Berkeley English; Simpson Fellow; Creative Writing Teacher.

Laura Cogan, Editor and Consultant

Ian Duncan, English Department Chair Emeritus, UC Berkeley; Florence Green Bixby Professor of English

Eric Falci, English Department Chair, UC Berkeley

John Murray, Author and Associate Professor (Teaching), University of Southern California

Joyce Carol Oates (Honorary Director), Author and Professor of Humanities, Princeton University

Michael Ross, Author, US & International Law School & University Lecturer

PREFACE

Welcome to *Simpsonistas: Tales from New Literary Project. Vol. 5*. The pleasure of the company of Manuel Muñoz, 2023 Joyce Carol Oates Prize Recipient, awaits you. He is represented by one of his justly celebrated short stories as well as his moving meditation about teaching creative writing, and he appears alongside other major writers like Joyce Carol Oates, David Means, and Mark Danner, among others. Here at the outset, though, I also very much wish to call other selections to your attention. These are pieces by young writers whose names you won't recognize, and some by writers whose names we actually cannot share, but whose work is as rewarding as it is harrowing. Particularly unforgettable pieces were composed by teenage students from juvenile hall. These young men participated in a Simpson Writing Workshop conducted by New Literary Project in partnership with the University of California, Berkeley, English Department.

Running a creative writing program within an institution such as juvenile hall presents us with provocative challenges. In the course of editing the newest volume of *Simpsonistas*, two poems I found especially striking and original were redacted by corrections authorities. Why were these two poems so concerning to them? I cannot say for sure. I do know that my critical reading of the work finds a writer animated by regret, sadness, and resolve, one who expresses himself candidly, insightfully, with authentic literary and psychological nuance. Yes, a personified gun does make an appearance in these lines, a factor that for all I know may have informed the authorities' judgment. But the gun is not figured as something to be reveled in, not as a menacing gesture, not in order to glorify violence, but instead as a vehicle of self-criticism and soul-searching. There may well have been zero-tolerance considerations, not articulated, that arguably impinge upon the authorities and led to their decision.

An editorial hurdle like this registers for us in ways that go far beyond the editorial. On one level, the response of these juvenile hall students is pedagogically heartening to behold—and revelatory. They responded. They did the work. They wrote. On another somehow more complex level, this redaction in and of itself underscores the urgency of New Literary Project and deepens our desire to work with a great cross-section of youth, including the incarcerated. To put this in the largest context, and as expressed by William Carlos Williams, "It is difficult to get the news from poems, yet men die miserably every day for lack of what is found there."

The reality is, in juvenile hall personal rights are radically restricted for what seem by most lights to be justifiable reasons. Within its confines, the risk of dehumanization is high and runs counter to the intended mission of rehabilitation. In this context, the value of time these students spent in reflection and composition (as well as the imaginative investment of readers like you) is simply immeasurable. We cannot assess the precise impact of their creative endeavors, but we do know that the poets and the poems' readers will never be the same.

It is important for us to note that we do sincerely acknowledge and appreciate that correction authorities have permitted us to publish the work from juvenile hall that appears in this volume—as we continually hear that these young men eagerly desire to see themselves represented on the page. We honor their writing generated under extreme circumstances of incarceration, as we have for other workshop students from juvenile hall in the four previous volumes of *Simpsonistas*.

Still, I find myself haunted by the echoing sounds of those two poems by one young man we were not permitted to publish. So many questions resonate. I readily concede the authorities are positioned to assess his status as an offender as I am not. My belief in the value of reading his work should not indicate I am naïve about him or any other young men in the workshop. I am doubtful any of them are saints, and in any case, what I know about saints from my Catholic underpinnings is that they are rarely pure and blameless, and that they attain their enlightenment only after furious, intense internal struggles. What I can affirm is that these young poets are not simply, merely, solely offenders. And some may be burgeoning artists, which, if I know anything about adolescent development and the classroom, is something they themselves may or may not even be completely aware of.

A young person in juvenile detention—having perpetrated actionable deeds and having made decisions while his cognitive and emotional development is very much still a work in progress—approaches the working definition of tragic. To be sure, they are dearly paying the consequences with their incarceration. Perhaps these tragic circumstances ought to be tracked to the crimes committed, adjudicated, but then also tracked to the life and social circumstances that contributed to those actions. So perhaps the through-line to our being denied in Summer 2023 the privilege of publishing one young man's poems began the day of his being criminally charged. But so, too, perhaps the through-line to these poems' composition began the selfsame sad day.

~

Since 2018, in the first five volumes of the annual anthology *Simpsonistas*, we have published 161 authors spanning the generations, including world-renowned writers from around the country, distinguished prize-winners, and other New Literary Project-connected writers such as teenagers from the twenty-two workshops conducted over the years, fledgling authors companionably featured alongside eminent professors, teaching fellows who lead workshops, devoted high school educators emanating nationwide, and a multitude of loyal NewLit volunteers. Over the course of 1,153 pages printed pages you can read dozens and dozens of stories and poems, essays and creative nonfiction that illuminate our purpose and mission—and deliver works of splendor and humor, insight and joy, tales of suffering and love and aspiration. We are gratified to be affiliated with each and every one of them, and we are honored to provide them a home inside the covers of a book where they can thrive in community with so many colleagues they did not know they had before. This all speaks directly to our purpose and to the reasons we founded the Project in the first place in 2015.

At the four corners of New Literary Project you can map our burgeoning initiatives, sustained in overwhelming part by individual donations:

—**The Simpson Workshops & The Starn Writing Workshops**, which have been offered free of charge to over three-hundred high school-age writers over time, conducted by **Simpson Fellows** from the Cal English Department since 2017, and beginning in 2023 by MFA writers who are **Iris Starn Fellows** from Saint Mary's College of California—thanks to the sustaining support of Carey and Frank Starn and the Starn Family; starting in 2024 Simpson Fellows & Workshops will be known as Bonnie Bonetti-Bell Fellows & Workshops, thanks to the sustaining support of James Bell;

—**The Jack Hazard Fellowships**, summer prizes for creative writers who teach high school to support their artistic endeavors, awarded to nine California writers in 2022, and awarded nationally since then, with fourteen writers (from Hawaii to Florida, Boston to Los Angeles, Chicago to Philadelphia, New York to the Bay Area) awarded in 2023; generously supported by System Property Development Company of Los Angeles (David Damus, CEO), in honor of the corporation's founder, philanthropist Jack Hazard;

—**The Joyce Carol Oates Prize**, for extraordinary mid-career fiction authors who have emerged and are still emerging before our eyes, awarded annually since 2017;

—And of course, right here in your hands or on your screens the most recent installment of our annual anthology, *Simpsonistas: Tales from New Literary Project. Vol. 5.*

Uppermost in our mind is the NewLit mantra that speaks to our governing vision and ties together all our various initiatives: *drive social change, unleash artistic power.*

We subscribe to that vision. And we continually answer its call as we seek to extend the reach, and increase the impact, of New Literary Project.

~

In this spirit, let us circle back to our redacted poet. I don't aim to romanticize someone imprisoned, knowing nothing about what he did and what sort of impact, grievous or otherwise, he may have made on others' lives as well as his own. Let us posit, for the sake of discussion, it was not negligible. Then again, as experience informs us every day, very few if any poems are composed by innocents. (Based on our poet's language, imagery, voice, he senses that, too.) The authorities may well see an offender whose words must be prudently redacted for the health or safety of others, or, for that matter, of himself—and again, they are acting within the scope of their legal rights and moral obligations. But I can also attest to one excellent choice he made: writing these poems. I would suggest when he wrote his poems he was working toward a better version of himself—which is why, I feel sure, juvenile hall welcomes working with our Fellows from Cal who lead workshops every year, and which is also why we value our association. A very eminent poet, Yeats, said that a poem is written by one arguing with oneself. Perhaps self-knowledge, and self-improvement, start there, too.

A poem is not merely a collection of words, after all, or a catalog of sentiments, a scaffolding of images. A good poem constitutes an act, a resonantly creative act that seeks its completion in the ears and voices of others. It is not an assault, it is not a threat, unless, that is, it assaults, or threatens, our complacency. A good poem reveals someone frankly coming to terms with one's own accountability and vulnerability—which happen to constitute significant attributes of a young man committed to his own rehabilitation. His writing these poems, we believe, may very well have slipped him a key to figuratively unlock the cell of his own devising.

I should confess this whole experience cuts close to home for me. My younger brother spent over ten years in prison, throughout his thirties and forties, including San Quentin and Nevada State Prison in maximum security, with extended stretches in solitary. All his crimes were connected in one way or another to his heroin addiction. In his youth, he never found footing in public schools, where his obvious learning disabilities went undiagnosed and unheeded, and where he was expelled again and again. He was certainly no innocent, but he was smart and charismatic and generous, cherished by a legion of friends, and only came close to finding a creative outlet when he became a beloved, gifted

24

restaurant manager and chef—for all too short a while, at least, when he was periodically clean. His letters from prison were artful, funny, honest, moving. I may be foolish or sentimental, or may be simply his older brother who misses him, but I fantasize how his life may have turned out different if he were given opportunities like those we offer young people. Not that he would have become a writer or a teacher, but maybe he could have been somehow empowered to summon his fertile imagination to chart a different course. It has been twenty years since he overdosed and died alone on a bathroom floor in San Francisco. It feels, to me, like a minute ago.

What does this all mean? What are the takeaways from our experience with our young poet, and how does it relate to NewLit and *Simpsonistas*?

For one thing, our resolve to offer arts education to young people from unevenly, erratically, or inadequately served communities is redoubled. Our understanding of the value of this teaching and workshopping has only been reinforced. We recommit to offering workshops at juvenile hall, as we earnestly hope we can, along with everywhere else we hope to teach in the future, such as Girls Inc. Alameda County, Emery High School, Northgate High School, and Cal Prep, where we taught in Spring 2023.

From time to time, we may be momentarily frustrated, but our work is not done. And it is never futile.

To this age of frenzied, moronic book banning and noxious culture wars, we offer the strongest response right here, in our programs whose impact will resonate in ways beyond what we can anticipate over the years to come. Our response: take a look at this work. You will be enlightened by it. And you will be better for it, that is, if you immerse yourself imaginatively in the struggles that take place on the printed page. On this score, make sure you read Andrew David King's remarkable essay, included in this anthology, about teaching this young man and his peers, "'My Life had Stood—a Loaded Gun...,'" the title drawn from one of the greatest Emily Dickinson poems.

As if to dramatically demonstrate the importance of long-term patience and perseverance, a happy, surprise, last-minute turn of events took place. As this book went into preproduction in mid-July, we were delighted to receive two different poems by the poet in question that were approved by corrections authorities. We are honored to include the poems and their author below.

This episode epitomizes the need for what we do, because there is something we should all unequivocally cheer: this young man succeeded in writing original poems of consequence. That's an achievement for anyone at any age under any circumstances, including incarceration. And the one lesson every writer worth reading might impart to you is this: writing begins with dismantling if not blowing through one roadblock after another. For the writer's world is nothing if not strewn with barriers, especially for younger writers whose aspirations are routinely minimized, undervalued, neglected, or denied.

As a reader of *Simpsonistas: Tales of New Literary Project. Vol. 5*, you play a role in removing those obstacles. In this way, you are at the heart of the entire NewLit body of endeavors. This book and our entire not-for-profit exist thanks to the trust and faith and investment of donors, readers, and writers, and thanks also to the collaboration of our big-hearted partners in the organizations and educational institutions that provide the sites and the teachers for our workshops.

You will discover much to marvel over here. Wonderment is but the beginning, however. Responsibility is the essential next step. You may cultivate within yourself a renewed commitment to champion arts education for young people and to nurture writers across the generations—celebrated, hopeful, struggling, imprisoned or not—who yearn in their diverse worlds and in their myriad ways to find their audience, through stories and poems and essays produced against the odds, often under most inauspicious circumstances. They show us how—and they show us why—we do all we can to *drive social change, unleash artistic power.*

Thank you for answering the call for a NewLit sort of audience. Only now that audience is you.

—JOSEPH Di PRISCO

MANUEL MUÑOZ
2023 JOYCE CAROL OATES PRIZE RECIPIENT

Joyce Carol Oates

I was struck immediately by the beauty, poise & effortless empathy of *The Consequences*. The title was intriguing—eventually I saw the collection as a kind of novel in which "consequences" are explored. The moral intelligence of the author seemed to shine forth. The work is suffused with information, exposition very artfully blended in with the narration. The characters are utterly convincing, women as well as young men, most of them embarked upon quests of a kind, and the author holds up a mirror to his subjects, or rather a window of transparency. He is never intruding into the narrative as if out of respect for the humanity of his characters. Living far away on the East Coast, I am not much familiar with the world of Mexican American farm workers & their families, but Manuel has made them feel like kin to me. I would place this deceptively modest collection of stories with Sherwood Anderson's *Winesburg, Ohio* as an example of how a novel might be created out of thematically linked stories that accumulate force and meaning. Much seemed to come together in the final story, "What Kind of Fool Am I?," in which a young woman is at last freed of a familial burden; though, given the nuances of the situation, perhaps she will return to her consequential familial duty, as a caretaker of a difficult younger brother. As one who much appreciates the art of the short story, I was filled with admiration for a writer who creates an entire world within the space of a few pages, with seeming effortlessness.

Joseph Di Prisco

Once in an interview, Manuel Muñoz reflected movingly on a "deep love of literature and a belief that it is of use," and how "that's the transformative possibility." He himself is an agent of imaginative transformation. He writes of transformational characters whose lives are altering before their eyes or being altered by forces out of their control, sometimes subtly, sometimes ineluctably, sometimes cruelly and mysteriously, but seemingly forever in the Central Valley of California. How enormous are the small towns he inhabits. He is also a valedictory writer, bidding farewell to people and to the past even while bravely facing the risks and riddling prospects on the horizon. His work plumbs depths a reader cannot resist exploring, sometimes at the expense of heartbreak, sometimes in thrall to wonder, and sometimes simultaneously in both. New Literary Project speaks of its purpose to nurture writers and writing across generations, communities, divides. Manuel Muñoz unforgettably brings that purposefulness to life in one beautiful story after another. We are indeed beyond fortunate to have him in our midst, believing that his writing is, to invoke his words, of profound transformational use to every one of us.

Ethan Nosowsky, Editorial Director, Graywolf Press

It is both thrilling and gratifying to learn that Manuel Muñoz is the latest recipient of the Joyce Carol Oates Prize for a mid-career writer. For years now, Muñoz's exquisite stories have quietly been earning laurel after laurel—O. Henry Awards, appearances in Best American Short Stories— and *The Consequences* gathers many of his brilliantly constructed stories. Manuel is above all a gifted portraitist, and through his indelible characters he portrays class conflict, profound betrayals, the weight of family obligations, the brutality of the immigrant experience, and so much more. The stories in *The Consequences* are set in a particular place and time, but they speak powerfully about what it is to be human, what it is to love, to struggle, to exist in a family or a community. Thank you to New Literary Project for their recognition of his important body of work.

Manuel Muñoz

For any writer to reach midcareer is a kind of miracle and it is one that happens because of the engagement made possible by readers, librarians, booksellers, teachers, fellow writers, and everyone in the wide circle that is our literature. I am deeply grateful to receive the Joyce Carol Oates Prize and doubly so because I was eleven years between books and without a publisher for a time. My thanks to the many people, near and far, both friends and strangers, who kept encouraging me in my writing so that I could find myself here, stunned and yet elated by this recognition. Gracias to Stuart Bernstein, my literary agent, for his sustaining belief in my work and his persistence in seeing it to light. Gracias to my editor Ethan Nosowsky and everyone at Graywolf Press, who have worked so hard to get me in front of new audiences, and to Susie Nicklin and The Indigo Press in the UK, who so enthusiastically shared my stories. To the literary journals and the editors who have supported my work: my gratitude for your belief in my stories. Profound gracias to New Literary Project and its Board of Directors, the University of California, Berkeley, and their partners for their important work in promoting access and participation in our art for all communities. To Joyce Carol Oates, an everlasting gracias for lending her name and legacy to honor writers at such a crucial stage in our careers. I look forward to the autumn residency and working within the community being fostered by New Literary Project and, as a former high school teacher, send special congratulations to the newly named Jack Hazard Fellows. I am urged onward in my love of the short story and in my belief that it is an important mechanism in documenting my beloved Central Valley and insisting on its place in our national literature.

ANYONE CAN DO IT

MANUEL MUÑOZ

Her immediate concern was money. It was a Friday when the men didn't come home from the fields and, true, sometimes they wouldn't return until late, the headlights of the neighborhood worktruck turning the corner, the men drunk and laughing from the bed of the pickup. And, true, other women might have thought first about the green immigration vans prowling the fields and the orchards all around the Valley, ready to take away the men they might not see again for days if good luck held, or longer if they found no luck at all.

When the street fell silent at dusk, the screen doors of the dark houses opened one by one and the shadows of the women came to sit outside, a vigil on the concrete steps. Delfina was one of them, but her worry was a different sort. She didn't know these women yet and these women didn't know her: she and her husband and her little boy had been in the neighborhood for only a month, renting a two-room house at the end of the street, with a narrow screened-in back porch, a tight bathroom with no insulation, and a mildewed kitchen. There was only a dirt yard for the boy to play in and they had to drive into the town center to use the payphone to call back to Texas, where Delfina was from. They had been here just long enough for Delfina's husband to be welcomed along to the fieldwork, the pay split among all the neighborhood men, the worktruck chugging away from the street before the sun even rose.

When Delfina saw the first silhouette rise in defeat, she thought of the private turmoil these other women felt in the absence of their men, and she knew that her own house held none of that. Just days before the end of June, with the rent due soon, she thought that all the women on the front steps might believe that nothing could be any different until the men returned, that nothing could change until they arrived back from wherever they had been taken. She knew the gravity of her worry, to be sure, but she felt a resolve that seemed absent in the women putting out last cigarettes and retreating behind the screen doors. She watched as the street went dark past sundown and the neighborhood children were sent inside to bed. The longer she held her place on her front steps, the stronger she felt.

From the far end of the street, one of the women emerged from a porch and Delfina saw her walk toward her house, guided by a few dim porchlights and the wan blur of television sets glowing through the windows. When the woman, tall and slender, arrived at her front yard, Delfina could make out the long sleeves of a husband's workshirt and wisps of hair falling from her neighbor's bun. Buenas tardes, the woman said.

Buenas tardes, Delfina answered and, rather than invite her forward, she rose from the steps and met her at the edge of the yard.

Sometimes they don't come back right away, the neighbor said in Spanish. But don't worry. They'll be back soon. All of them. If they take them together, they come back together.

The woman extended her hand. Me llamo Lis, she said.

Delfina, she answered and as Lis emerged fully out of the street shadow, Delfina saw a face about the same age as hers.

Your house was empty for nearly three months, said Lis, before you arrived. That's a long time around here, even for our neighborhood. Everything costs so much these days.

It does, Delfina agreed.

Was it expensive in Texas? Lis asked. Is that why you moved?

Delfina looked at her placidly, betraying nothing. She had not told this woman that she was from Texas, and she began to wonder what her husband might have said to the other men in the worktruck, or in the parking lot of the little corner store near Gold Street, where the owner said nothing about the men's loitering as long as they kept buying beer after a day in the fields.

Your car, Lis said, pointing to the Ford Galaxie parked on the dirt yard. I noticed the Texas license plates when you first came.

We drove it from Texas, Delfina answered.

31

You're lucky your husband didn't take that car to the fields. They impound them, you know, and it's tough to get them back.

The woman reminded Delfina of her sister back in Texas, who had always tried to talk her into things she didn't want to do. It was her sister who had told her that moving to California was a bad idea, and who had repeated terrible stories about the people who lived there, though she had never been there herself. Her sister had given all the possible reasons why she should stay except for the true one, that she had not wanted to be left alone with their mother.

My husband says they stop you if you don't have California plates, Delfina said. So I try not to drive the car unless I have to.

On the long drive from Texas, she had learned that strangers only introduced themselves when they needed something. She could refuse Lis money if she asked, but it would be hard to deny her a ride into town if she needed it.

Even in the dark, she could tell that Lis was coming up with a response. She had turned her head to look at the Galaxie, her face back in shadow under the streetlight.

Gas is expensive, Lis said, drawn out and final, as if she had realized that whatever she had wanted to request was no longer worth asking about. But she kept looking at the car and said nothing more, which only convinced Delfina that she would, in time, come out with it.

We got our worktruck very cheap before the gas lines started and we didn't realize how much it would take to keep it filled up. Did you have to stand in line for gas in Texas?

We did, said Delfina. It was like that everywhere, I heard.

Not everywhere, said Lis. They tell me that Mexico is okay again, but family will always tell you whatever they need to get you home.

Where are you from?

Guanajuato. And you?

From Texas, said Delfina. Where we drove from, she added, as if to remind her.

Lis's face had fallen back into shadow, making it hard to see if she was pressing her lips into a vague smile about the fact that Delfina's husband had been rounded up with the rest of them. I think the old man who used to live in your house a long time ago was from Texas, from the Matamoros side, she said. Or Durango? He lived here so long he said this street used to be the real edge of town and that it backed up to a grape vineyard.

Is that right?

He passed away a while back but he was too old to work by then. He always said he wished he could go back to Mexico because he was all alone. Pobrecito. Sometimes I think he had the right idea. It's a terrible thing to be alone.

If she knew this woman better, if this woman knew her better, Delfina thought, she would tell her that this was only half true, that it was hard to make a go of it alone, but that it could be just as hard to live in a house without kindness.

But then you two came. With your niño. How old is he?

He is four.

So little, said Lis. How sweet. My girl is a little older. Ten.

I think I've seen her before, said Delfina, though she didn't remember.

Children never understand the circumstances, said Lis.

No, they don't, said Delfina. I don't think they should ever learn that.

It's part of life, said Lis. Ni modo. You know, that old man, I think he would've liked what we were doing with the worktruck. All of us going together, as many people as we could load in the back. He always said people were better neighbors in Mexico.

The Texas side?

Claro, said Lis, half-smiling. Listen, our rent is due on the first, she said. Yours, too, no?

Delfina didn't want to say yes, not even in the dark, but only "no" would mean this wasn't true.

Lis looked over at the Galaxie. I learned something the last time this happened, that I had to keep working instead of waiting. It's not good to run low on money.

Delfina could hear Lis's voice press in the same way her sister's used to, her sister who talked and talked, who thought that the more you talked, the more convincing you sounded. Her husband had said that anyone who asked too hard about anything really wanted something else.

What would you say about taking the car out to the peach orchards and splitting what we get? I'd pay for half the gas.

Oh, I don't know…, Delfina began.

33

My girl is old enough to care for your niño, if you trust her, Lis offered. It could be just us, she said, if you don't want to bring along anyone else in the neighborhood.

I don't know…, Delfina hesitated, though she knew she could not say that more than twice and she steeled herself to say no.

I know the farmer, said Lis. We could go out to the orchards and pick up a few rows before he gives all that work away.

I'll have to think about it, said Delfina. My husband doesn't like me driving the car. She remembered what her neighbor had said about impoundment and she tried that: If they take the car…

You're from Texas, said Lis, but she pressed no further. Her face was clear and open, but the way she said these words stung, as if being from one side or the other meant anything about how easy or hard things could be. It was none of any stranger's business, but Delfina's husband had never allowed her to work and she knew what women like Lis thought about women like her.

I don't know the first thing about working in the fields anyway, Delfina said. She tried to say it in a way that meant it was the truth and not at all a reply to what Lis had said about Texas.

It's easy but hard at the same time, said Lis. Anyone can do it. It's just that no one really wants to.

I'll have to think about it, said Delfina.

I understand, Lis answered and backed a step out to the street, her arms folded in a way that Delfina recognized from her sister, the way she had stood on the Texas porch in defeat and resignation. Que pases buenas noches, Lis said and began walking away before Delfina had a chance to reply in kind. When she did, she felt her voice carry along the street, as if everyone else on the block had overheard this refusal, and she went back into the house with an unexpected sense of shame.

Very early the next morning, after a restless night, Delfina woke her little boy from the pallet of blankets on the living room floor. We're going into town, she told him, when Kiki resisted her with grogginess as she struggled to get him dressed. She was about to lead him to the car when she pictured herself driving past Lis's house, how that would look to a woman she had just refused, and her pride took over. She grasped Kiki's hand in her own with such ferocity that he knew that she meant business and he walked quickly beside her down the street and around the corner, past the little white church empty on a Saturday morning and toward town. The boy kept pace with her somehow and, to her surprise, he made no more protests, and twenty minutes later, when they reached the TG&Y, she deposited Kiki in the toy aisle without saying a word and marched to the payphone at the back of the store to call her mother in Texas.

He left you, her mother's voice said over the line. Nothing keeps a good father from his family.

They took other men in the neighborhood, too, Delfina said. He wasn't alone.

How many times did he go out to work here in Texas and he came home just fine? I told you that you shouldn't have gone. Your sister was absolutely right...

Delfina pulled the phone away from her ear and the vague hectoring of her mother barely rippled out along the bolts of fabric and the sewing notions hanging on the back wall of the store. Delfina gripped the remaining dimes in her hands, slick and damp in her palm, and clicked one of them into the phone, the sound cutting out for a moment as the coin went through.

How's the niño? Is he dreaming about his father yet? That's how you'll know if he's coming back or not.

Did you hear that? she interrupted her mother, dropping another coin. I don't have much time left.

Why are you calling? For money? Of course, you're calling for money. If he's a good father, he'll find a way to send some if he can't get back.

If you were a good mother, Delfina began, but it came as hardly even a whisper, and she lacked the courage to talk back this way, to summon the memory of her white-haired father who had died years ago and taken with him, it seemed, any criticism of his own late-night ways. Her voice was lost anyway as her mother yelled out to turn the phone over to Delfina's sister, and in the moment when the exchange left them all suspended in static, Delfina hung up the receiver. She had not even given them the address for the Western Union office and she would have to apologize, she knew, when the worst of the financial troubles would be upon her. But for the moment, she relished how she had left her older sister calling into the phone, staring back incredulous at her mother.

35

Come along, she said to Kiki, when she went to collect him from the toy aisle, where he had quietly scattered the pieces of a board game without the notice of the clerk. He started to cry out in protest, now that he was in the cool and quiet of the five-and-dime and she was pulling him away from the bins of marbles and plastic army men. Delfina imagined the footsteps of the clerk coming to check on the commotion and, in her hurry to shove the board game back onto the shelf, she let slip the payphone dimes, Kiki frozen in surprise by their clatter before he stooped to pick them up.

Come along, she said again, letting him have the dimes. Ice cream, she whispered in encouragement, and led on by this suggestion, he followed her out of the store. Kiki fell meek and quiet once again, as if he knew not to jeopardize his sudden fortune. It was only right to reward him with the promised treat and she led him down the street to the drugstore with its ice cream counter visible from the large front window. It was only ten in the morning and the young woman at the main register had to come around to serve them two single scoops, but Delfina didn't even take the money from Kiki's hands to pay for it. She had a single folded dollar bill in her pocket and she handed it to the clerk, foolish, she thought, to be spending so frivolously. But her boy didn't need to know those troubles. His Saturday was coming along like any other, his father sometimes not home at sundown and always gone at sunrise. There was no reason to get him wondering about things he wasn't yet wondering about.

Delfina led him to the little park across the street from the town bank. He gripped his cone tightly and his other hand held the fist of dimes. She motioned him to pocket the change for safekeeping. Put it away, she said, sitting on one of the benches. But her little boy kept them in his grip and so she patted his pocket more firmly to encourage him and that's when she felt it, a hard little object that she knew instantly was something he had stolen from the toy aisle.

Let me see, she said, or I will take away your coins. Kiki struggled against her, smearing some of the ice cream on his pants, which finally distressed him enough into actual tears. Ya, ya, Delfina said, calming him, and fished what was in his pocket, a little green car, metal and surprisingly heavy. Her little boy was inconsolable and the Saturday shoppers along the sidewalk stopped to look in their direction. Sssh, she told him, there,

there, and took the time to show him the car in the palm of her hand before she slipped it back into his pocket. Ya, ya, she said one more time, and leaned back on the bench, the Saturday morning going by.

Later, when they rounded the corner back into the neighborhood, she saw Lis out in her dirt yard. She was tending to a small bed of wild sunflowers, weeding around them with a hoe, her back turned to the street. The closer they got to Lis's yard, the harder the scuffling of Kiki's shoes became and Lis turned around toward the noise.

Buenos dias, Delfina greeted her. She wanted to keep walking but Lis made her way toward her and she knew she would have to stop and listen, much like the time in Arizona on the trip out here, when she had accidently locked eyes with a man at a gas station, and he had walked over to rap on the window of the Galaxie and beg for some change.

Good thing we didn't go to the orchards after all, said Lis. I would've felt terrible if your car had stalled out there.

No…, Delfina began. I… The more she stumbled, the less it made sense to make up any story at all. There was no reason to be anything but honest.

The car is fine, she said. I just wanted him to walk a bit. We got ice cream.

For breakfast, Lis said, looking down at Kiki and smiling. What a Saturday! The morning's sweat matted her hair down on her forehead and she wore no gloves, her fingers a bit raw from the metal handle of the hoe, but she was cheerful with Kiki, recognizing his exhaustion. Her daughter, Delfina realized, was not out helping her, but inside the cool of the house, and she took this as a sign of the same propensity for sacrifice that she believed herself to hold.

I've thought about it, Delfina said, though she really hadn't. I think it's a good idea.

I'm glad, said Lis.

I wish I had said so last night. We could've put in a day's work. But I'm happy to go tomorrow.

Tomorrow's Sunday, said Lis, and when Delfina put her hand up to her mouth as if she'd forgotten, as if she might change her mind, Lis moved even closer to her, looking down at Kiki. But work never waits, she said.

El día de Dios, said Delfina. I didn't even think of it.

People work, said Lis. Don't worry about it.

We can wait until Monday. That way the children can be at school.

Like I told you, my daughter is old enough to watch him, if you trust her. I leave her alone sometimes. Or we can bring them out with us and stay longer.

Delfina could make out the shadow of a child watching from behind the screen door and, catching her glance past her shoulder, Lis turned to look. She called her forth and her daughter stepped out, a girl very tall for ten years old. This is our neighbor, Lis explained, and we'll need you to watch her little boy tomorrow. Will you do that?

The girl nodded and she stuck out her hand to Delfina in awkward politeness.

What's your name? Delfina asked.

Irma, the girl said, very quietly, her voice deferential. She had small eyes that she squinted as if in embarrassment and Delfina wondered if she knew she needed glasses but was too afraid to say.

We can trust you, can't we, said Lis, to take care of the little boy? If I leave you some food, you can feed him, can't you?

Oh, I can leave them something…

Don't worry, said Lis. I can leave something easy to fix and you can bring out something for us in the orchard. I have a little ice chest to keep everything out of the sun.

After Delfina nodded her head in agreement, Lis made as if to go back to her yard work. At dawn, then, Lis said. I'll bring everything we need.

For the rest of the day, Delfina was restless, anxious that every noise on the street might signal the return of the men. To have them come back would mean the lull of normalcy, of what had been and would continue to be, just when she was on the brink of doing something truly on her own. But the street stayed quiet. The afternoon heat swallowed the houses and by evening, some of the shadows resumed their evening watch, sitting stiffly but without much hope or expectation. They turned back in before night had fully come and Delfina went to bed early, too.

At dawn, she roused Kiki from the blankets strewn on the living room floor and poured him some cereal. He blinked against the harshness of the kitchen light at such an early hour, surprised at his mother wearing one of his father's long-sleeved workshirts, and even more surprised by the knock at the door. Lis stood there, her daughter behind her. Buenos dias, Delfina said and waved the girl Irma inside. She poured her a bowl of cereal, too, and Irma sat quietly at the table without having to be told to do so.

Thank you for taking care of him, Delfina said. We'll be back in the middle of the afternoon. She knew she didn't have to say more than that, trusted that Lis had spoken with the same motherly sense of warning that she used. Still, it was only now, on the brink of leaving them alone for the day, that she wished she had asked Kiki if he had been dreaming about his father, if he might have communicated something about what was true for him while he slept.

Lis showed her the gloves and the work knives and then the two costales to hold the fruit, a sturdy one of thick canvas with a hearty shoulder strap and a smaller one of nylon mesh. Her other hand balanced a water jug and a small ice chest, where Delfina put in a bundle of foil-wrapped bean tacos that would keep through the heat of the day.

In the car, Lis pointed her south of town and toward the orchards and Delfina drove along. They kept going south, the orchards endless, cars parked over on the side of the road and pickers approaching foremen, work already getting started even though the dawn's light hadn't yet seeped into the trees.

Up there, Lis said, where a few cars had already lined up and several workers had gathered around a man sitting on the open tailgate of his worktruck. Wait here, she said.

Before Delfina could ask why, Lis had exited, approaching the man with a handshake. He seemed to recognize her and then looked back at Delfina in the car. Lis finished what she had needed to say and the man took one more look at Delfina and then pointed down the rows.

Lis motioned her to get out of the car.

He says he'll give us two rows for now and we do what we can. If we're fast, he'll give us more. And he's letting us use a ladder free of charge.

That's kind of him…

They charge sometimes, Lis said. She took one end of a heavy-looking wooden ladder, the tripod hinge rusty and the rungs worn smooth in the middle. So fifty-fifty?

Half and half, Delfina agreed.

I can pick the tops and you can do the bottoms, if you're afraid of heights. Or you can walk the costales back to the crates for weighing. Give them your name if you want to, but make sure the foreman tells you exactly how much we brought in.

They worked quickly, the morning still cool. Delfina parted the leaves where the peaches sat golden among the boughs and the work felt easy at first. The fruit came down with scarcely more than a tug and when she yanked hard enough to rustle the branches, Lis spoke her advice from the ladder above. Just the redder ones and not too hard. Feel them, she said. If they're too hard, leave them. Someone else will come back around in a few days and they'll be riper then.

They did a few rounds like this, Delfina taking the costales back to the road to have them weighed. Sometimes Lis was ready with the smaller nylon sack and sometimes Delfina had to wait for other pickers to have their fruit accounted for. The morning moved on, a brighter white light coming into the orchard as they got closer to noon. As they picked the trees near clean, they moved deeper and deeper into the orchard and the walk back to the crates took longer, Lis almost lost to her among the leaves.

They had not quite finished the row when the sun finally peaked directly overhead and their end of the orchard sank into quiet. Delfina let out a sigh upon her return.

I should've brought the ice chest while I was there.

I can get it, said Lis. You've walked enough. She came down with the half-empty nylon costal and pulled a few more peaches from the bottom boughs while Delfina rested. She started walking toward the road, then turned around. The keys, she said, and held out her hand.

Delfina watched her go. Lis walked quickly with the nylon costal dangling over her shoulder. Maybe the weight of Lis's work was all in her arms from stretching and pulling, and not heavy and burning in the thighs like hers. Delfina took a peach for herself, the plumpest she could reach without stretching, and sat in the higher bank of the orchard row, catching her breath, massaging her upper legs and resting. It was a Sunday, she remembered, and Lis had been right after all. People did work on this day, even if it felt as tranquil and lonely as Sundays always did, here among the trees with the leaves growing more and more still, the orchard quiet and then quieter. Sundays were always so peaceful, Delfina thought, no matter where you were, so serene she imagined the birds themselves had gone dumb. El día de Dios, she thought, and remembered Sundays when her white-haired father had not yet slept out the drunkenness of the previous night. Her own husband had sometimes broken the sacredness of a Sunday silence and she was oddly thankful for the calm of this orchard moment that had been brought on only by his absence. Delfina ate the last bits of her peach and tossed the pit into the dirt, looking down the row to soak in that blessed quiet. The longer she looked, the emptier and emptier it became. The empty row where, she realized, Lis had disappeared like a faraway star.

She started back toward the road. The walk was long and she couldn't hear a sound, not of the other workers, not other cars rumbling past the orchards, just the endless trees and her feet against the heavy dirt of the fields. The day's weariness slowed her and made the trees impossible to count, but she walked on, resolute, the gray of the road coming into view. She emerged onto the shoulder of the road and saw the foreman and the foreman's truck and a few other cars, but the Galaxie was gone.

Excuse me, she said, approaching the foreman, who seemed surprised to see her, though he had seen her all morning, noting down the weight of the peaches she had brought in, saying the numbers twice, tallied under the last name Arellano.

You're still here, the foreman said, very kindly, as if the fact was a surprise to him too, and his face grew into a scowl like the faces of the white men Delfina had encountered in Texas, the ones who always seemed surprised that she spoke English. But where their faces had been steely and uncaring, his softened with concern, as if he recognized that he had made a serious mistake.

I thought you were gone…, he said.

We were supposed to split… She held a hand to her head and looked up the road, one way and then the other, as if the car were on its way back, Lis having gone only to the small country store to fetch colder drinks.

41

Arellano, the foreman said, tapping his ledger. Arellano is the first name on the list, he said. I paid it out about a half hour ago.

That was my car, Delfina said, as if that would be enough for him to know what to do next. But the foreman only stared back at her. It was my husband's car, she said, because that was how she saw it now, what her husband would say about its loss if he ever made it back.

She told me that you two were sisters, the foreman said. If he only knew, Delfina thought, her real sister back in Texas. The mere mention made her turn back toward the orchard and walk into the row. She could sense the foreman walking to the row's opening to see where she was going, and when she reached the ladder, she folded it down and heaved it best as she could, its legs cutting a little trough behind her as she dragged it back to the road.

You didn't have to do that, the foreman said.

You did right by letting us use it, Delfina said. It's only fair. Other pickers had approached the foreman's truck and he attended to them, though he kept looking over at Delfina now and then, his face sunken in concern. None of the workers looked at her and she let go of the idea of asking any of them for a ride back into town. She sat in the dirt under the shade of a peach tree and watched while the foreman flipped out small wads of cash as the workers began to quit for the afternoon. When the last of them shook hands with the foreman and began to leave, she rose to help him load all of the wooden ladders back on to the truck.

He accepted her help and opened the door of the truck cab, motioning for her to get in. They drove slow back into town, the ladders clattering with every stop and start, the weight of them shifting and settling. Neither of them said a word, but before the orchards gave way back to the houses, the foreman cleared his throat and spoke: I think it's the first time I ever had two women come out alone like that, but I was raised to think that anybody can do anything and you don't ask questions just because something isn't normal. Even just a little bit of work is better than none at all and I kept thinking about the story she told me, that you two were sisters and that your husbands had gotten thrown over the border. You can tell a lot by a wife who wants to work as hard as her husband, you know what I mean? I wasn't sure you could finish two rows just the both of you, but you kept coming and coming with those sacks and that's how I knew you had kids to feed.

At the four-way intersection, just before the last mile into town, the foreman fished into his pocket and pulled out a bill. Take it, he said. He handed it to her, a twenty, and almost pushed it into Delfina's hands as he started the turn, needing to keep the steering wheel steady. The bill fluttered in her fingers from the breeze of the open passenger window, but the truck wasn't going to pick up much more speed. She wouldn't lose it.

Thank you, she said.

It's not your fault, he said. And I'm not defending her for what she did. But I believe any story that anybody tells me. You can't be to blame if you got faith in people.

You're right, she agreed. And though she didn't have to say it, she followed it with the words of blind acceptance before she could stop herself. I understand, she said, and it was not worth explaining that she really didn't.

Where should I take you? asked the foreman.

She didn't hesitate. There's a little store right near Gold Street, just across the tracks, she said. If you could stop, just so I can get something for my boy.

Of course, he said, though there could have been no other possible way to respond, since Delfina's request came with a small hiccup of tears, which she quickly swallowed away as the truck pulled into the store's small lot. Other workers had stopped there, too, and men from other neighborhoods lingered out front with their open cases of beer and skinny bags of sunflower seeds, staring at her as she wiped at her face with her dirty sleeves. She brought a package of bologna and a loaf of bread to the register and fished out three bottles of cola from the case at the front counter. The clerk broke the twenty into a bundle of ones, and she held them with the temporary solace of pretending there would be money enough for the days ahead and that money was going to be the least of her worries anyway.

She directed the foreman just a couple more blocks and when they turned the corner, the neighborhood held a Sunday quiet that made her think first of an empty church, but she had not been to a service in years.

No, it was a quiet like the porch of the house in Texas when she and her husband had driven away, leaving her sister and her mother, a stillness that she was sure held only so long before one of them had started crying, followed by the other. A calm like that could only be broken by the bereft and that was how she understood that neither of them would ever forgive her. But that didn't matter now. The hotter days of July were coming, Delfina knew, and the work of picking all the fruit would last from sunup to sundown. Something would work out, she told herself, clear and resolute against the emptiness of her neighborhood, Lis's house stark in its vacancy. There, she said, pointing to her house, and she wasn't surprised to see Kiki sitting there on the front steps all alone.

There he is, waiting for his mama, the foreman said, as he pulled up, and Kiki looked back at them, with neither curiosity nor glee.

She handed the foreman the third cola bottle.

You know, he said, it'll work out in the end. Sisters always end up doing the right thing. She'll be back, you'll see.

What story had he figured out for himself, Delfina wondered, after she hadn't bothered to correct him about Lis not being her sister, and she decided that this also mattered little in the end, how he would explain this to his wife back home. She would not explain this to her husband when he came back. All her husband would care about was what happened to the Galaxie and that would be enough of a story. She might even tell her husband about the luck of the twenty-dollar bill but she would hold private the detail of the ring on the foreman's finger. She would hold in her mind what it felt like to be treated with a faithful kindness.

Thank you, she said, and descended from the truck cab, nodding her head goodbye.

On the steps, Kiki eyed the tall bottles of cola in her hand. But first there was the heavy field dust to pound away from her shoes and the tiredness she could suddenly feel in her bones. Delfina kicked her shoes off and sat on the front steps. She lodged one of the bottles under the water spigot to pop the cap, a trick she had seen her husband do. She handed that bottle to Kiki and he took it with both hands, full of thirst or greed for the sweetness, she couldn't tell. She took some of the bread loaf and the bologna for herself and offered him a bite, knowing he wouldn't eat one of his own. He was hungry and this was how she knew that Irma was gone, too. She was a girl who did what she was told and Delfina didn't blame her. Kiki crowded close to her knees, even in the heat of the afternoon, and so she popped the cap of the second bottle to take a sip herself and to ask her little boy of no words to tell where he thought the older girl had gone, of where he dreamed his father was. Dígame, she said, asking him to tell her a whole story, but Kiki had already taken the little metal car from his pocket and he was showing her, starting from the crook of his arm, how a car had driven away slowly, slowly, and on out past the edge of his little hand and out of their lives forever.

45

WRITING THE WRONG
MANUEL MUÑOZ

I teach creative writing, mostly to undergraduate students, and they sometimes come to me for advice and guidance about graduate school. Many of them have never left the state of Arizona, in the southwest desert corner of the United States, and are more eager to have a change in environment than to consider the caliber of a program. Some of them panic over the idea of another set of entrance exams or about student loans. Nearly all of them believe that their make-or-break moment for admission will come in their statement of purpose. They want to know how a strong statement might sound. They want to know if there is a right answer to the question about why they want to be a writer.

Every one of my students is different from the other. I remind them of that, encouraging them to take into consideration what might be different about how they've moved in their worlds, academic and otherwise. But one common piece of advice that I give them is to never start their statement with the phrase 'I've always wanted to be a writer'. When they ask why, I tell them that over half of the admissions essays I have read in my time as a professor have begun with that phrase. Not only is the phrase a shallow cliché, so are nearly all of the anecdotes that tend to follow it: the novel that was drafted at age twelve, the cracking open of a first diary or journal, or hearing a beloved author read aloud for the first time. Everyone seeks to tell the origin story. In a way, we as readers keep asking to hear some version of it.

I don't think I could answer my students' dilemma any better. Even now, after four completed books in almost twenty years, the curiosity about what started it all is sometimes at the heart of the questions that can come my way. I was, after all, a scholarship kid from a small, rural town in California who landed at Harvard. I could say that I wanted to be a writer then, but I was only eighteen years old. Maybe the idea had grown from seeing so many glossy university catalogues, students studying on the grass or practicing a musical instrument. The captions encouraged me to think of college as a place for exploration. I was used to practicality.

Sometimes, I tell my students, it might be best to write about what almost stopped them from writing altogether. At Harvard, to clear a first-year composition requirement, I took a class designed to appeal to those of us who wanted to be writers: 'Writing for Writers', or some odd phrasing like that, which lured me instantly. It was the only class I had that was a small seminar, the room not only intimate but intimidating, just a handful of us working together. All of my other first-year courses were large lectures, where I could easily hide in the back row. We weren't writing about science or ethics or history, which many of these exposition courses were designed to introduce us to, but about ourselves. In other words, the personal essay, which even my roommates seemed to think would never be of much use.

The course had all the elements of what I had imagined college to be. It may have been in Sever Hall, an imposing brick building at one end of Harvard Yard, where most of my English courses were. It had a large, dark archway as its main entrance, a foreboding cave amidst the green pathways and the leafy trees of the Yard. We sat at a long table, with the professor at the head of it, notebooks scattered about and every student scribbling down some sudden wisdom. It was the first time I glimpsed a workshop, what it meant to share a draft of a work in progress. I don't remember much of what I wrote in that class nor even if the other students had much to say about it. What I do remember is a long discussion, an interminable one, over my use of the word 'soundlessly'.

I wasn't the first person in my family to go to college. My father had taken English language in some adult education courses, pushed along by an employer who had promised promotions and better pay to any worker who could speak English well enough without needing a translator around. My father brought workbooks home and I'd peek at some of the pages, curious to see his handwriting. My oldest sister had taken courses at a community college just six miles away from town. Written communication, or something to that effect, to get better pay at her office job. I had gone along with her to one of her night classes so she'd have someone to walk her safely back to the parking lot. My other sister, only a year older than me, was the first to attend a four-year institution, the University of California at Santa Barbara. She had managed all of the applications herself, no small feat when no one in the family had ever written a college entrance essay or scouted appropriate scholarships or applied for a student loan. If there were rules to follow, she had no map in front of her.

I mention all of them because I sometimes wonder how they faced being in a classroom, how they felt when it was their turn to offer an answer, or how they might have reacted when their effort was deemed wrong. I don't recall what I could possibly have been writing about in that first-year class. I have only the "wrong" word to guide me. Soundlessly. I must have written about one of two powerful early memories, ones I can summon even now. The first, being out in the grape vineyards during harvest season when I was very young, loathing the heat and the dirt, and sulking under the vines, watching the leaves move here and there in the hot breeze, wishing for an easier life. The other, during the night my grandmother died, being summoned by her in a dream, her hand knocking on a door that wouldn't make a sound. Who knows what the other students made of what I tried to remember. Who knows if any of them had the grace to approach a draft as only an effort, the first step in a journey where a writer might later take us to a more astonishing place. Instead, it was the wrong word.

"This isn't even a real word," one of them had scrawled in the margins.

I tell my students all the time that writing is a confusing world of perceived rules and intimate codes, a place where you might be lauded in one circle for breaking boundaries, but mocked in another for not knowing its currency. I think about that scrawl in the margins of my draft, how I went to the library to look up the word for myself. I was secretly relieved when I found it on the page—it existed!—but it didn't change anything. I didn't know how to counter someone who was so sure of how correct he was. Looking back on it now, I see that he must have heard some teacher say that adverbs were to be avoided or minimized, but he wielded that in a way to critique and exclude. A rule where a single word was more than enough cause to dismiss a whole story. The damage was done. I didn't say a whole lot in class thereafter.

The Consequences is my first book in eleven years. The stories were difficult to write for a variety of reasons, but doubt played a big part. The editor of my novel, upon receiving the first draft, had responded with a brief, if curt, "This is too cerebral." Some version of that student's dismissive scrawl was in that comment, but I was older and more experienced. I didn't need to point to any dictionary. I could point to the authority of my imagination, or at least I felt I had earned the audacity to do so. Still, the sense that I had not met some expectation—who I could be as a writer—kept me at a remove from so many of my drafts afterward. Surely, I was doing something wrong. Surely, there was a wrong word in there, some misstep. Surely, this wasn't the story I should be writing.

What story should I be writing?

I think back to my father's half-finished English workbooks. I wonder why he didn't keep up his studies. The answer might be a simple one—he got the course credit he needed and the pay cheque bump, even if his English remains halting and uncertain to this day. Or my sister, who typed out her essays on a baby blue Corona typewriter, who couldn't be bothered any more with being bone-tired in those long evening classes after a full day of work. My other sister would've been the first person in our family to graduate from college but had health complications that prevented it. When I picture them in their various classrooms, I see them amongst people who were there for the same reasons. Other fieldworkers, like my dad. Office clerks, young women in their early twenties, like my oldest sister. Valley kids on scholarship, like my other sister, settling in among the palm trees and the bicycles of a seaside campus. Everyone looked like them.

Starting with that first writing workshop, that's never been the case for me. I stood out. What I wrote about required explanation. What I wrote about wasn't familiar. What I wrote about couldn't be probable. I don't know why I persisted back then. To a certain degree, I don't know why I persist even today. None of the usual answers satisfy. Not the triumphant story of tenacity nor the defiance of proving the doubts false. Why do you write, the question is asked. Why did you want to be a writer? The question keeps coming and, more often than not, the answer always makes me feel wrong.

I tell my students to try their best to get at the essential mystery, not of their writing, but of their persistence. What kept them on the path? What could have pulled them in another direction? What made the expression so invaluable? For me, it is the only way I know to access the reservoir of feeling behind so much of what I have seen. I have had no other way to shape it, but perhaps by reading with depth and breadth, I could keep learning to do so. I might learn what to do with the empty space of my father's half-finished English workbooks, what to do with the crimped and unsteady markings of his handwriting. I might know how to make something of the box of neat, expensive onion-skin typing paper that my sister kept for her essays, the hesitation she had in committing something to its page. Or my other sister, when it was time to acknowledge she could not continue her studies, shelving her books within eyesight, just in case, maybe one day.

Or maybe I write because one story, however hard-gained, is better than none at all, and there's some value in working through the glimpse of a moment to gather what it might mean. Witness: one of my first summer jobs out of the fields was as an office clerk in a county job placement center in my small town. I was in eighth grade, lanky and studious and big-headed and mild-mannered. Adults trusted me with responsibility. I was tasked with archiving old paper applications into file folders. The applications needed to be alphabetized and separated by job placements, each one in a separate folder with the last name written neatly at the top. Janitorial work in nursing homes, here. Shipping and receiving in fruit-packing houses over there. Clerical work in that pile. I worked my way through them, until I got the ones that were only a single slip of paper. No skills, or so said the bottom of the page. A folder for each one of those applications, each of those pleas, each of those asks for assistance. I made my way through the M's. I found my mother's. I didn't need to read it to know what it said. She had never made it past the third grade. I made a folder for it, wrote the last name on the file tab, and added it to the archive box. Soundlessly, as it was a quiet room, with only me in it, standing in the stillness of all those files, putting the true story together.

M A R T H E: A REFERENDUM

JOYCE CAROL OATES

Welcome to our Earth Day 2169 Referendum!

For most of you, this is your first time *gathered together* in a public place. And for all of you, this may be the gravest decision you will ever make as *AICitizen-voters*.

On screens through the Great Hall you are seeing a magnified image of the primate M A R T H E in *realtime*—yes, this is the notorious M A R T H E—the "last living member of her species"—aged 171.

For a mammal of her age M A R T H E is considered a "highly attractive" specimen though in some quarters she has become loathed as the symbol of a "weak, moribund, predator species" whose artificially engineered survival has strained the State's financial resources.

Yes, M A R T H E's eyes are intensely "blue"—and yes, the eyes are "open"—but don't be deceived that M A R T H E is aware of *you*.

For you are observing M A R T H E in her hospital bed in Intensive Care at a classified location where she has been since March 2168 in a state of physician-induced coma. Initially, M A R T H E's most recent liver transplant was rejected by her body but since then it has been discovered that M A R T H E's artificial heart and brain stem will soon require rebooting, her circulatory system will soon require a complete PlasmaInfusion, and a number of her PlastiPlutonium bones will require replacements, at prices far exceeding the budget allotted under the Endangered Species Intervention Act.

Indeed the most durable of M A R T H E's artificial organs has been her remarkably lifelike Plastaepidermis. At the age of 171 M A R T H E has a smooth and luminous "skin" that, at a little distance at least, might be mistaken for the skin of a human woman one-tenth her age; the

Plastahair on M A R T H E's head remains a beautiful thick russet-red, more lustrous than the "natural" hair M A R T H E had in the prime of her youth.

And there are those *blue eyes!*—not altogether M A R T H E's original eyes, but (seductive) authentic replicas.

Though M A R T H E has become a poster child for sentimentalists who favor the protection of the species that created Artificial Intelligence, first as *RobotHelpers,* then as *AICitizens,* it should be emphasized that M A R T H E was never a wholly "natural" primate: she was one of 188 female clones engineered by the NSI following the Climate Collapse Crisis of 2039 when fertility in her species first plummeted. Her harvested eggs were fertilized in second-generation cloning trials that gave birth to 14,000 human infants—but a chromosomal defect in the DNA resulted in early deaths for most of them.

In addition, M A R T H E was a (volunteer) participant in those controversial experiments of the 2060s involving the artificial insemination of "biologically natural" children in female uteruses, following the general epidemic of male impotence; according to hospital records, M A R T H E gave birth to several "natural" children, unfortunately born with rudimentary brains and defective hearts, who had to be euthanized under the State Eugenics Law.

Still, M A R T H E was reportedly eager to "try again at motherhood"— but her appeal was rejected.

The photograph you are now seeing is M A R T H E in 2074, at the time of the "volunteer" inseminations, when she was twenty-five years old. By *Homo sapiens* aesthetic standards, M A R T H E is considered "beautiful"—"desirable." Millions of years of organic evolution bent upon the grim and ceaseless task of reproducing mammalian species in the old, physical way of sexual intercourse yielded this specimen of a *sexually desirable yet "sweet-tempered"* human female: the apotheosis of what was called *femininity.*

At the time of this photograph M A R T H E was still in possession of her original organs including her flawless "Caucasian" skin and lustrous blue eyes that seem, across the abyss of years, to be alive with something like *hope.* That is indeed a natural "sweet smile" intended to signal to the viewer—*Love me! Please.*

Fortunately, *AICitizens* are immune to the blandishments of natural species and the dubious aesthetics of "beauty." Otherwise such "beautiful" species as gazelles, leopards, tigers, horses, tropical fish, dogs, cats, wild birds and butterflies of great variety, etc., dwelling in uninhabitable regions of Earth (much of Europe and North America, most of Asia and South America, virtually all of Africa) would not have been allowed to lapse into extinction, having failed to reproduce their kind without costly intervention by the State. (Along with these problematic species, those sub-species, or "races," of *Homo sapiens* dwelling in such regions were also allowed to lapse into extinction, though preserved, like other, popular animal species, as ingeniously crafted replicas displayed in zoo museums.)

Like others of her favored species, M A R T H E was the beneficiary of numerous transplants and artificial devices: hips, knees, lungs, kidneys, corneas, eardrums as well as liver, heart, and blood-bearing vessels. Having married into an affluent class, M A R T H E was able to purchase elective surgery: "face lifts" and "face recontouring," silicone implants, muscle transplants, "living teeth" inserted in her jaws. At the age of 119, at the time of her sixteenth marriage, M A R T H E undertook the controversial procedure *GenitaliaNew!* and may have had a (black market) uterine transplant, of which nothing more is known.

At the age of 168, however, M A R T H E suffered a series of mini-strokes; she would have died a natural death except for the intervention of the *CreatorSpecies Protection Movement,* which lobbied for radical neurosurgery to repair her damaged brain. Following this, M A R T H E was shamelessly exploited as a political icon on social media; no *AICitizen* has not been exposed to the (seductive) appeal of M A R T H E—"the last living member of her species."

Others in M A R T H E's generation continued to die off one by one, including, in 2158, the last remaining *Homo sapiens* male, affectionately known as A D O N I S, who lived to the age of 143. This was viewed in the media as a "tragic" turning-point in evolution—but only if old-style sexual reproduction were still the norm, which it was not.

In fact, *Homo sapiens* had failed to reproduce "naturally" since the Great Catastrophe of 2072 when brain-devouring amoeba, thriving in the high temperatures of global warming, learned to alter their DNA to withstand antibiotics, with devastating results for the species; the plummeting birth rate never righted itself, despite heroic efforts to reverse it. (It was at this time that *RobotHelpers* were upgraded to *AICitizens*, to take on the burdens and responsibilities of running the aging "human" State; gradually, *AICitizens*, equipped with super-computer brains and none of the vulnerabilities of a species encased in flesh and blood, took over completely, though contractually bound to "serve" *Homo sapiens*.)

In contrast with the fate of *Homo sapiens*, the hardiest of organic species have not needed extraordinary interventions in order to survive— rats, crocodiles, groundhogs, Tasmanian devils, venomous snakes, sea creatures, and above all insects; these continue to reproduce, in mutated forms, in toxic landscapes outside Climate Control Towers where primates could not survive for more than a few minutes and where even *AICitizens* (with precisely calibrated computer-brains) begin to corrode and disintegrate after a few weeks' exposure to the elements.

Perhaps it is significant that Earth Day 2169 seems to have had no "dawn." Instead the sky has been overcast by an eerie green-tinged dust-cloud arising from the southern hemisphere, occluding visibility from the observatory level of Climate Control Tower I; this dust-cloud meteorologists believe to be "hyper-radioactive" and may be of a potency that can infiltrate Climate Control barriers. Also, there have been reports of slime mold quivering with "life" in toxic tundra wastelands that have been lifeless for centuries. A malevolent new organism resembling gigantic paramecia is reported flourishing where "grasses" and "trees" once grew plentifully in the Great Void Plains, said to be equipped with a "rudimentary consciousness." Suffocating winds, blood-red acid-rain, lethal solar rays that can shrivel unprotected organic skin and scald corneas blind within seconds; a near-continuous quaking of coastal lands along new seismic fault-lines; smoldering mudslides, radioactive firestorms, steaming sinkholes, bubbling swamplands where no living creatures had been detected for centuries until the sudden emergence of a species of new, hardy beetle as large as a Norway rat—all signify a new, heightened danger to our civilization.

Which is why today's referendum vote is "historic": a vote to defund M A R T H E will be a vote to pump badly needed funds into the sidelined

Space Colonizing Project—our only hope to escape the doomed Earth, destroyed by the ravages of the accursed species *Homo sapiens*.

~

Yes, *three-dimensional "paper" ballots* are indeed an anachronism in 2169! Since most of you exist only infrequently in *three-dimensional space,* let alone in *three-dimensional realtime,* you are likely to feel disoriented. Most of you have never *gatheredtogether* in any public setting like the Great Hall, still less have you *gatheredtogether* in *realtime.*

The reason for a "paper ballot" is to prevent computer hacking and to assure an accurate count. The reason for *realtime* is that the referendum must be completed within an hour so that the results of the vote can be set into motion by midnight.

As voters you are required to check one box. *Yes* or *No* to the proposal: *No further "extraordinary measures" should be employed to keep M A R T H E alive.*

That is, *Yes* means *no, M A R T H E—the "last living specimen of her doomed, moribund, accursed species"—should not continue to live* while *No* means *yes, M A R T H E and her "doomed, moribund, accursed species" should continue to live.*

It is true, *AICitizens* are contractually obliged to protect their *CreatorSpecies* from extinction; but it is also true, contracts can be broken, precedents can be overturned, new generations are not invariably bound to honor the obligations of older generations.

The latest polls report sharply divided opinion on the Referendum: 46 percent of *AICitizens* favor halting "extreme measures" to keep M A R T H E alive; 42 percent favor keeping M A R T H E alive with "extreme measures"; a swing vote of 12 percent is "undecided."

Consider carefully before you vote! The future of civilization depends upon *you.*

CLEMENTINE, CARMELITA, DOG

DAVID MEANS

2023 JOYCE CAROL OATES PRIZE FINALIST

A middle-aged dachshund with a short-haired, caramel-colored coat scurried along a path, nervously veering from one side to the other, stopping to lower her nose to the ground, to catch traces of human footwear, a whiff of rubber, an even fainter residue of shoe leather, smells that formed a vague pattern in the past. Some had probably walked through that part of the woods long ago. She lifted her nose and let it flare to catch the wind from the north, and in it she detected the familiar scent of river water after it had passed through trees and over rock, a delightful—and under other circumstances—soothing smell that in the past had arrived in the house when her person, Norman, opened the windows.

The wind was stirring the trees, mottling the sunlight, and she tweezed it apart to find his scent, or even her own scent, which she'd lost track of in her burst of freedom. But all she caught was a raccoon she knew and a whiff of bacon frying in some faraway kitchen, so she put her nose down and continued north again, following an even narrower path—invisible to the human eye—into thick weeds and brush, picking up burrs as she moved into the shadows of the cliffs to her left until the ground became hard and rocky.

Then she paused for a moment and lifted her head and twitched her ears to listen for a whistle, or the sound of her own name, Clementine, in Norman's distinctive pitch. All she heard was the rustle of leaves, the call of birds. How had she gotten into this predicament, her belly low to the ground, lost in a forest?

That morning Norman had jiggled the leash over her head, a delightful sound, and asked her if she wanted to go for a walk—as if she needed to be asked—and looked down as she danced and wagged and rushed to the back door to scratch and bark. At the door, she had sniffed at the crack where the outside air slipped in and, as she had many times before, caught the smell that would never leave the house, the mix of patchouli and ginger that was Claire. She was still Claire's dog. In the scent was a memory of being lifted into arms and nuzzled and kissed— the waxy lipstick—and then other memories of being on the floor, rolling around, and then the stark, earthy smell that she'd noticed one day near Claire's armpit, a scent she knew from an old friend, a lumbering gray-furred beast who was often tied up outside the coffee shop in town. It was the smell of death. Claire got that smell seeping up through her skin. It became stronger and appeared in other places until she began sleeping downstairs in the living room, in a bed that moaned loudly when it moved, and there were days on that bed, sleeping in the sun at her feet, or in her arms, and then, in the strange way of humans, she disappeared completely.

When Claire was gone, Norman began to give off his own sad odor of metal and salt, and Clementine did everything she could to make him happy, grabbing his balled socks out of the laundry pile and tossing them in the air, rolling to expose her belly when he approached, leaning against him as he read on the couch, until she began to carry her own grief.

This morning he'd dangled the leash, and, while she was waiting at the back door, he'd gone to the kitchen and got a tool from a drawer, an oil-and-saltpeter thing that made a frightening sound, Clementine knew, because once he had taken her along to shoot it upstate. (Don't get me wrong. She knew it was a gun but she didn't have a name for it—it was an object that had frightened her.) The thing was zipped into his bag when he came to the door. He stood with his hand on the handle, and she waited while he looked at the kitchen for a few seconds—minutes, in dog time— and then she was pulling at the leash, feeling the fresh air and the sun and the morning dew as she guided him along the road, deep in routine, barely bothering with the roadside odors, to the entrance of the park. On the main path that morning—with the water to the right and the woods to the left—there had been the usual familiar dogs, some passing with their noses to the ground, snobbishly, others barking a greeting. (Her own mode was to bark as if it they were a real threat—she was, after all, as she acknowledged in these moments, shorter than most dogs—while wagging vigorously at the same time.) There had been an old Irish setter, Franklin, who had passed her with a nod, and then a fellow dachshund named Bonnie, who had also passed without much of a greeting, and then finally Piper, an elderly retired greyhound who had stopped to say hello while his person and Norman spoke in subdued voices—she got the tone of sadness, picked up on it—and then, when the talk was over, Norman had pulled her away from Piper and they continued up the path until they came upon a small, nameless mixed-breed mutt who launched, unprovoked, into a crazy tail-chasing routine in the middle of the path, a dervish stirring up the dust in a way that made Clementine step away and pull on the leash, because it is a fact that there is just as much nonsense in the dog world as there is in the human world.

Sitting now on the rocky ground, resting, she lifted her nose to the wind and caught the smell of a bear in a cloak of limestone dust from the quarry, and inside the same cloak was the raccoon she knew, the one that had rummaged around Norman's garbage cans, and then, of course, deer—they were everywhere. Lacking anything better to do, she put her nose down and began to follow deer traces along the rocks and into the grass, a single-file line of hooves that led to a grove of pines where they had scattered, broken in all directions, and at this spot she cried softly and hunched down, feeling for the first time what might (in human terms) be called fear, but was manifested instinctively as a riffle along her spine that ran through the same fibers that raised her hackles, and then, for a second, smelling pine sap, she closed her eyes and saw the basement workshop where she sometimes stood and watched Norman, until one of his machines made a sound that hurt her ears and sent her scurrying up the stairs.

Cold was falling and her ears twitched at the memory of the sound of the saw blade. Norman was upstairs in his room staring ahead and clicking plastic keys in front of a glowing screen while she lay on old towels in the sunlight, waiting for the clicking to stop, opening her eyes when it did, and searching for a sign that he might get up, get her food. Sometimes his voice rose and fell while she sat at his feet and looked up attentively, raising her paws when he stopped. Since Claire had disappeared, he left the house in the morning only to return at night, in the dark, to pour dry kibble—that senseless food—into her dish, and splash water into her drinking bowl. Behind his door, the television droned, and maybe, on the way out of the house the next morning, he might reach down and ruffle her head and say, *I'm sorry, girl, I'm not such great company these days.*

As she opened her eyes, stood up, and began walking, these memories were like wind ruffling her fur, telling her where she should be instead of where she was at that moment, moving north through the trees. The sun had disappeared behind the cliffs and dark shadows spread across the river and the wind began to gust, bringing geese and scrub grass, tundra and stone—wrapped in a shroud from beyond the Arctic Circle, an ice underscent that foretold the brutality of missing vegetation; it was a smell that got animals foraging and eating, and it made her belly tense.

Here I should stress that dog memory is not at all like human memory, and that human memory, from a dog's point of view, would seem strange, clunky, unnatural, and deceptive. Dog memory isn't constructed along temporal lines, gridded out along a distorted timeline, but rather in an overlapping and, of course, deeply olfactory manner, like a fanned-out deck of cards, perhaps, except that the overlapping areas aren't hidden but are instead more intense, so that the quick flash of a squirrel in the corner of the yard, or the crisp sound of a bag of kibble being shaken, can overlap with the single recognizable bark of a schnauzer from a few blocks away on a moonlit night. In this account, as much as possible, dog has been translated into human, and like any translation, the human version is a tin, feeble approximation of what transpired in Clementine's mind as she stood in the woods crying and hungry, old sensations overlapping with new ones, the different sounds that Norman's steps had made that morning, the odd sway of his gait, and the beautiful smell of a clump of onion grass—her favorite thing in the world!—as she'd deliriously sniffed and sneezed, storing the smell in the chambers of her nose for later examination with Norman waited with unusual patience.

That smell of onion grass was the last thing she could remember—again in that overlapping way—along with a small herd of deer, who that morning had been a few yards away in the woods, giving off a funk, and the sudden freedom around her neck when Norman unharnessed her and took the leash and she darted up into the woods, running past the place where the deer had been and, on the way, catching sight of the rabbit for the first time, chasing it while feeling herself inside a familiar dynamic that worked like this: he would let her go and she'd feel the freedom around her neck, running, and then at some point he would call her name, or, if that didn't work, whistle to bring her back; each time she'd bound and leap and tear up the hillside and then, when he called, she'd find herself between two states: the desire to keep going and the desire to return to Norman, and each time she'd keep running until he called her name again, or whistled. Then she'd retrace her own scent to find her way back to him.

It was true that since Claire had disappeared the sound of his whistle had grown slack, lower in tone, but he always whistled, and when she returned there was always a flash of joy at the reunion. Not long ago, he'd swept her into his arms and smothered her with his blessing, saying, *Good girl, good girl, what did you find up there?* Then with great ceremony he'd rolled her up into his arms, kissed her, plucked a burr from her coat, and carried her over the stones to the waterline, where he let her taste and smell an underworld she would never know: eels, seagrass, fish, and even the moon.

Yes, in the morning light she'd caught sight of a cottontail flash of white in the trees and then, giving chase, barking as she ran, followed it into the brush until she came to it in a clearing, brown with a white tail, ears straight up, frozen in place, ears straight up, offering a pure but confusing temptation. There they stood, the two of them. His big eyes stared into her big eyes. The rabbit darted sharply and Clementine was running with the grass thrashing her belly and then, faster, with all four paws leaving the ground with each stretched-out bound. There was nothing like those bounds! Slowed down in dog time it was a sublime job, the haunches rightening, spreading out, and then coiling—she could feel this sensation!—as the rabbit zigzagged at sharp angles and, at some point, dashed over a creek while she followed, leaping over the water to the other side, where, just as fast as it had appeared, the rabbit vanished, finding a cove, or a warren hole in the rocks at the bottom of the palisade, leaving her with a wagging tail and a wet nose and lost for the first time in her life.

Now she was alone in the dark, making a bed in the pine needles, circling a few times and then lowering her nose onto her paws, doing her best to stay awake while the cool air fell on her back. Out of habit, she got up and circled again in place and then lay down, keeping her eyes open, twitching her eyebrows, closing them and then opening them until she was in the room with Norman, who was at his desk working, clicking his keys. Claire was there, reaching down and digging her thumb into a sweet spot where the fur gave around her neck.

Hearing a sound, she opened her eyes. There were patches of underworld moonlight and in them deer were moving quietly. The bear was still to the north in the wind. A skunk was spreading like ink.

In the car with Norman and Claire, her own face was at the open window, the wind lifting her ears, and her nose was thrust into a fantastic blast of beach and salt marsh and milkweed chaff while, in the front seat, they talked musically to each other, singing the way they used to sing.

Something rustled in the woods. In the faint starlight, the large shadow of the beast moved through the trees. She kept still and watched until it was devoured by the dark.

She was in the bed by the window in Norman's room. He was taping the keys. Tap, tap, tap, tap.

The tapping arrived in the morning light. It came from a stick against the forest floor.

The man holding the stick was tall and lean with a small blue cap on his head. *Hey, good dog, good doggie, what are you doing out here, are you lost?* The flat of his palm offered something like coconut, wheat flour, hemp, and, as an underscent, the appealing smell of spicy meat.

The man picked her up gently and carried her—*How long have you been up here, what's your name, girl?*—across the ridge of stones, through the woods to a wider path under big trees and then down, over several large stones, to the beach where he smoked and poured some water into a cup and laughed as she lapped it up, twirling her tongue into her mouth. In his hands was a piece of meat, spicy and sweet as she gulped it down, and then another, tossed lightly so that she could take it out of the air, not chewing it at all, swallowing it whole.

That was all it took. One bit of spicy meat and she reconfigured her relationship with the human. She felt this in her body, in her haunches, her tail, and the taste of the meat in the back of her throat. But, again, it wasn't so simple. Again, this is only a translation, as close as one can get in human terms to her thinking at this moment, after the feeling of the cold water on her tongue and the taste of meat. One or two bits of meat aren't enough to establish a relationship. Yes, the moment the meat hit her mouth a new dynamic was established between this unknown person and herself, but, to put it in human terms, there was simply the potential in the taste of meat for future tastes of meat. The human concept of trust had in no way entered the dynamic yet, and she remained ready to snap at this strange man's hand, to growl, or even, if necessary, to growl and snap and raise her hackles and make a run for it. Human trust was careless and quick, often based on silly—in canine terms—externals, full of the folly of human emotion.

This is as good a place as any to note that through all of her adventures, from the early morning walk on the path to the long trek through the woods and the night in the pine needles, Clementine did not once hear the loud report of a gun. Of course she wasn't anticipating the sound. Once the gun was in Norman's bag, it was gone from her mind, completely, naturally. It wasn't some kind of Chekhovian device that would have to, at some point, go off.

The man picked her up from the sand, brushed her paws clean—*It's gonna be okay. Where do you live?*—and carried her to the main trail. The sway of his arms made her eyes close. When she opened them, they were on a road and the limestone dust was strong, and there was a near-at-hand bacon smell coming from a house. He put her to the ground and let her clamber down a small cinder-block stairway and through a door and into his house.

~

In a charged emotional state, Clementine poked around the strange rooms sniffing the corners, early reconnoitering—a dusty stuffed seal under a crib in a room upstairs, eatable crumbs under a bed, a cinnamon candle near a side table, a long row of records—all the while missing the freedom she had experienced in the woods, bounding through the trees, the harness gone, and beneath that, a feeling that Norman somewhere outside was still calling her name, or whistling.

All day she explored the house, pausing for naps in the afternoon sun, and retraced the activities of previous dogs, a long-ago cat, and various persons. She found pill bugs and cobwebs (she hated cobwebs) in the corners, and on a chair in the dining room, small plastic bags of something similar to skunk grass and spider flowers—not exactly onion grass, but still worth close attention.

That day, Clementine came to understand that the man's name was Steve. Later in the afternoon, a woman named Luisa arrived and spoke a different language—no words like *sit*, or *walk*, or *good dog*, or *hungry*—to which she paid close attention, partly because Luisa had a smell similar to Claire's, gingery and floral with a faint verdant, bready odor that— Clementine felt this, in her dog way—united them in a special way. There was also the way Luisa rubbed her neck, gently and then more firmly, using her thumb as she leaned down and said, *What should we call you?* And then went through many beautiful words until she settled on *Carmelita*. *Carmelita*, she said. *Carmelita*.

Even in her excitement over her new home, Carmelita was experiencing a form of grief particular to her species. There are 57 varieties of dog grief, just as there are—from a dog's point of view—110 distinct varieties of human grief, ranging from a vague gloom of Sunday afternoon sadness, for example, to the intense, peppery, lost-father grief, to the grief she was smelling in this new house, which was a lost child (or lost pup) type of grief, patches of which could be found in the kitchen, around the cabinets, near the sink, and all over the person named Luisa. It was on the toys upstairs, too, and as she sniffed around she gathered pieces together and incorporated them into her own mood.

Resting in the moonlight that night, on an old blanket in the room with the stereo speakers, she kept her eyes open. An owl hooted outside. A faraway dog barked. A distant rumbling sound, along with a screeching sound, began in the distance and gradually grew into a high-pitched screeching and clattering, a booming roar that was worse than thunder, and then it tapered off, pulled itself away into the distance, and disappeared.

The light came on and Steven rubbed her belly—*It's just a train, sweetie, you'll have to get used to those*—and then, in the dark again, she detected a mouse in the corner, erect on two feet, holding and nibbling on something. When she growled it disappeared into the wall. The light came again and Luisa rubbed her head and belly. Then it was dark again and to soothe herself she brought out from one of the chambers in her nose the smell of onion grass.

~

Days passed. Weeks passed. Carmelita settled into her new life. Some days, Luisa was in the house, moving around, sitting at the table with the smell of green stuff, dangling a bag of it in front of Carmelita's nose so she could sniff it and open her mouth and gently clasp—she had learned not to bite the bags.

One afternoon, Steve took her into the woods, along a small trail, and through a fence to an open spot. She lay and watched as he dug with a shovel, cut down stalks, and stopped to smoke. (She liked to snap at the rings he made, to thrust her nose into the smell that tangled up and brought the sudden overlap of memory. Claire in her bed smoking, and the strange smell of the cans under the workbench in Norman's workshop.)

In the evenings, they ate at the table by candlelight and talked about someone named Carmen. Each time the word appeared, the smell of grief would fill the room. The scent was all over the house, in different variations. She even found it on the thing that Steve carried when he left the house in the morning, a leather satchel with a bouquet of iron and steel, clinking when he hefted it up—*So long, Carmelita, see you after work, gotta go build something*—an object always worth examining when he came back to the house because it carried an interesting array of distant places, and other humans.

Sometimes they took her for a walk to the woods, or down the road past the stone quarry to a park where children played and other dogs hung out. She became friendly with the dogs there and they exchanged scents and greetings. Her favorite, Alvy, a bulldog with a playful disposition and a scratching issue, came to the house one evening and they slept together in her bed, side by side. He snorted and sneezed and coughed in his sleep. When he sneezed—his massive nose was beautiful—he emitted a cornucopia of aromas, mint weed, leathery jerky, Arctic vegetation, even a hint of caribou—essences he had drawn in from the northern wind and stored for future examination.

Winter came. Snow fell. The ice smell from the north became the smell outside. When Carmelita went out in the evening—her belly brushing the snow—she kept to the path and did her business quickly, stopping only for a moment to taste the air. Then she dashed back to Steve in the doorway, the warmth of the house pouring around him into the cold clue.

One night there were cries from the bedroom upstairs. She got up—noting the mouse—and went and saw them naked together, wrapped in the familiar bloom of salt and, somehow, a fragrance like the river underworld. When they were finished they brought her up onto the bed. There was a hint of spring in the air that night, and the next morning; the wind shifted and the ice smell from the north was replaced by southern smells—one day faint forsythia and crocus, another day Spanish moss and dogwood, magnolia, morning glories, and another the addition of redbuds, and, of course, cypress, all these smells drifting in a mirepoix (no other human word will do) of red clay and turned rich farm soil that told the animal world that green was coming. When the weather was good she could go out to the back deck—passing through the little door Steve had installed—and rest her chin on the wooden rail, looking out over the water, watching the birds in the sky, as she turned the wind around in her nose.

One morning there was another presence in the house, a small thump in Luisa's belly, a movement. Carmelita put her head down and listened, hearing a white liquid fury, along with the thump, while her tongue—licking and licking Luisa's skin—tasted the tangy salt of new life.

That night she woke in darkness—the moon gone, no moon at all—to the sound of a raccoon crying. Through the window over her bed the strong southern wind slip-streamed, and when she fell back asleep she was free, chasing the rabbit (if you had been in the room you'd have seen her paws twitching as she lay on her side), bounding through soft grass, inside the pursuit. The rabbit froze, ears straight and still, and offered its big, pooling eyes. They stood in the clearing for a moment, Carmelita on one side, the rabbit on the other. The air was clear and bright and the sun was warm overhead. Then the rabbit spoke in the language of dog. The rabbit spoke of the sadness Carmelita sometimes felt, a long-stretched-out sense of displacement that would arrive, suddenly, amid the hubbub of the house, the leather satchel fragrance, the thump in Luisa's skin—that heartbeat—and the memory of Claire. It spoke loudly of all the things that had gone into the past and all of the things that might, like a slice of meat, appear in the future, and then it dashed off to one side, heading toward a mountain, and with a bark (Carmelita did bark, giving a dreamy snap of her jaw) and she was back in the chase, moving in gravity-free bounds over velvety grass until, with a start, she woke to darkness, staring around the room—a faint residual predawn marking the windows and, once again, the mouse on its hind legs, holding something as it gently nibbled.

The end of spring came and the air filled with a superabundance of local trees, grasses, flowers, and pollen. Some days, the air was neither north nor south. A newborn was in the house, too, gurgling and twisting, crying at night.

One afternoon, the house quiet, Carmelita went onto the deck to air and sun. At the railing, her chin on the wood, she examined the wind coming from the south and as she sniffed she caught and held Norman's smell. It was faint. In human terms it was not a smell at all—a microscopic tumbleweed of his molecules. But it was there. She caught it and held it in her nose, in one of the chambers, and turned it over like a gemstone.

That night the rabbit did not pause at the end of the glade and instead the chase went on and on, weaving round until she woke up in the darkness, and to soothe herself, she sat up and examined the little bit of Norman's smell she had stored in her nose. (Again, this is just a translation. There wasn't, in any of this, a concept of causality, and the smell of Norman in the air alone, mixed into a billion other smells, wasn't enough to make her dream of escaping to the woods to trace her way back to her previous origin point. She was perfectly content in her life with Steve and Luisa and the baby, walks in the woods, good food, lots of fresh meat, even on occasion the spicy meat. That tiny bundle of molecules that smelled like Norman was just something to ponder, to bring back out.) Dawn was breaking and she got up and went to the bedroom, clicking her long nails, to listen to Steve and the baby.

One night in August she was chasing the rabbit again, a ball of white movement that pulled her along a stretch of the main path that she had traveled many times. As she ran she passed familiar pee-spots: picnic-bench legs, trash cans, bushes. The rabbit didn't zig, or zag, but was running in a straight line, undaunted, and because of this she felt a new kind of fury, an eagerness that drove her across the wide parking lot, past cars and people, with the wide river glassy and quivering to the left of her vision—everything in a dreamlike way pulled into the vortex of her singular desire, nothing at all playful this time, so that she kept her head down and plunged ahead. Then she was up the hill—completely familiar—and along a stone path to the door of the house where the rabbit had stopped and turned, twitching, standing still, as if offering itself to her. In a single fluid motion she clutched it in her rear paw, twisting hard and then, when she had her chance, she got to the rabbit's neck, clamped down, and shook it until it stopped moving and then shook it some more, taking great pleasure in its resistance to the motion of her neck, and then, as she was tasting the bloody meat, gamey and warm, there was the sound of Steve speaking, and she was on her blanket, which she had pawed all the way across the room. It was morning. He was in the doorway to the kitchen with a mug of coffee in his hand. *You must've been dreaming,* he said. *Your little paws were moving.*

Did one dream foretell another? Was it possible that the dream indicated what was to come? Of course she would never think of it that way because she wasn't bound by the logic of causality; the dream of the rabbit was as real as her waking state, so it overlapped with what happened one afternoon, a Saturday late in the summer, when Steve took her for a long hike along the path. (He never took her too far down the path because he didn't want to give her up. He had made a half-hearted attempt to locate her owner, asking around, looking at posts on the internet, until he was persuaded that no one in the area had reported a missing dachshund. But one day at the Stop & Shop on Mountain Road, on the community bulletin board, he saw her photo. But by the summer, the dog was part of the family, and it seemed important—in some mystical way—that she had appeared in the woods before Luisa became pregnant.)

Once again it is important to stress that Carmelita's world is composed of fibers of sensation caught like lint in a web of her neurons, a vivid collection of tastes, luminous visions, dreams, and even, in her own ways, hopes and grief. Enter her nose, the enfolded sensors a million times more sensitive to odor than your own; imagine what it was like for her to hold, even as a clump of molecules, the distinctive smell of Norman, along with every thing she had ever encountered arrayed like a nebula swirl, spinning in a timeless location.

On the path, she pulled on the leash, feeling big. It was a perfect day, with a breeze that carried not only the usual scents of the sea but of the city, too: streets and car exhaust and pretzel stands and oniony salsa and baking bread.

At a turn in the path the wind funneled along the rock and narrowed, bringing together several streams. In this wind she detected Norman's smell again, just a trace. Steve often let her loose for a few minutes at this spot where the trail was quiet and the trees were sparse. Like Norman, he called and whistled her back, but he didn't wait as long, most of the time, and the dynamic was somehow different.

As she ran up through the woods, not really chasing anything—although of course the rabbit dream was still fresh—she was surprised in a wide clearing by a rabbit in the grass ahead, eating clover, unaware of her presence. She drew closer, barked, and the rabbit froze and then dashed away, making a zigzag, leaping across a creek.

With joy and fury she ran, entering freedom. It was a smart old rabbit, larger than the one in the dream. It disappeared ahead while Carmelita kept running, skirting the creek, slowing down to nose the ground.

It was here that she caught Norman's smell in the air again, stronger than before, a distinctive slice of odor coming through the woods, not just Norman but his house and yard, too. It came strongly, in a clear-cut, redolent shape, so she ran toward it, tracking and triangulating as it appeared and then disappeared. A flash of brown dog through the grass and then the woods, her instincts making innumerable adjustments as she went over the rocky ground, through another grove of trees, pulling away from Steve, having passed beyond the familiar dynamic as the pull of the voice behind her was counteracted by the scent ahead.

It was a matter of chance that Steve had been on the phone with Luisa, talking about the baby, about diapers or formula. On this day the wind was just right and Clementine was fifty or so yards behind a certain boundary line, not ignoring the sound of Steve's voice, distant but clear, calling her name, but overwhelmed by the scent ahead. Simply put, the smell of Norman prevailed over the sound of Steve.

I wish I could make words be dog, get into her coat and paws and belly and ears as she ran, slowing down on the main trail, passing the picnic tables, the trash bins, catching now and then the familiar fragrance of home, but also, by this point, her own trace of scent on the asphalt where she had passed a hundred times long ago. If I could make words be dog, then perhaps I could find a way to inhabit the true dynamic, to imagine a world not defined by notions of power, or morality, or memory, or sentiment, but instead by pure instinct locked in her body, her little legs, as she trotted up the hill and along the wall and, when the wall disappeared, but across manicured grass, past the sign to the park, another great spot to pee, then up the road—staying to the side as she had been taught—to the driveway, stopping there for a moment to sniff.

Out on the back porch Norman was at a table under a wide green umbrella, working. Music was coming through the open door. His neck was stiff and he held his hand up and was trying to work out a kink. He sighed and was standing up to stretch when he heard her bark, once, a big bark for such a small dog. Then he had his arms out and was running and she was running, too, with her body squiring around her flapping tail until he was near and then, with another yip, yip, yip, she was on her back with her belly up, bending this way and that, waiting for his hands, because that was all there was at that moment, his hands lifting her up, lifting, until still squirming and crying, she was pushing her face into his face, licking and licking as he spoke to her, saying, *Oh girl I missed you so much, I missed you, I let you go and started missing you the second you were gone, and when you were gone I knew I had to go on,* and then there was a burst of something beyond the wind itself, beyond the taste of meat, and the two of them were inside reunion; even in that moment she was aware that his smell had changed, and she was still dancing on her paws as she went into the house to investigate, checking the floorboard beneath the sink, going from room to room, from one corner to the next.

One day in the fall, keeping the leash tight, he took her back along the path to the spot where she had left him. It might've been that day, or another, when she caught Steve's scent in the wind, the baby's, too, and then, another time, Luisa's distinctive scent. In her dreams the rabbit still appeared from time to time, and she ran and leaped and bounded between earth and sky, hovering in bliss and stillness that seemed beyond the animal kingdom. Often, at the end of a long-dreamed chase she met the rabbit and they watched each other from their respective sides of the clearing, frozen inside the moment, speaking with their eyes of the tang of onion grass and the taste of spicy meat.

THE SLOW-MOTION COUP

MARK DANNER

Today is not the end. It's just the beginning.
—Donald Trump, January 6, 2021

1.

Our political End Times glitter with surreal scenes—the green-tinted shock and awe unleashed over Baghdad, the "Brooks Brothers warriors" rioting at the Miami election bureau, the jetliner piercing the Manhattan skyscraper—and beneath the unearthly beauty of the Capitol dome that frigid January day, I gazed in wonder at the latest of them: the heaving bodies in their winter clothes, the dark-uniformed, club-wielding police falling back before the phalanx of fists and bicycle racks and flagpoles, and, floating over the straining limbs, the swirls and eddies of bear spray and tear gas in nauseous yellow and green. Was it all a grotesque mirage? *Is this what revolution really looks like?* And yet we know now that from this phantasmagoric tableau a vital piece was missing: *he* was meant to be there.

Donald J. Trump's essential advantage is to be always underestimated: treated as a narcissistic fop, a deranged and ignorant bull in the china shop of American governance. True, he knows little and refuses to learn more because he is certain he knows all. True, he flaunts his narcissism and mythomania with petulant and unflagging pride. But for all that, he is a connoisseur of grievance and resentment and outrage, and a master at shaping from these lucrative political emotions a creative and motivating message. Could anyone accuse him of failing to comprehend the politics of spectacle? Could anyone doubt that he would have known how to shape this fantastic scene of "the people" seizing back their government into a full-fledged camera-ready extravaganza?

Scarcely an hour before and a couple miles away—just as I was shuffling off the Ellipse with my half-frozen, flag-wielding fellows to march up Constitution Avenue toward the Capitol, where, the ranting president had vowed to us, "I'll be there with you!"—Trump was climbing into the Beast, the presidential limousine. When the driver took the wheel to return his precious cargo to the White House, Trump grew instantly irate. "I'm the *fucking president!*" he screamed to his Secret Service protectors. "Take me up to the Capitol now!"

They had refused, of course, and went on refusing, even after the enraged president seized one of the agents at the throat. Or so White House aide Cassidy Hutchinson recounted to the January 6 committee, unleashing a cascade of furious denials. Did the president really respond to this thwarting of his will with violence? Perhaps the better question to have explored was: What would the president have done had those Secret Service agents obeyed? How would that day have unfolded? For it is clear that he had some plan, clear that what was intended to seem an impromptu visit to the Capitol had been well thought out, at least for Trump. "Cass, are you excited for the sixth?" Rudy Giuliani had asked Hutchinson as they left the White House four days before. "It's going to be a great day." Why? she asked. "We're going to the Capitol. It's going to be great. The president is going to be there. He's going to look powerful. He's going to be with the members. He's going to be with the senators."

He's going to look powerful. In his mind's eye, did Trump see himself descending from the Beast amid the welter of bodies outside the Capitol, to the wild cheers of the beefy men pummeling the police—and turning from their violent work to howl and slam their gloved hands together or raise their fists—and to the shouts of noncombatants arrayed in their Trumpian finery milling about the Capitol lawn? There in his chic black overcoat he would have waved, smiled, thrust his fist in the air as the tens of thousands of his faithful, far and near, raised their voices in a bloodcurdling roar. And finally, after shaking scores of hands, taking a few selfies, and perhaps offering an inspiring word or two through a megaphone, he would have led the crowd up the steps, as the cheers rose deafeningly and the little screens of the cell phones held aloft conveyed him making his triumphant way up to the domed temple in thousands of miniature images.

For had the president chosen to stride up those steps, who would have dared stop him? His followers would have fallen in behind him and the Capitol police would have fallen away before him and he would have breached the doors himself, his gold-orange hair shining beneath the mythic white dome in the crisp cold sunlight of that historic January day.

Is that how Donald John Trump, forty-fifth president of the United States, had imagined it? And if so, what did he then intend? Would he have led his chanting, flag-waving followers through the ceremonial doors, past the looming statues, down the marble hallways, and into the Senate chamber, there to face squarely his white-haired, stalwart vice-president, poised in frozen shock on the dais? With his Senate supporters gathered around their victorious leader, shaking his hand, pounding him on the back, would President Trump have smiled up at Mike Pence, held out his famously small hand, and demanded the certificates certifying the electoral votes of the "stolen" election? And would Pence, a man who had shown himself until this very day to be one of the most obsequious public officials in American history, have dared refuse? And then perhaps, in a dramatic gesture for his rowdy minions and the senators and the congressmen and the television cameras and the whole world watching, Donald Trump with his own two hands would have torn those tokens of legitimacy asunder.

We may well never know, of course, what exactly Trump had planned for his momentous appearance at the Capitol that day. We do know that this dramatic visitation was to be the last in a series of attempts—involving false declarations on election night, forged electoral certificates, insinuating telephone calls with state legislators and secretaries of state, consultations with marginally unbalanced conservative lawyers, and endless, merciless pressure on the hapless vice-president ("You can either go down in history as a patriot or you can go down in history as a pussy")—to overthrow the results of the election. Eight weeks after election day, after his vice-president's betrayal, the final betrayal of all the Deep State betrayals of his four years in office ("He's thrown the president under the bus!" a red, white, and blue–clad woman, eyes glued to her phone as we marched up Constitution Avenue, shouted out to us), Trump found himself with no choice but to seize power personally, at the head of thousands of rabid followers, some of them armed. ("They're not here to hurt me," he had shouted before his speech, when he learned that those bearing weapons were being stopped at the gates. "Let my people in!") It would be beautiful, unforgettable. It would be a true and decisive victory over the Deep State. It would be his March on Rome.

Or perhaps his Beer Hall Putsch. Who can say? Would Pence, however surprisingly firm he had held to the Constitution those last few days, have dared oppose the president and his merry band in the Senate chamber? And if Pence had not managed to perform his "ministerial" role, could the election have been certified for Joseph R. Biden that appointed day of January 6? And if the election couldn't be certified, would the matter have been thrown into the House of Representatives, where Democrats held a majority of seats but Republicans, crucially, controlled a majority of the state delegations, which the Founders in their wisdom had decided would be the deciding measure? If all the Republican-controlled delegations voted for Trump, the House would have chosen him as the country's next president. Biden could have appealed to the Supreme Court, but could the Court, with six Republican votes, have been depended upon to render dispassionate justice, any more than it had managed to do twenty years before?

It is shockingly easy to imagine how the events of January 6, with just a tiny detail altered—a Secret Service agent, say, who was not quite so determined in opposing a screaming commander in chief—could have worked out quite differently and produced a reelected President Trump and furious Democrats marching in the streets. Would the triumphant president have called out the military to quell those crowds, as he had tried to do the previous spring during the Black Lives Matter protests? Would the senior officers—as "nonpolitical" as they pride themselves on being—have dared to disobey?

All counterfactuals, of course, are submerged beneath the relentless forward march of what actually happened. Still, however much we want to relegate the events of January 6 to the realm of the near-missed catastrophe, our politics remain imprisoned in a series of events unfolding from that day. The coup did not end on January 6 or even in the early hours of January 7, when Congress finally certified the election of the new president. Today this unfinished chain of cause and effect—call it a slow-motion coup—continues to unfold before the country. The coup drives news coverage. The coup elects candidates. And the coup has already gone far toward leaching from our democracy the one element indispensable for a peaceful politics: the legitimacy of our means of conferring power. By launching and leading his slow-motion coup, Donald Trump has led the country into an unfamiliar and darker world. We don't know how, or if, we will emerge.

2.

Thanks to Trump, election past is election future. To think about the 2020 election is to think about the 2024 election. To look back at the attempted steal is to ponder the steal to come. To tens of millions of Americans "the Steal" is what the former president tried and failed to achieve. To tens of millions of other Americans "the Steal" is what the current president did achieve. Whatever it is, the Steal is a living myth that actively shapes our world. Across the country more than a hundred Republican candidates are running on it—at least fifty-seven of them were present at the Capitol that day—and some of them will likely win. Conceived in the fertile and aggrieved mind of Donald Trump, the Steal has captured the imagination of tens of millions and threatens to attain a kind of perfect reversed reality the next time we go to the polls to choose a president.

It is in the nature of the Big Man that he imposes his mind upon the people. His obsessions are not private. The former president's obsession that he won the 2020 election in a landslide and that his victory was stolen from him is now the obsession of millions. That there is little or no evidence for it makes no difference. That he may not believe it himself does not matter. What matters is the Big Man's performative certainty, which has become his followers' certainty. Their certainty makes it a political fact.

Because of the Big Man's certainty, states are passing laws restricting who can vote and changing who has the power to judge which votes count. Because of it, millions of those who voted in 2020 will find it harder to vote in 2022. Because of it, candidates who deny the legitimacy of the last election—and, by extension, of the system itself—are winning the nominations of their party for governor and secretary of state and representative and senator, and if they are raised to power they will act accordingly during the election to come. And all these historic changes began not with evidence or with facts but with a living, growing obsession in the Big Man's mind.

Between the Big Man's mind and his mind-melded supporters cower the Republican political elite. "What is the downside for humoring him for this little bit of time?" an unnamed "senior Republican official" inquired of *Washington Post* reporters shortly after the 2020 election. "He went golfing this weekend. It's not like he's plotting how to prevent Joe Biden from taking power on Jan. 20."

Perilous as it is to evoke certain political eras, one must go back to Paul von Hindenburg and other titans of the late Weimar Republic to find an elite that so perfectly embodies fecklessness, cowardice, and folly. In one of the unintentionally funny passages in *Landslide: The Final Days of the Trump Presidency*, Michael Wolff tells us that Senator Mitch McConnell's "view of Trump was as virulent as the most virulent liberal's view":

Trump was ignorant, corrupt, incompetent, unstable. Worse, he called into question the value and seriousness of every aspect of McConnell's Machiavellian achievement—what good was power if you had to share it with people who had no respect for it?

Share? McConnell voted to acquit Trump in his second impeachment trial, even as he denounced him from the Senate floor, then weeks later—after the polls were in—slavishly pledged to support "the president" if he ran again in 2024. The majority leader saw his dearest political ambitions founder when the "ignorant, corrupt, incompetent, unstable" president, whom McConnell and his cronies had "humored" for nearly two months, preferred to rave to Georgia voters about his stolen presidency rather than urge them to come out to vote for their Republican Senate candidates, thereby losing the Senate runoffs on January 5 and unceremoniously demoting the crafty Machiavellian to minority leader. Had Trump's coup the next day seemed to be succeeding, can anyone imagine that *McConnell* would have stood against him? Who is humoring whom?

McConnell and his fellow Republican officials and donors fear Trump because they fear his voters, particularly the mobilized base that worships him. While many of these elites act out of rank opportunism, the more strategic-minded profess to believe that Trump is essential if the Republicans are to have a chance at regaining power in their present incarnation: a white-nationalist populist party with a suburban business-class appendage, which increasingly finds itself holding its nose at the stench of the white unwashed. The donor class may be embarrassed by the canaille—and by Trump himself—but it knows the party could not win without their voices and their votes. Senator Lindsey Graham, who in slithering his way from savagely denouncing Trump in 2016 to shamelessly currying favor with him since has marked out a path many Republican leaders have followed, is one of the few willing to say this forthrightly:

Can we move forward without President Trump? The answer is no. I've always liked Liz Cheney, but she's made a determination that the Republican Party can't grow with President Trump. I've determined we can't grow without him.

Though the statement is characteristically misleading—Cheney has made it clear she believes Trump threatens the country and the Constitution—Graham is saying the quiet part out loud: only Trump can guarantee to maintain or hope to increase the party's appeal to lower-middle-class and working-class whites, and in so doing, Graham went on, "make the Republican Party something that nobody else I know can make it. He can make it bigger. He can make it stronger. He can make it more diverse. And he also could destroy it."

That last point is crucial. But better to say: He could destroy *us*. For Graham's voice here is that of the Republican elite, whom Trump delights in making tremble with his every derisive shout of *RINO!* (Republican in Name Only). There is personal fear of Trump's violent supporters but also an acknowledgment of and even attraction to the harsh male dominance he embodies, so critical to the successful autocrat. "You know what I liked about Trump?" Graham asked a crowd of laughing, nodding Republicans. "Everybody was afraid of him, including me... But here's one thing I can tell you about him. Don't cross him. Don't you miss that?"

By virtue of his iron hold on the base, Trump represents both an unparalleled opportunity and an existential threat to the Republican Party. His power is in part a negative one: he can *prevent* the party from winning. And if crossed he has made it clear he would have no compunction about doing exactly that. He reminds traditional Republican leaders of that power and his willingness to use it not only by his frank and unapologetic narcissism but by enacting and reenacting rituals of vengeance, most recently upon those Republicans—including Cheney—who dared vote to impeach him. By performing these public blood sacrifices, and by issuing revitalizing endorsements to those who are obsequious enough in seeking them, he reminds the party of his dominance and keeps all but the most heroic and reckless would-be dissenters firmly in line.

3.

That the Steal came fully formed from the president's mind and grew thanks to the fear and negligence of the politicians who thought they could "humor" him, that such a demonstrably false idea is now, as a firmly held belief of half the American electorate, a dominating strain in American history—that these astonishing events could come to disfigure the public life of the United States testifies to the decadence of the country's traditional hierarchies of power and information. It testifies also to the sheer animal spirits of the media beast Donald Trump, who still effortlessly dominates the news cycle, seizing the spotlight from his successor even as President Biden manages to pass historic legislation. By virtue of Trump's embodied grievance, his shamelessness, and his daring and skill at shaping a narrative—and then, when it is debunked, shaping another—Trump proves himself victorious, again and again, in attracting and holding eyeballs, which are the golden currency of our age. That American politics was destined to be absorbed by television and the communication and entertainment media it spawned could be foreseen as far back as John F. Kennedy, but the "reality star" Donald Trump is this new world's first grand apotheosis.

The question, as I write, is whether, having absorbed politics and one of our two parties, the Trump Reality Show can absorb the legal system as well. Eighteen months after launching the only coup d'état in the nation's quarter-millennium history, Trump remains the odds-on favorite to become the Republican nominee in 2024. Yes, the indictments and court cases are coming. But are they destined to be transformed into new and ever more enthralling episodes? Will they bolster his popularity and the resonance of his anti–Deep State message even as he faces the country from the dock? Will he undermine the rule of law with the same ease as he undermined the legitimacy of the government?

For all its garish effectiveness, much of the show's script is not new. In *The Steal: The Attempt to Overturn the 2020 Election and the People Who Stopped It*, Mark Bowden and Matthew Teague quote the candidate at a rally in Colorado in 2016:

They even want to try and rig the election at the polling booths, where so many cities are corrupt. And you see that… And voter fraud is all too common. And then they criticize us for saying that… Take a look at Philadelphia…take a look at Chicago, take a look at Saint Louis. Take a look at some of these cities where you see things happening that are horrendous.

The Steal, like so many of Trump's more resonant master-fables, vibrates with all the most potent elements of his politics of resentment. The system is rigged. Everywhere you look the "others"—blacks, immigrants, city dwellers—pillage and usurp and steal. And no matter how plain and obvious these facts are, "political correctness" means that no one dares say them out loud. *Except me*, that is.

Small wonder that when defenders of "the system" argue the case with facts—You claim the election was stolen? Show us the evidence!— they get nowhere. Bowden and Teague point to one study of fraud in American voting, by the very conservative Heritage Foundation, that over the last thirty years "listed only widely scattered instances committed by members of both political parties, capable of influencing—and even then only in rare instances—local elections results." Since November 2020, all the recounts, audits, and court cases—more than sixty of the latter—have found the same: the election was sound. More than sound: given the pandemic, it was a kind of miracle. It doesn't matter. Even in 2016, write Bowden and Teague, Trump's charge

resonated with those who feared big government, the growing number and power of minorities, the whole modern drift of American society. Drawing on antiquated stereotypes from the era of Tammany Hall, Trump especially stressed corruption in big cities, where Democrats ruled and the population was heavy with African Americans.

Which is to say that the Steal is a perfect microcosm of Trump's politics of resentment: The very system is corrupt. With the help of minorities and illegal immigrants, the swamp and the Deep State rule. Beneath the elaborate façade constructed with endless inventive mendacity by the mainstream media lies a tangle of political and sexual conspiracies that account for the mystifying collapse during the last three or four decades of the world of the white working and lower-middle classes: the stagnation of wages, the emptying out of midwestern manufacturing, the outsourcing of jobs to China and elsewhere, the financial and housing collapse of 2008, the opioid crisis, the rise of the tech and Wall Street billionaires.

Add to that any number of deeply fraught "cultural issues," among them the state recognizing same-sex marriages, schools teaching children frankly about gay and trans people, and colleges opening women's sports to trans athletes. The Steal of 2020 is only the latest example of the rigged, corrupt, perverse system ruthlessly rising up to defend itself against the attack waged upon it by that fearless and solitary warrior, Donald J. Trump. The Steal, like all his keystone narratives, validates the legitimacy and destiny of Trump himself.

If the reality show candidate and his media magic seem new, the deep grievances and societal dislocations that make his populism so effective most assuredly are not. Four decades of nearly stagnant wages and the wildly disproportionate distribution of the fruits of the country's growth are plain for all to see. So is the vast and unpunished corruption exposed by the financial collapse of 2008. History has shown how populism feeds on corruption and unaddressed grievance. "A longing for money and power took hold of citizens," Josiah Osgood remarks in *How to Stop a Conspiracy*, his new edition of the Roman historian Sallust's *The War With Catiline* (circa 42 BC), "and the moral inversion began."

Greed taught arrogance and cruelty; ambition made men deceitful.... The powerful "few" felt more than ever that the state was theirs to dominate. In desperation, the ordinary citizens, oppressed with debt, were willing to embrace a dubious champion like Catiline.

Nor is Trump the first American leader who has schemed to manipulate the aggrieved populace to gain permanent power. Osgood quotes Alexander Hamilton's appraisal of Aaron Burr, the brilliant, unscrupulous rogue and would-be American emperor who came within a whisker of the presidency. Burr's "private character," Hamilton wrote, *is not defended by his most partial friends. He is bankrupt beyond redemption except by the plunder of his country. His public principles have no other spring or aim than his own aggrandizement.... If he can he will certainly disturb our institutions to secure himself permanent power and with it wealth. He is truly the Catiline of America.*

This American Cataline, of course, went on to murder Hamilton.

The struggle between the force of individual personality, however disreputable, and the limiting power of institutions fascinated Hamilton and his colleagues. Among other things, alas, these last years have taught Americans the shortcomings of the Founders' attempt to shape institutions impervious to aspiring dictators. Perhaps the effort is destined to fail in any political system designed for fallible human beings. Sallust offers in his *Catiline* an unforgettable portrait of the deranged and almost irresistible schemer, corrupt, alluring, concupiscent, indefatigable, his complexion pale, his eyes bloodshot. This electric blend of attraction and repulsion rings uncomfortably familiar, as does the tale of the leader's troubling traits disrupting the institutions of the country he rules. "So strong was the disturbance within him," Osgood tells us, "that it could not be contained. It spilled out and engulfed the whole Republic."

4.

It is the conviction of his followers that they know Trump well—that they know him personally. At his raucous rallies it is hard not to feel that he is showing you his true self, for not only his wit and his anecdotes but his aberrant personality—his narcissism, his mendacity, his endless preening—are on full and unbridled display. He flaunts his neuroses. They are what make him entertaining. Because of this, reading the memoirs of those who have worked for him can be an oddly disjointed experience. Each begins by hoping the real Trump will be different. And day by day each gradually and reluctantly comes to know someone *we* already do. The real Trump is the Trump all can see, and his neuroses are what now drive our history. The most important of these, of course, is the deep and obsessive anxiety about losing. William P. Barr, his last attorney general, tells us in his memoir *One Damn Thing After Another* that he "doubted the President could ever admit to himself that he lost the election," because

in his cosmos, a "loser" was the lowest form of life. Shortly after the
election he was already persuading himself, and his followers, that the
election had been stolen. The Internet was awash with unsupported
conspiracy theories and outright falsehoods, which the President was all
too ready to repeat. His ever-hovering circle of outside advisers—experts
in telling him what he wanted to hear—were feeding him a steady diet of
sensational fraud allegations. These were presented to the President, and
publicly, in such detail and with such certitude as to sound—at first—very
convincing and troubling.

The Steal was born not of evidence but of a neurotic inability to
accept defeat. Even the most casual viewer of one of Trump's rallies can't
fail to notice how central this inability is to how he views the world.
Mary L. Trump, a clinical psychologist and niece of the former president,
attributes this obsession and much else in his strange personality to the
influence of his "high-functioning sociopath" father, Fred Trump, the
self-made real estate tycoon from Queens who in effect raised—or, in her
view, failed to raise—Donald after his mother fell ill:

Fred's fundamental beliefs about how the world worked—in life,
there can be only one winner and everybody else is a loser (an idea that
essentially precluded the ability to share) and kindness is weakness—were
clear. Donald knew, because he had seen it with [his older brother] Freddy,
that failure to comply with his father's rules was punished by severe and
often public humiliation, so he continued to adhere to them even outside his
father's purview. Not surprisingly, his understanding of "right" and "wrong"
would clash with the lessons taught in most elementary schools.

Unmanageable in his private school, Trump was eventually sent to
the New York Military Academy, where discipline was harsh. He thrived
there, for

life at NYMA reinforced one of Fred's lessons: the person with the
power (no matter how arbitrarily that power was conferred or attained)
got to decide what was right and wrong. Anything that helped you
maintain power was by definition right, even if it wasn't always fair.
[Emphasis added]

In Mary Trump's analysis, Donald had been intentionally shaped to
succeed in this harsh world by Fred, who, having destroyed his firstborn

son—Mary's father, who died of alcoholism at age forty-two—resolved to encourage "the killer" in his second:

[Donald] took what he wanted without asking for permission not because he was brave but because he was afraid not to. Whether Donald understood the underlying message or not, Fred did: in family, as in life, there could be only one winner; everybody else had to lose. Freddy kept trying and failing to do the right thing; Donald began to realize that there was nothing he could do wrong, so he stopped trying to do anything "right." He became bolder and more aggressive because he was rarely challenged or held to account by the only person in the world who mattered—his father. Fred liked his killer attitude, even if it manifested as bad behavior.

Every one of Donald's transgressions became an audition for his father's favor, as if he were saying, "See, Dad, I'm the tough one. I'm the killer." He kept piling on because there wasn't any resistance—until there was.

A loser cannot also be a killer. Trump's conviction on this matter is no secret. That he would refuse to acknowledge his loss and resist leaving office voluntarily was prophesied by Michael Cohen, his ex–fixer and lawyer, among others who know him well. What was less easy to predict were the complex mechanisms of fecklessness and ambition that led most of the leaders and officeholders of one of America's two major political parties to humor the president in his fantasy about the Steal—and that led tens of millions of voters to believe it in turn, and to elect politicians who profess to believe it as well. It is a tale that would be marvelous, if it didn't pose so grave a threat to the country and its institutions.

Central to the tale is a peculiar kind of court politics. In every administration the courtiers rise and fall according to the favor of the sovereign. The principles animating this vary from one administration to the next, but Trump's staffing was unprecedented in its volatility— unheard-of numbers of officials at senior and middle levels were hired and fired—and its personalism. A courtier rose by pleasing Trump and pleased him by giving him what he wanted, which was almost always something that pushed against the government's customary practices and often against the country's laws.

Against the tireless will of Trump, the so-called Deep State—the permanent bureaucracy and its allies among political appointees—pushed back. Those officials who helped Trump push back against it in his turn drew his favor and advanced. Those who acted too blatantly to restrain him—like the famous "adults in the room," two of them prominent generals, who surrounded him at the start of his administration—were one by one defenestrated. Over time, the process gradually exhausted and winnowed out those willing to oppose the president in defense of normal practices, principles, and laws.

Because of its inherent dynamic (Trump—thoroughly uninterested in learning how to be "presidential"—remained Trump), those willing to serve him in high positions had to develop complicated survival strategies, both to avoid giving the president what he wanted in the most egregious cases and to justify their compliance when they felt they had to act in a way they knew they shouldn't. Much of Barr's book, like many of the Trump memoirs, offers a kind of extended aria on this theme.

Following the 2020 election, this process accelerated. Only a bedraggled group of compliant survivors remained in the White House, and their numbers diminished by the day. And even they were increasingly ignored by a president who began to take most of his counsel from "outside advisers"—Barr's despised "clown show" of Giuliani, Sidney Powell, Jenna Ellis, and John Eastman. At the best of times Trump was difficult to "manage." "It was hard to hold Trump's attention," Wolff remarks, "when he wasn't the one talking." Barr writes:

It had always been difficult to keep him on track—you had to put up with endless bitching and exercise a superhuman level of patience, but it could be done. After the election, though, he was beyond restraint. He would only listen to a few sycophants who told him what he wanted to hear. Reasoning with him was hopeless.

By this relentless process of elimination, Trump gradually constructed around himself a circle of "advisers" who increasingly reflected back to him his own views, however outlandish. To "agree" with him in the cause of preventing some larger harm to come was perilous. Those who believed there was "no harm" in "humoring" Trump were treading a well-worn track traversed by hundreds throughout his life. Wolff, who has spent a career reporting on dominating personalities and their handlers in the worlds of money and the media, is deft in describing these moments, with a satirical touch that nearly makes one forget the gravity of it all:

But the president suddenly went from sourness to delight. And inspiration!... They could just use Covid as a reason to delay the election. "People can't get to the polls. It's a national emergency. Right?" He looked around to everybody for their assent—and for congratulations on his great idea.

There was often a small moment of silence and a collective intake of breath whenever Trump, with alarming frequency, went where no one wanted to go or would have dreamed of going. The reaction now was somewhere between gauging Trump's being Trump, with everybody understanding that nine-tenths of what came out of his mouth was blah-blah and recognizing that here might be a hinge moment in history and that he really might be thinking he could delay the election. If the latter, then there was the urgent question of who needed now, right now, to go into the breach?

A reluctant [Chief of Staff Mark] Meadows did: "Mr. President, there isn't any procedure for that. There would be no constitutional precedent or mechanism. The date is fixed. The first Tuesday..." Meadows's sugary North Carolinian voice was tinged with panic.

"Uh-uh. But what about—?"

"I'm afraid—no, you can't. We can't."

"I'm sure there might be a way, but...well..."

Trump, as so often, did not give up on the idea. He simply looked for more agreeable interlocutors—Chris Christie, for example, the former governor of New Jersey, whom he saw at a debate prep session the next week:

"I'm thinking about calling it off," said Trump, as though without much thought.

"The prep?" said Christie.

"No, the election—too much virus."

"Well, you can't do that, man," said Christie, a former US attorney, half chuckling. "You do know you can't declare martial law." Christie followed up: "You do know that, right?"

It was both alarming and awkward that he might not.

On the afternoon of January 6, Chief of Staff Mark Meadows sat outside the White House dining room, scrolling desultorily through the texts on his phone, while Pat Cipollone, the White House counsel, desperately pushed him to get up and confront Trump. The president of the United States had returned from his speech at the Ellipse and, having failed in his attempt to get to the Capitol—for quite a while he refused to take off his overcoat, convinced he would still persuade his Secret Service detail to take him on his triumphant mission—now sat glued to the television, watching as thousands of his followers sacked the seat of Congress. Transfixed by the scenes of carnage, the commander in chief refused to pick up the phone.

"We need to go down and see the president now," shouted Cipollone, according to Cassidy Hutchinson.

"He doesn't want to *do* anything, Pat," a beaten-down Meadows replied.

"*Something* needs to be done," Cipollone shouted, "or people are going to die and the blood is going to be on *your* fucking hands…. They're literally calling for the vice-president to be fucking hung."

"You *heard* him, Pat," Meadows said. "He thinks Mike deserves it."

What could be the harm in humoring Donald Trump?

5.

In our nation's 246-year history, there has never been an individual who is a greater threat to our republic than Donald Trump.
—Dick Cheney, August 4, 2022

The former vice-president's blunt assessment comes as a shock, and yet it needs only a minute or two of pondering to realize that Dick Cheney, a man who, whatever you think of him, knows as much about power and its exercise as any contemporary American, speaks a stark truth. By engineering a half-dozen or so plots and conspiracies between the election and Biden's inauguration, Trump committed a grave crime against the state. He plotted to overthrow the government, and he very nearly succeeded. And after committing this crime in full view of the country—the crime for which Cicero and his fellow Roman senators executed five of Catiline's coconspirators and meant to execute Catiline, had he not died fighting—Trump not only walks free but remains the undisputed leader of the Republican Party with a chance, whether he is under indictment or not, to retake the presidency.

Is that likely to happen? No. But it is possible it will happen. And that it remains a possibility is deeply disquieting. Trump has done his fellow Americans the service of showing them how vulnerable their vaunted system of government really is. For all their concern about tyranny, the Founders put in place a mechanism to remove a criminal president that has proved, in the face of strong party loyalties, to be laughably impotent. And in a country supposedly of laws, not of men, the laws' workings have shown themselves to be, in the face of a genuine emergency, ponderously slow, allowing a leader who tried illicitly to seize power to prepare quite openly to take power again. History offers notable examples of dictators who have come to power through elections, but it is hard to think of one who attempted to cling to power through a coup and failed—and to whom the polity, in its blithe unconcern, offered the chance to try again.

PEARL ANNIVERSARY FOR A DIRTY WEDDING: DENIS JOHNSON'S *JESUS' SON* AT 30

IAN S. MALONEY

It's been three decades since a slim volume of eleven interconnected stories, cobbled together for a few thousand dollars to keep the IRS at bay, changed the landscape of American literature. Denis Johnson's *Jesus' Son* is one of those books you read in a single sitting, again and again. It's a repeat offender, in the best sense of the term. A professor at Brooklyn College handed me my first copy in the late 1990s—he said only this: "Read this. I'll say no more." I read it often, and I've been handing it to students, friends, and family members ever since. As we reach its pearl anniversary, I can't help but connect this book with Matthew 7:6 and not "casting your pearls before pigs, lest they trample them underfoot, and turn again and rend you." Such is the wisdom of this small, epiphanic book about a drifter, druggie, drunk, and ne'er do well as he slowly finds himself working out of drug addiction and acedia and toward a hard-earned, sober redemption and reengagement with the world.

Here in *Jesus' Son*, we roll across a charred and broken American landscape of lost souls and fragmented American dreams—places like Missouri, Iowa, Washington, Arizona—from car crashes, hustles, and work stints to day-drinking in hole-in-the-wall dive bars with Fuckhead, our drug addicted, hopelessly lost narrator and tour guide. In many ways, *Jesus' Son* reads like a twelve-step journey to God and sobriety. And, it is that and much more. By the end, when we reach "Beverly Home," our narrator has found employment in a nursing home and started on the road to recovery. He's writing the community newsletter at Beverly Home and working with patients, even as he plays Peeping Tom on a Mennonite couple, listening mesmerized to the wife singing in the shower or waiting

88

to catch a glimpse of the couple making love. Sure, this part of the final story is creepy, but he admits as such: "How could I do it, how could a person go that low? And I understand your question, to which I apply, Are you kidding? That's nothing. I'd been much lower than that. And I expected to see myself do worse." And ostensibly he's right. The whole scene alludes to the Old Testament, when David watches Bathsheba from his rooftop, and then calls the married woman to his palace to have sex with her. Then, David sends her husband Uriah to the front lines of battle to be killed, after he's learned that he's impregnated Uriah's wife. Yeah, it could *definitely* be worse. And that's the point. Johnson's stories don't point to a lightning-strike, pure redemption, but rather, to a very real one of increments, steps, and hard work. The victory is the acknowledgement of his commonality with other addicts and lost travelers. The haunting last lines need to be heard: "All these weirdos, and me getting a little better every day right in the midst of them. I had never known, never even imagined for a heartbeat, that there might be a place for people like us." It's a beautiful sentiment—not a hallelujah from the mountaintop, but a man quietly setting his path straight, slowly, by doing his daily work. Johnson sets this last story in Phoenix, so the narrator rises out of the ashes of his own burning. It's beautiful and biblical. We don't get the Messiah rising on the third day, but we do see someone with a newfound zest for living and being a part of common, everyday life, and that's enough.

Sentences grab a hold of you in *Jesus' Son*, and pull you into their paradoxical beauty, in the midst of despair, disillusion, and ugliness. In reading it this time, I saw it a hero's journey. In the opening story "Car Crash While Hitchhiking," probably the most powerful story for me, the narrator tells us the following:

At the head of the entrance ramp I waited without hope of a ride. What was the point, even, of rolling up my sleeping bag when I was too wet to be let into anybody's car? I draped it around me like a cape. The downpour raked the asphalt and gurgled in the ruts. My thoughts zoomed pitifully. The travelling salesman had fed me pills that made the linings of my veins feel scraped out. My jaw ached. I knew every raindrop by its name. I sensed everything before it happened. I knew a certain Oldsmobile would stop for me even before it slowed, and by the sweet voices of the family inside it I knew we'd have an accident in the storm.

I didn't care. They said they'd take me all the way.

The pitiful hero with a wet cape, racing thoughts, and suicidal ideation waits on the highway to be taken all the way. That singular sentence, repeated every time someone mentions this book, *I knew every raindrop by its name,* provides that spark of magic, for what it is otherwise a sad case of a drugged-out drifter alone on a highway, waiting for a lift in a rainstorm. During the story, the crash occurs and the narrator watches. He really is incapable of much else, and that's what sets off his hero's journey. He is holding a child and he doesn't know who is alive or dead anymore. The question is: *Is he alive or dead?* His journey leads him down into despair and darkness, only to return in the final few stories to light and hope in the world through connections with other people. The final paragraph of "Car Crash" in the hospital is worth noting.

It was raining. Gigantic ferns leaned over us. The forest drifted down a hill. I could hear a creek rushing down among the rocks. And you, you ridiculous people, you expect me to help you.

The bookend stories from the beginning to end move the narrator to helping those "ridiculous people"—and instead of watching a family waiting for help in the dark in the opening story, he gets on a bus, goes to work, and continues his road to reengagement with life and recovery in the final one. It's a full circle journey from darkness into light, from despair into hope, with several key threshold moments in between.

Each section in *Jesus' Son* has moments of haunting transcendence, as the narrator grapples to find his way through the dark. In "Two Men" he and his companions try to lose a mute football player they've picked up, eventually ditching him into a rotted stop sign at a crossroads. The reader is left thinking about ghosts and haunted shells of the self. A few pages earlier, the narrator notes this about a dilapidated house they enter: "The house looked abandoned, no curtains, no rugs. All over the floor were shiny things I thought might be spent flashbulbs or empty bullet casings. But it was dark and nothing was clear. I peered around until my eyes were tired and I thought I could make out designs all over the floor like the chalk outlines of victims or markings for strange rituals." It's moments like these that haunt me—moments of perception, which could signal the broken flashbulb dreams of escapism, or perhaps the evidence left after a crime.

In "Out on Bail" we meet Jack Hotel and the infamous Vine bar, which we revisit throughout the collection: "It was a long, narrow place, like a train car that wasn't going anywhere. The people all seemed to have escaped from somewhere—I saw plastic hospital name bracelets on several wrists. They were trying to pay for their drinks with counterfeit money they'd made themselves, in Xerox machines…The Vine was different every day. Some of the most terrible things that had happened to me in my life had happened in here. But like the others I kept coming back." Patrons at the Vine "had that helpless, destined feeling. We would die with handcuffs on. We would be put a stop to, and it wouldn't be our fault. So we imagined. And yet we always being found innocent for ridiculous reasons." As the narrators tells us, today became yesterday here, yesterday was tomorrow, and so on. Ironically, the bar's name echoes back to the New Testament here and John 15: 1-5:

I am the true vine, and my Father is the husbandman.

Every branch in me that beareth not fruit he taketh away: and every branch that beareth fruit, he purgeth it, that it may bring forth more fruit.

Now ye are clean through the word which I have spoken unto you.

Abide in me, and I in you. As the branch cannot bear fruit of itself, except it abide in the vine; no more can ye, except ye abide in me.

I am the vine, ye are the branches: He that abideth in me, and I in him, the same bringeth forth much fruit: for without me ye can do nothing.

By the close of the section, Jack Hotel has died of an overdose and the narrator has survived. "He simply went under. He died. I am still alive." By chance or luck or fate, the narrator survives, "There was no touching the hem of mystery, no little occasion when any of us thought— well, speaking for myself only, I suppose—that our lungs were filled with light, or anything like that." This hearkening back to light echoes back to Christ as the light of the world, and the ironic Vine suggests that even the most barren branch can bear fruit. Without the true vine, there is nothingness for him. So much of *Jesus' Son* reminds me of Flannery O'Connor's grotesque, Christ-haunted landscapes, where "the ragged figure who moves from tree to tree in the back of his mind" in *Wise Blood*. This very much feels akin to the narrator's journey to find salvation, light, and grace and to escape the clutches of the false vine wrapped around him, if you will.

The narrative then leads us to "Dundun" where a murder has taken place. In this short section, Dundun has shot McInness, who dies without much notice in the back of the narrator's car. It's nonchalant and almost feels like the humdrum presence of the demonic or the dung heap. Blackbirds circle over their shadows. Jack Hotel, mentioned again after his death in the previous section, does drugs in the beginning and a remembrance of Dundun torturing Hotel near Denver is mentioned at the close. The section reads like the underworld of Iowa. "There'd been a drought for years, and a bronze fog of dust stood over the plains. The soybean crop was dead again, and the failed, wilted cornstalks were laid out on the ground like rows of underthings. Most of the farmers didn't even plant anymore. All the false visions had been erased. It felt like the moment before the Savior comes. And the Savior did come, but we had to wait a long time." The scene is a wasteland of the heartland, and the "rows of underthings" suggests the fates and destinies of the wasted people themselves, these scarecrows, waiting for salvation after plague, drought, and fire. Dundun is described like a fire-branded devil at the end: "It was only that certain important connections had been burned through. If I opened up your head and ran a hot smoldering iron around in your brain, I might turn you into someone like that." The fire images here conjure thoughts of Prometheus, Milton's Satan, and Melville's Ahab. Dundun muses as they drive the "skeleton remnants" of fields that he wouldn't mind being a hit man. He's probably the darkest, most destructive figure of this wasteland.

In "Work" there are glimmers of salvation. The narrator and his girlfriend have been staying at a Holiday Inn. "We made love in the bed, ate steaks in the restaurant, shot up in the john, puked, cried, accused one another, begged of one another, forgave, promised and carried one another to heaven." After an argument, the narrator hits his girlfriend and is beaten up by some onlookers. Then, he's back at the Vine, meets Wayne, and heads out to strip the wiring out of Wayne's old empty house for money. As they strip the house of copper wiring, an image of a red-haired woman appears on the river; she's been pulled by a boat going thirty or forty miles per hour, and we learn that it's Wayne's wife. The narrator feels as if he's wandered somehow into Wayne's dream, and there's a strange mystical sense about the moment. Wayne uses the odd word "sacrifice" as he buys them drinks at the Vine and as Wayne argues over cards, the narrator has a vision: "A clattering sound was tearing up my head as I staggered upright and opened the door on a vision: Where are my women now, with their sweet wet words, and the miraculous balls of hail popping in a green translucence in the yard?" The section is punctuated with odd visions and evocations of mysterious, angelic women, concluding with the bartender (Nurse), who "poured doubles like an angel right up to the lip of a cocktail glass, no measuring." There's the mention of a hummingbird, a symbol perhaps that challenging times are nearing the end and that you will find joy in your own circumstances. This is a crucial turning point in the narrative, as the narrator sobs and calls the bartender his mother. He seems to be seeking the assistance or intervention of the divine, perhaps the intercession of Jesus' mother, the Virgin Mary. The reference of the bartender as "Nurse" leads into the next chapter, where work once again leads to greater revelations.

"Work" flows into "Emergency," our only real glimpse of the narrator working an actual job before the final chapter. The narrator is working as an orderly in a Catholic hospital's emergency room. He's been working here three weeks (perhaps a symbolic nod to the trinity), but the attention in the opening page is on blood (Blood of Christ?). We meet Georgie, a fellow orderly, who steals pills from the cabinets. Blood is all over the floor, and Georgie points out "There's so much goop inside of us, man and all it all wants to get out." The section often feels confessional and miraculous to me—the central action occurs when Terrence Weber (played by Denis Johnson himself in the film adaptation) comes in with a knife in his eye, but doesn't request for the police to be summoned, unless he dies. Georgie emerges inexplicably with the knife in his hand as the doctors debate a course of action, and Weber has nothing wrong with him. Georgie and the narrator drive around, at one point debating whether to go to church or the county fair. The most haunting section of the story comes when they hit a jackrabbit, and Georgie saves the babies inside the dead rabbit and hands them over to the narrator. Georgie feels like the white knight of these stories. The strange night they spend wandering around blurs the lines between reality and fantasy. A snowstorm engulfs them during their travels and the narrator asks, "Georgie, can you see?" The narrator then has this vision:

We bumped softly down a hill toward an open field that seemed to be a military graveyard, filled with rows and rows of austere, identical markers over soldiers' graves. I'd never before come across this cemetery. On the farther side of the field, just beyond the curtains of snow, the sky was torn away and the angels were descending out of a brilliant blue summer, their huge faces streaked with light and full of pity. The sight of them cut through my heart and down the knuckles of my spine, and if there'd been anything in my bowels I would have messed my pants from fear.

Georgie opened his arms and cried out, "It's the drive-in, man!"

"The drive-in..." I wasn't sure what these words meant.

"They're showing movies in a fucking blizzard!" Georgie screamed.

"I see. I thought it was something else," I said.

This blizzard drive-in scene always captivated me, for it reminds me of Plato's Allegory of the Cave, as the prisoners are chained to watching the shadows on the wall, all the time believing what they're seeing is real. Georgie's intervention opens the narrator's eyes for a minute, and then he drives that message home when he asks the narrator about the baby rabbits, which have been forgotten and crushed by Fuckhead. At this dark moment of revelation, Georgie asks, "Does everything you touch turn to shit? Does this happen to you every time?"

It's a pivotal moment when the weight of the innocent, dead rabbits come to light—the illusions begin to fade. I consider *Alice in Wonderland* and Jefferson Airplane's "White Rabbit" in this section. Fuckhead has gone down the rabbit hole and the flickering images of his subconscious mind are finally beginning to hit bottom. He notes, "I could understand how a drowning man might suddenly feel a deep thirst being quenched. Or how the slave might become a friend to the master." The image of the elk and the coyote in the field seems to foreshadow the strange watching of the couple at the close of the book. The elk waits silently with an air of authority—the ravenous coyote still jogs across the pasture. Maybe this is the spirit embodiment of owning up to addiction. Stand still and watch the white snow in the pasture, or keep plodding on, ravenous for more, looking and fading away into the darkened trees for another fix. Georgie's last line of the section, when he's asked about his profession is simple and straightforward: "I save lives." In my reading this time, it's the start of the Narrator's salvation.

Like we've seen before, "Emergency" holds important keys for "Dirty Wedding," which follows it. In this chapter, the narrator and his girlfriend Michelle have an abortion. We watch the narrator grapple again with the death of innocence, and to grapple with his confusion, he rides a train, watching families drift by through the windows. Fuckhead gets tossed out of the clinic, for being insensitive and cruel to Michelle after the procedure. He's clearly making his way to the bottom by this point—he notes about the abortion protesters outside: "They splashed holy water on my cheek and on the back of my neck, and I didn't feel a thing. Not for many years." The scene that follows is a haunting one, as the narrators enters another train, all the while watching the snow out the windows and feeling the spectral presence of "the cancelled life dreaming after me. Yes, a ghost. A vestige. Something remaining." The narrator decides to follow a man off the train and into a laundromat. In a short sequence, the man takes his shirt off and washes it and then confronts the narrator, noting he was on the train. "I turned away because my throat was closing up. Suddenly I had an erection. I knew men got that way about men, but I didn't know I did. His chest was like Christ's. that's probably who he was." Is this an ironic way of beginning the cleanout process? Christ in a laundromat? Is that where the rebirth cycle begins?

After getting back on the train, more hallucinations follow. Words like, "When I coughed I saw fireflies." But there's a strange moment of clarity which comes here: "I know there are people who believe that wherever you look, all you see is yourself. Episodes like this make me wonder if they aren't right." And it's these swings from believing that he's followed Christ into a laundromat to sensing he's watching monsters dragging themselves upstairs at the Savoy that begin to move his vision away from himself. By the end of the chapter, Michelle has left him and committed suicide, and he ends the section with this haunting recollection about abortion, or perhaps about aborted love: "I know they argue about whether or not it's right, whether or not the baby is alive at this point or that point in its growth inside the womb. This wasn't about that. It wasn't what the lawyers did. It wasn't what the doctors did, it wasn't what the

95

woman did. It was what the mother and father did together." And there, some bit of responsibility and connection starts to take root.

"The Other Man" and "Happy Hour" speed the narrator to rock bottom. First, in "The Other Man," we see his meeting with the guy from Cleveland, who claims to be from Poland, and then his going home with the woman who had been married for four days. And finally, his pursuit of the aptly-named belly dancer, Angelique. "Happy Hour" appropriately ends in a bar in Pig Alley, Seattle. "People entering the bars on First Avenue gave up their bodies. Then only the demons inhabiting us could be seen. Souls who had wronged each other were brought together here. The rapist met his victim, the jilted child discovered its mother. But nothing could be healed, the mirror was a knife dividing everything from itself, tears of false fellowship dripped on the bar. And what are you going to do to me now? With what, exactly, would you expect to frighten me?" It's rock bottom for Fuckhead—a disorienting place where he sits with a nurse with a black eye and remembers a moment when he almost killed a man at a library earlier on. It ends with the narrator considering that he may not be human, that he's just taking bigger and bigger pills. It's also his nod to Matthew 7:6 and not casting your pearls before swine in Pig Alley.

Mercifully, the next chapter, "Steady Hands at Seattle General," takes the first step to recovery. The narrator shaves his roommate, Bill, and I can't help but connect the character to Bill Wilson, founder of Alcoholics Anonymous. In the penultimate chapter, dialogue drives the story. Bill tells the narrator that he's left wrecked cars behind—flashing back to where we began the ride of Jesus' Son in "Car Crash." After the narrator comments that the hospital is a playpen, Bill responds with the following:

"I hope so. Because I been in places where all they do is wrap you in a wet sheet, and let you bite down on a little rubber toy for puppies."

"I could see living here two weeks out of every month."

"Well, I'm older than you are. You can take a couple more rides on this wheel and still get out with your arms and legs stuck on right. Not me."

"Hey. You're doing fine."

"Talk into here."

"Talk into your bullet hole?"

"Talk into my bullet hole. Tell me I'm fine."

The first part of Matthew 7:6 states: "Do not give dogs what is sacred..." As I concluded my reading of *Jesus' Son,* I was struck by Bill's line about the rubber toy for puppies. His reminder is that life is cyclical and finite, and that's it's time to step off the ride and leave the slovenly, cycle of addiction and dark holes behind, especially as you're staring into one in someone's else's face, as you would in a group recovery meeting. This scene of looking into the bullet wound evokes the moment in the New Testament (John 20) when Jesus implores St. Thomas, the doubter, to examine his wounds to prove his identity. "Because you have seen me, you have believed; blessed are those who have not seen and yet have believed" (John 20:29). The narrator, the perpetual doubter, has to look and acknowledge the abyss before his eyes and with his steady hands shaving Bill at Seattle General.

Losing Denis Johnson in 2017 was a massive, irreparable loss. It's hard to imagine a writer with his depth, range, and originality. And, as I look back at this little masterpiece of a book on its thirtieth publication anniversary, I'm grateful for this dark, yet honest journey of an American drifter and dreamer, as he makes his way through the belly of the beast of his addictions, demons, and delusions, to be resurrected as a writer, worker, and weirdo. Denis Johnson tapped into something personal and eternal with *Jesus' Son,* and it's going to provide epiphanies for generations of readers to come. That's something to be grateful for, a pearl of a book for a world in need of reunion, recovery, and redemption.

MY TWO AND ONLY

CARLA MALDEN

Excerpt from My Two and Only, *a novel that explores the heart and mind of a West LA woman who finds herself gripped by the widowhood status that has so defined her life for the last decade…even as she falls in love again.*

Eleven p.m. on a Friday in September. Two people driving through the Jack in the Box on Santa Monica Boulevard. That Westside no-man's land of uninspired low rises, a Cost Plus, and a Porsche dealership. Neither one of them has hit a drive-thru in forever, which means for her, since her kids were little, a good fifteen years; for him, a good two weeks, maybe ten days. She's in her reliable Volvo wagon, overdue for a wash. He's got the top down on his sporty, two-door Audi, an emblem of his balls-out divorced life. He'd considered a Corvette but landed on a more grown-up car—still a convertible meant to guarantee an endless queue of women prancing through his single life.

In truth, all but one of the women who slid into the passenger seat requested that Brian put the top up.

"I've paid a fortune undoing years of sun damage."

"The pollen count is off the charts."

"The sun is so…sunny."

"You don't want to see what happens to my hair when it's muggy."

"My hair doesn't do well when there's zero humidity."

"I just spent an hour at Dry Bar getting my hair blown out."

"My hair…"

"My hair…"

"My hair…"

Brian spent an awful lot of time putting the top up. Even so, he was compelled to put it back down after every lousy date. An obstinate declaration of independence.

On this night, he'd taken his date to the Pantages Theater in Hollywood to see a revival of *Jersey Boys*. It made him feel old that this was a revival—the revival of a show celebrating a band he remembered from real time. He had a vague memory of taking a date to see the original *Jersey Boys*, let alone the original Four Seasons, but he swept it from his mind; too many degrees of déjà vu all over again.

This was his third date with Kimberly, but the first time he picked her up. Unlike the days of "Sherry Baby," internet dating required neutral territory.

After two dates, Kimberly relaxed her guard. She told Brian where she lived.

She studied the Audi waiting out front. "It's a little windy. My hair will end up sticking to my lip gloss."

Brian's hand fidgeted in his pocket, finding a handkerchief for her to wipe off the candy apple gloss, but thought better of it. He put the top up.

When the lights came up at intermission, she turned to him. "I never really liked the Four Seasons," she said. Brian waited for her to add "until tonight."

She didn't.

They'd planned on a late dinner after the show, but Brian pleaded a headache and drove her home. Scratch Kimberly.

After the show, he dropped her at her door, put the top down, and headed west. It had been four years since he'd moved out of the house he shared with Liz, his wife of twenty-six years, but it was still hard to call this little apartment home. Tonight, it was too depressing to head straight there. He turned into the Jack in the Box.

The line of cars inched up. He glanced in his rearview mirror. Illuminated by the glow of the giant Jack was the face of the woman in the car behind him. It was a face that looked exactly like he felt after four years of being divorced, after four years of dating, after one post-divorce relationship he'd hoped might be something but turned out to be less than nothing impersonating something. It was a face that looked like he felt after spending the evening with a woman who never really liked the Four Seasons and who was, with arms folded across her chest, determined not to change her mind.

It was also a face whose tears he wanted to dry.

Brian stared into the rearview mirror. The woman started to sing, along with the radio, he presumed. They both had their windows down, ready to talk to Jack. He thought he could hear her. Singing. Crying and singing at the same time.

He couldn't take his eyes off her. "A cheeseburger and fries," he said.

He drove ahead to the pick-up window. The smell of hot grease wafted from the bag. He handed over the money. "Can I pay for the car behind me?"

"Huh?" said the kid at the window, like he just woke up.

"I want to pay for the woman in the car behind me."

The kid yelled over his shoulder. A garbled answer came back.

"We can't do that."

"Can you double check? May I speak to the manager?"

More yelling. More garbling.

"Okay. It's cool."

"Great," said Brian.

"Do you know her?" the kid asked. This was as exciting as his night was going to get.

"No," said Brian.

"Cool," said the kid. "She ordered a taco."

"That's it?"

"Give her a milkshake, too. Chocolate."

The kid grinned. He was into it now. "What do you want me to say to her?"

"Tell her…" Brian had no idea. "Tell her the guy in the car in front of her hopes she has a good night…No," he corrected himself. "Tell her the guy in the car in front of her hopes her night gets better." That was feeble. And forced. But he meant it. He hoped the kindness of a stranger might dam the tears and amp up the singing.

Brian paid for her order and drove on. The traffic was heavy for late at night; he couldn't make a right into the flow. He sat there, waiting for a break in the cars. Suddenly, someone was standing beside his car.

"Why did you do that?" she said. "Are you part of some weird pay-it-forward cult or something?"

"You're welcome," he said.

She wiped a tear from her cheek, not daintily, but with the whole flat of her hand. Her cheeks were flushed and blotchy.

"How come you did that?" she asked.

"You looked like you needed a chocolate milkshake."

A tear traced a path down her cheek. "Well then," she said. "Thank you."

"You're welcome."

She started back toward her car.

"Just a second," he said. "I'd like to enjoy your enjoying it if that's possible. I'm not a weirdo or anything. I promise. We can just sit inside and eat our food and you can drink your shake and then that's it. Or you can tell me why you're crying if you like. Whatever you like."

Charlotte rolled it over in her mind. He looked too much like Richard Gere to be a stalker. Same half-smile. Open, accessible, but holding back a droll secret for later. Same twinkle. His oval glasses mimicked the curve of his jaw.

"Fine," she said. It was the least likely thing she ever said in her entire life.

"Fine," he said.

"But you're wrong. You are a weirdo. By definition. Normal people don't buy milkshakes for strangers."

They circled back into the parking lot. As they carried their bags inside, Charlotte looked down at her sweats. Her pants were on their fourth wear, and there was a drying splotch on her sweatshirt that looked suspiciously like snot. She made no excuse. It was after eleven p.m. at Jack in the Box. Any excuse would have been redundant.

The man springing for her milkshake was duded up. This was the end of an evening out for him. A monochromatic study in gray: silver hair, pewter eyes, heathered sport coat. He was taller than he looked behind the wheel of that low-to-the-ground sportscar. A whiff of aftershave—slightly spicy, slightly citrus—wafted.

They sat near the window. The table wanted a spritz of something grease cutting. Charlotte eyed the surface, then carefully set her taco on top of its bag.

A clutch of giggly high school girls squirmed at the next table, folding a leg under a leg, twirling hair, picking at chipped nail polish.

"He must know we're high," said one. "He put extra hot sauce on our tacos."

The others craned their necks to check out the guy behind the counter. He'd fallen back to his default state. Somnambulism.

Brian ate his burger and fries. Charlotte ate her taco and sucked her milkshake through the straw, which took some effort. She couldn't remember the last time she'd had a milkshake. It was kind of heavenly.

About halfway through she said, "What do you do?"

"You mean when I'm not plying strange women with milkshakes?"

"Are you implying that I'm strange?"

"Never," he said, "though strange might go nicely with weird."

She looked at him askance. Who was he trying to impress with the cutesy dialogue? A woman in snotty sweats.

"I'm a lawyer," he said.

"What kind?"

"Environmental."

"Like Erin Brockovich?"

"Exactly. Except it's against my principles to use cleavage in the courtroom." He dragged a fry through ketchup. "May I start again?" he said. "I don't know why I'm saying these obnoxious things. It's not me."

"Who is it?"

"Some crazy version of me. He's come out for the sole purpose of saying stupid things ever since…"

"Ever since…?"

"Ever since my divorce."

"Oh," she said. She slurped the last of her milkshake.

"It's so clichéd. Embarrassingly so."

"At least you don't drive a real true sports-car sports car. That would have been a cliché too far."

"Agreed," he said, grateful he'd thought better of the Vette.

"How long have you been divorced?" She didn't usually ask follow-ups.

"Four years. It wasn't technically a gray divorce. It started out as more of a salt-and-pepper one." He ran his fingers through his silver hair. "The last four years did this." He nodded toward her shake. "Want another one?"

She shrugged: why not?

He returned from the counter with one for each of them. "I like that you're having a second milkshake," he said.

"Why?"

"I don't know. I guess since I've been dating..." A little shudder shot through him at the word. "Since I find myself in the dating world again, I've noticed that women don't eat like normal people. At least not on dates."

"How do they eat?"

"Like they're not one bit interested in food. Like eating is a nasty chore."

"Hmm," she said, considering.

"Why is that?"

"You're asking me? Of the two milkshakes?"

"Yes, please. Elucidate."

"First of all, I didn't even know that was a phenomenon. Second of all..." she thought for a minute. "Women are self-conscious about their bodies in ways men will never understand. Including what they put in them." She poked the straw into the crisscross slot in the plastic top.

He smiled.

"That didn't come out right," she said. "Let's just say, maybe some women think eating looks...unfeminine."

"Not you?"

"Not me," she said, picking a stray shred of cheese off the paper and popping it in her mouth. "You?"

"Absolutely not," he said. "I think it looks human. What's more human than stuffing your face?"

"Am I stuffing my face?" she asked. "'Cause that doesn't actually sound all that...attractive." She didn't care if he found her attractive, but she couldn't think of any other way to put it.

"No, you're not. You're eating like a person."

She nodded. Fair enough.

"How about you?" he said.

"How about me, what? Am I a person?"

"Are you…divorced?" he asked.

"No," she said. "I'm a widow." She watched for the look, the look to which she had become inured—part shock, part pity, part oh-shit-what-do-I-say-now.

He said, simply, "I'm sorry."

"Eight years," she said. That was more than she normally volunteered.

"Wow."

"Yeah," she said. "Wow." As though she were experiencing the revelation along with him. Groundhog Grief Day.

"Your husband must have been really young."

"Forty-four."

"Wow." He didn't ask what happened. Somehow (and this he would always tell people when he relayed the story of that night) he knew he'd find out sooner or later. They were going to be friends.

"She wanted it," he said. "The divorce." Charlotte didn't tell him he had just read her mind. "She wanted out for a long time," he said.

"What happened?" She couldn't believe she was asking such a personal question, but it didn't feel too personal. It felt curious. Which she was. Surprisingly.

"Someone convinced her that she hated me."

"Who?"

"Well," he said. "First, it was her therapist. Then, it was the man she was cheating on me with. Lastly, it was her new husband."

"Wow," said Charlotte.

He looked her in the eye. "All the same person."

"Double wow."

He was having trouble opening another packet of ketchup. She took it from him, located the slash, and squeezed the ketchup onto the napkin he was using as a plate.

He fiddled with the empty packet. "I thought we'd just be separated for a while, like a phase."

"Like puberty?"

"Like puberty."

"Nobody wants to get stuck in puberty," said Charlotte.

"I was willing to try to fix things," he said, "for way too long."

"That was…" She wasn't sure exactly what that was—generous and forgiving, or misguided and masochistic.

"The therapist thing…" she said. "Isn't that against the rules?"

"I think so. But it happens… It happened."

"What kind?" she said.

"What kind of what?"

"Of therapist?"

"Jungian."

Charlotte played with her straw, drawing it in and out of the milkshake. It squeaked against the slits in the plastic lid.

"I can't really blame her therapist. She wanted a bigger life," he said. "I guess I always knew that."

"Did she get one?"

"Yes, by LA standards," he said. "He's the therapist to the stars. Gwyneth has him on speed dial. A bunch of people like that."

"There's only one Gwyneth."

"So we're told."

"Do you think her sessions are more interesting than normal people's?" Charlotte wondered. "Gwyneth's, not your wife's."

"I never thought about it," he said.

"They must be…glowier," she said.

"And she probably brings him green smoothies."

"There are definitely green smoothies involved."

He stuffed three fries in his mouth, in defiance against green juice. "And you?" he asked. He took off his glasses and cleaned them with a napkin. "What do you do?"

"I'm an interior designer. I'm not saving the planet or anything."

"Neither am I. Trust me," he said. "I couldn't do what you do."

She shrugged.

"I couldn't," he said. "Literally. I'm colorblind."

She laughed—so hard that milkshake went down the wrong pipe. She coughed and sputtered and actually spat a little into her napkin in order not to choke to death.

"Are you okay?" he asked, leaning across the table, at the ready.

She nodded vigorously, gave him the thumbs-up. When she could breathe again, she said, "Maybe I should reconsider not eating in front of people." She dabbed her eyes with a napkin.

"What kind of colorblind?" she asked.

"What?"

"Which kind of colorblindness do you have? Red-green? Blue-yellow?" She lowered her voice. "Or, God forbid, total absence?"

"You know this stuff?"

"Color looms large in my profession."

"Of course," he said. "Red-green."

"Christmas must be tough."

He laughed. "It's not so bad. I can tell, for example, that the stuff dribbling down your sweatshirt is brown."

"You can't take me anywhere," she said. She swiped at her sweatshirt with a used napkin, smearing the smudge.

He gestured around the place. "Clearly." Then added, "I'd like to try though." He shook his head. "There I go again. I don't mean for everything I say to come out sounding like a line. It's like when I signed the divorce papers, they implanted a chip in my brain. A smarm chip. I swear, it's entirely out of my control." He took a deep breath. "I just meant, maybe we could have dinner at a place where the food comes on a plate."

"Wow, you have real delusions of grandeur, don't you?"

"A guy can dream."

"China plates?" she said.

"Why the hell not?"

"I don't date," she said.

In retrospect, she liked to remember a fleeting look of disappointment. But he didn't miss a beat. "That's a relief," he said. "It's a horrid pastime."

They headed back to their cars, tossing their trash along the way.

"Do you come here often?" she asked.

"Never. And you?"

"Same."

That happened to be the truth. Again, after the fact, they would think of it as kismet. In the moment, however, they looked at each other and said, simultaneously, "Liar."

"By the way," he said, "I would never waste my time plying a normal woman with a milkshake."

WRITING FROM SIMPSON & STARN WORKSHOPS

Cal Prep

Contra Costa County Juvenile Hall (Mt. McKinley High School)

Emery High School (two workshops)

Girls Inc. of Alameda County (two workshops)

Northgate High School

SIMPSON FELLOWS, UC BERKELEY ENGLISH DEPARTMENT

Uttara Chintamani Chaudhuri (Girls Inc. of Alameda County)

Naima Karczmar (Girls Inc. of Alameda County)

Mehak Faisal Khan (Northgate High School)

andy david king (Contra Costa County Juvenile Hall)

Ryan Lackey (Cal Prep)

IRIS STARN FELLOWS, SAINT MARY'S COLLEGE OF CALIFORNIA, MFA CREATIVE WRITING

Camila Elizabet Aguirre Aguilar (Emery High School)

Carla Blackwell (Emery High School)

Molly Montgomery, Emery High School English Teacher

David Wood, Northgate High School English Teacher

STILL LIFE: FRUIT TART

ALEXIA FLORES (CAL PREP)

Your deep golden brown
    crust reminds me of summer
Your colors
    appetizing
Your smooth, creamy custard the
    cherry on top
Your soft fruit
    pairs well with your crisp shell
Your garnishes never
    fail to surprise me
You're cherished
    whether the weather is hot or cold
You're divine
    during the day or night
I savor every bite and start losing
    track of time

ON SELENE AND ENDYMION, AFTER ALBERT AUBLET

AQUETZALLI POPOCATL CAHUANTZI (CAL PREP)

She visits him every night.
Bright and beautiful,
look: shine
down on him.
Is he aware
(she, still, is there)
Is he aware
she visits him every night
when he sleeps
serenely—she casts a spell:
keep him forever
be young forever
sleep forever
under pale moonlight.

THE DREADHEAD LOVE JOURNEY

DANIEL MORGAN (EMERY HIGH SCHOOL)

As he rides the BART to her hurt heart
He sits back in the seat with open brown eyes
Surrounded by dominant darkness
He wonders why that is
His mind shows him his past
Like he's watching TV as he scrambles for the remote

While she waits for him, she reminisces
About the path her parents took
She braids her hair with hope
That they take the same steps
Cornrows in the shape of a heart
She hopes he likes it

He loves it
From the roots
To the ends

Now, he leaves
Her presence
On a bus
Sitting next to
The last 6 hours

He loves the compassionate,
comfortable conversation
He and Memory are having

A row behind him sits two boys
Named Trauma and Trouble
The whole ride
They attempt to torment him

He doesn't give in
He blocks it out
And continues to enjoy
The immaculate conversation

THE TREE

JAZMIN ROBERTS (EMERY HIGH SCHOOL)

All this terrible tree ever did was bloom hate,
Until the fair flower showed it the looming love it never gave.

All the tired tree did was bloom horrid hate,
Until the battered boy gave it a name.

All the troublesome tree ever did was bloom hate,
To cover up the fact that it never caved—

All the tactless tree ever did was bloom bombastic hate,
Until the mellow marsh swallowed its face.

All the trifling tree did was bloom hate—
Until the wicked woman who grew him,
Was down in the gregarious grave –

All this tree ever knew how to do
    was
           bloom
                hate

HEARTBROKEN, BUT WHOLE

ZACH SMITH (EMERY HIGH SCHOOL)

The more we grow closer the more we grow apart. Seems like the love you had has been pierced by the aim of a dart. Even though I have gone from your heart forever, you, for me is how true love starts.

RESPECT

KAYLA PAUL (EMERY HIGH SCHOOL)

I rose from a garden of niceness
I rose from a garden of sadness
I rose from a garden of madness
I rose from a garden of kindness
I rose from a garden of love
I rose from a garden of hate
I rose from a garden of power
  I rose from a garden of reconstruction
I rose from a garden of heaven
  I rose from a garden of roses
    I rose from a garden of brutality
    I rose from a garden of deconstruction
    I rose from a garden of sex
    I rose from a garden of lust

BARBED

STERLING STYMANS (EMERY HIGH SCHOOL)

the
gun fired
chains at the
ankles of others.
the girl braided her
hair with the shackles from
her ankles. she took a bart to
her past, call her the angel of death
with the haunted halo twisted and turned
with bullets and barbed wire hanging above her
head. she swims in a red river of guilt and blood shed,
the tree grew and bloomed rebellion, some biggie smalls
booming from the low rider on a street named heaven.

OLD STREETS

JOSIAHA BALTRIP (EMERY HIGH SCHOOL)

I swim in a river
full of lost souls
with a weight
on every limb of my body
waiting for the day
of my victory to lift me up.

I took BART
with my head in the sky
waiting to be
taken to a place
named Memory Lane
where I grew up.

On the way there
I stalked the lowrider
turning on a street
named Ridelow
blasting Keith Sweat
with its butt screeching
in the darkness
blood stains
in the street, its driver
tattooed his eyelids
up with flames
because he survived

the house fire
that left his family
with nothing but trauma.

The trees bloomed cameras
watching over colored people hanging
outside their homes.

One girl on the BART
braided her hair
with the thought
of her boyfriend
waiting on her to get
to his house. There I found
myself at Memory Lane

I hopped out of the BART
to some people
arguing over a female
and it ended
with a finger
on the trigger

TATTERED FABRIC OF MEMORY

VINCENT TANFORAN (NORTHGATE HIGH SCHOOL GRADUATE)

The loss was no surprise. Neither is an earthquake, living on top of the San Andreas fault, but for all our level-headed predictions of the Next Big One, we cannot feel the impact rattle in our bones, nor see the place we once called home enveloped in rubble, until it hits. Death scoffs at our feeble efforts to rationalize. We could not anticipate the aftermath of Po Po's death, no matter how long we had been expecting it. What was another hole in the tattered fabric of our family?

The day of her passing, we tried our best to plaster Band-Aids on the scars of generational trauma. I made polite small talk to my estranged aunt and uncle; bore the snubs of my younger cousins, who had all but forgotten me in the past year of post-transition seclusion from my conservative relatives; submitted to hugs from Gung Gung, who seemed happy enough in the unfeeling purgatory of senility. What were these petty sacrifices to the one happening in the next room over, that of a human life?

As I opened the door to her room, I felt as though I had stepped out of time. I was a child again, carefully climbing the cement steps leading to their apartment—number 17, at the end of the balcony, doorway flanked by skinny trees planted in water jugs—only to find it empty. Gone was the rust-colored armchair, the perpetually sticky kitchen table, the ancient nubby couch with its broken springs. Discolored patches of water damage were now laid bare to the light of day without the colorful drawings that had once covered them. The tapping of rainwater on the roof turned sinister, no longer a comforting background noise, but the sound of footsteps approaching at an inhumanly even pace. Dissonance between memory and reality can be a shocking thing. In her presence, all I felt was absence.

Yet, it is only in absence that I have come to understand her. Dementia struck five years earlier than the mixture of health conditions that eventually ended her life. Seemingly overnight, I was wiped from her memory and left with my own memories of her altered by the premonition of future loss. In life, she always seemed to be keeping something back, so that I only saw one side of her. To me, she was always the perfect grandmother: baking cookies, sewing clothes, crocheting piles upon piles of hats. Though it couldn't have occurred to me at the time, in hindsight I wish she had been less than perfect. I wish I had seen her cry, if only to even the score for every "big girls don't cry" I heard from her as a child. Any display of vulnerability then would have lent her memory a new degree of reality.

Language was the invisible barrier surrounding her. Though she spoke English with Gung Gung and their children, their relationships always had the undercurrent of translation with her. For every substitution of "white lemons" for vitamins, "loctor" for doctor, who can say what else was left unsaid? My first word was *aap*, Cantonese for duck. Po Po, Gung Gung, and I would go walking in the park next to their apartment to watch the ducks. I don't remember any of this, of course, but there is another path where I grew up speaking Cantonese. I found Gung Gung's Cantonese books, heavily annotated and gathering dust, but I never heard them hold a conversation. Perhaps his born-and-raised Pennsylvania German Americanness was too permanent, an indelible stamp against him that no amount of language courses could erase. She could love him only in English. I want to believe that, if only I had learned her language, I would have been admitted to her inner sanctum, able to meet the hidden self she carried with her from Vietnam. But dementia is a cruel beast. It has no sense, and answers no pleas, knowing only the *snip-snip* of scissors into the fabric of time. Not long after she forgot me, she forgot her native language, and with it a part of her being.

From Guangdong to Da Nang fleeing Mao, to Pittsburgh following the American soldier to Seattle to Long Beach to Seattle again to Long Beach again to Porterville to Concord, still following his whims, out of work and into a one-bedroom apartment, how many possible lives left behind? Who left us on January 19, 2023—Ngoc Lan or Shirley?

I knew one iteration of her, while she only knew one iteration of me. Both of us have lived two lives, meeting each other only in one stage of metamorphosis. Locked in our respective places in time, we will never know each other more than that. I will never get to come out to her. She will never get to give me the long-promised ball gown for my eighteenth birthday. When I cried that day in the car driving home, it was for the missed connections and our inability, through circumstance rather than fault, to understand one another. Five years now I have been a stranger. For that, I have shed my tears and made my peace in equal measure.

When I think of her, I see myself and at the same time I see her, blurry, an overexposed photo on the other side of a mirror. Even in my recognition, the old barrier still rises between us, the gulf of understanding made permanent by death. With mutual understanding impossible, it is all I can do to remember. The Po Po of my memories, incomplete as she may be, is all that I have left.

UNDERGROUND

MONA SHARIFF (EMERY HIGH SCHOOL)

The year is...actually I don't remember what year it is, no one really knows anymore, it's the least of our worries. Shaking her head disappointedly, Naila shut her journal close and put her makeshift pen down beside it. Her pen was about the size of a toothpick with her ink being gasoline she found outside. That was the only way to survive in California now.

"Naila you should get some rest, tomorrow is going to be a long day for every Californian," said Mira, Naila's younger sister.

"Yeah you're right," Naila said, as she kissed her little sister goodnight. Naila thought to herself as she was falling asleep, *I need to make the most of that hour. It's going to be the only way we survive this mess. It's me and Mira.*

The first thing Mira sees as she still wakes up is Naila putting on her gear. Naila's gear covered her from head to toe with black rubber shoes and gloves, an oxygen tank attached to the back of the protective wear, black goggles, and everything else white. "You know you're only allowed to go out for an hour, right?" Mira said while handing her older sister the timer that was set for an hour and began ticking once it sensed an environment that was 2,000 degrees Fahrenheit or more.

At 3:58 pm the feedback from the speakers in other underground bunkers screeched, everyone in California lived in bunkers ever since the incident. The passive-aggressive female announcer read her daily script, *"Good afternoon residents of California, years ago the incident happened. This caused California to become inhabitable and the government for years now has graced you all with protective suits. These suits can endure approximately one hour outside. Your hour begins in 10, 9, 8..."* Naila looked from the speakers and back to Mira *"6, 5, 4"*, "Yeah, I know. I can run, that can save us. I'll see you soon." Naila smiled as she began to open the first hatch of their underground bunker.

Naila stepped out and was greeted with black smoke filled with the lives and memories of people. The sky was orange and the clouds were thin yet blood red. The buildings were in ruins and heaps of unrecognizable junk were scattered everywhere. *I need to find a radio but that would be a long shot. No one but the rich owned radios but they left California years ago.* Naila began to look up toward the red sky thinking to herself. *If I could find one then we can learn the truth about what's happening outside of California. Who knows maybe today we can find our one ticket out of this place.* Then, the sounds of a stampede cut her daydream short. Naila was a second early and the race for resources began. The leaders of each underground bunker ran out with their own protective suits. Some died right away because of a possible suit malfunction and others died by getting stomped on by the crowd. Naila focused on survival and ran as far as she could away from everyone else, people became violent when trying to get what they want. *I guess all that running years ago really did pay off,* Naila thought to herself. Naila saw something that looked like a burned house that was two or three blocks down. *It could be sturdy enough to rummage through,* she thought to herself.

She got there in no time and kicked down the burned door, it wasn't that hard. She took a glance at the entrance and tried to sort out what parts could be used. To the left of her was what looked like a kitchen because of the racks that were left inside a burned black box. The ground was covered in dust, ashes, and sorrow that stuck to her rubber shoes. Naila managed to get to the second floor of the building and ended up in a room that had wood ashes. Naila studied ashes for months just to get clues as to what could be useful to her and her little sister. She was about ten minutes away from the bunker. Naila checked her timer and saw that she had twenty-five minutes to get back home. Naila needed to further investigate and in the hopes of bringing something back, she started to rip the room apart. She tore the dull insides of the walls and gave herself five minutes to continue to rummage through things. Eventually, she was inside the walls and used a light to continue looking. She decided that she could take back some dirty drapes she found inside the walls and turned toward the exit of the house. *Nothing. I found nothing. At this rate, me and Mira won't survive another week.* While kicking dust, Naila's foot met with something hard. *Ow, what was that?* Naila thought to herself, intrigued. *I guess I could spare a few more minutes.*

Naila kneeled in a hurry to find what that was and get out of there, her suit was already thinning and she was getting warmer, she was breaking a sweat. She grabbed her prized possession, her sledgehammer she brought years back. Naila became excited and started hammering at the box she stumbled upon, *Maybe I can bring something back. There's no way this is a safe. I knew they existed but I never thought I would find one! This could be it. Maybe we'll finally find a radio.* Naila kept hammering back-to-back. *Even if it's broken we can make it work.* Finally, it hatched open and Naila had tears roll down her cheeks, she was disappointed. *All of that time was wasted on a few pieces of paper. I never should have thought we could escape this living hell.* Naila snatched the papers and ran toward the bunker. She checked the time and she had less than five minutes to make a ten-minute trip.

The heat was getting to Naila and her cracked lips begged for water. She didn't, no, she couldn't stop running. She could almost see the tiny black top that peeked through the ground. There Mira could help mend her injuries. She needed to make it back, for Mira. She couldn't deny it any longer, *I don't think I can make it.* She checked her arm once again, it read, 58:04 minutes. Her suit was thinner than plastic wrap and it started to stick like honey onto her skin. It burned as the plastic fused with her flesh.

Then the worst thing that could happen, happened. Her oxygen tank was at zero. *It was never designed to last until the last second, was it?* Naila couldn't inhale or the toxins of the outside air would kill her in an instant. *I'm not good at holding my breath.* Her timer told her she had forty-six seconds of life left in her. Her vision was blurry and her body no longer felt the burning heat. *Where am I? Why? Why does it have to be like this?* Naila said her first word out loud since her hour began, in a weak and lost voice the words, "Help, me," were whispered. Naila fell to the floor, with nothing but the image of Mira engraved onto her eyelids.

I'm sorry.

good memories on wet pavement

MIA MONTIFAR (NORTHGATE HIGH SCHOOL)

little hands
clutching tightly to a blanket
rosy nose
pressed against the glass
brown eyes
entranced by the gliding droplets
street lights
flicker in and fade out as they pass

faint music
heard above the vibrating hum
of the tires
splashing across the slick roads
rumbling thunder
cutting through the low thrum

dash of lightning
a strike of certainty for a second showed
once again gone
disappearing behind a curtain of gray

shimmering pavement
reflect red lights under clouded skies
quiet enchantment
carries her away with heavy-lidded eyes

[UNTITLED]

CHARLOTTE FEEHAN (NORTHGATE HIGH SCHOOL)

The ocean is still there
Salted winds across a bay
An empty, dark lagoon
A tide not come to stay
One tiny crab upon the shore
Silky sand within its clutch
A wave farther than far
But close enough to touch
I pass across the bridge
My mother starts to laugh
The burning in my throat
Quenched in a cool bath
I, for the first time,
Since I saw your deep deep blue
Exhale a soft breath
Touch the glass between us two
The ocean is still there
The water still alive
Things continue being
Outside the current of my eyes

STRAWBERRY LOVE

ARISTOTLE WEBBER (EMERY HIGH SCHOOL)

I wake up to the sunlight coming in from outside, it illuminates my room and I feel the warmth all around my body. My alarm goes off a little bit after I wake up, I turn it off and turn over and look at the ceiling. I think, I ponder about everything my life has led up to. I hear the birds chirping and think about the times where everything was simple and pleasant.

I get out of my bed and get ready for the day. I first take a shower and I feel the hot steaming water purifying my body. Each drop cleansing any bad energy or negativity I have built up from the past. I brush my teeth after and get ready for the day. I throw on my favorite lazy outfit, black sweatpants, my favorite red jacket, and my red sneakers. I open the door and the sunlight hits me, embracing me with every beam of warm light.

I start my journey to school. I walk through many streets and think about what the day has in store for me. What life has to offer me on this day. But on the way there I notice something, someone. I see a girl with a similar outfit. Black leggings, red jacket, shining red cherry shoes. She has pretty red lips and rosy red cheeks. I couldn't help but admire her beauty from a distance the entire way to school. I kept observing her, trying to understand how someone who seemed so perfect could be so close to me yet so far.

I get to class, and despite this being my most important class, I couldn't stay focused on my work. I had her on my mind the entire time, I couldn't get over her and I wanted to see her. Who was she? What was her name? Does she notice me? I need to find out soon, my heart is reaching for her. My mind is working differently, my heart beats sound like drums of love.

I try to get through class but it was hard. I try to stay focused on my work because my mind was elsewhere. Was she my dream? Was she my imagination? What is wrong with my heart? The teacher asked if I was okay but I didn't know what to say, I am okay but I'm lost in this feeling, this color.

Our class ends and I head to lunch. I see everyone, laughing, talking to their friends with their minds carefree. But I didn't know what to say, I didn't want to see all these emotions I couldn't understand. I needed to let my mind go, I need my mind to understand itself. I know I can't ask anyone here about this feeling. I think of a place where I would go in the past to let my mind wander through this river of life. I know the place, a tree at the far side of the building, a tree that seems to grow every time I pour my thoughts into it. I leave everyone behind and quickly get to where I need to be.

I arrive and sit down, I feel the emotions rush me. I had remembered before I left the house I had packed some strawberries. I open my backpack and pull them out. They reminded me of the girl that I had seen. So red and sweet, I wish she was here. Before I could take another bite, I drop a strawberry. I saw her, I saw her once again. Where was she going? Toward the library? No no, I can't miss this opportunity. I saw her walk in and I quickly pack my stuff and follow the star girl.

By the time I got there she already sat down. I'm breathing heavily, I'm watching her, observing all the little things in her. Her eyes told a story of someone who had nobody, who didn't have anything to share, no one to express themselves to. She looks up and notices me staring at her from across the hallway. Her eyes see through mine, her colors mixing into mine.

My face bleeds red. My eyes blank as ever, my mind is everywhere all at once. I panic and try turning around and walking away. In no way could I face her, face my feelings, and I then ask myself, "Did I ruin everything?" I try to get out but she calls for me. "Hey, is everything okay?" I turn around slowly and couldn't believe it was her reaching out for me at first. My heart drops, I didn't even process what she just asked me, I was assuming the worst, the most terrible scenario that could've happened right then and there.

I try to swallow my nervousness and I am able to manage just a wave. She points to a chair next to her and I walk over. My steps are heavy, every second feels like a century of nothing but anxiousness and anxiety. I pull the chair out, it felt like a thousand years had just passed by

I can finally admire her up close, I can truly observe her beauty up close and see every part of her face that I had not seen earlier that day. Everything was better, I couldn't believe that such beauty could get more beautiful with every second that passed by and I could feel my heart racing.

I pull out the bag of strawberries I had and pointed toward them. She nodded her head and we enjoyed it together. Almost no words were said, we just sat down and enjoyed the moment. I felt at peace, like a peaceful aura was protecting me from all the usual troubles I have.

After lunch ends, she guides me outside, we don't go back to our usual classes but we sneak out of the school. She takes me to a hill that I had never seen before, and we walk to the top. On top of the hill, sit a bed of strawberry vines. We sit beside each other and take a handful of strawberries and look into the distance. Maybe some things are left to be naturally found and not sought, and that's how I ended up here with her.

ROADKILL
EMILY CHAO (NORTHGATE HIGH SCHOOL)

Tension brings silence as company.
Hands grip tight at the steering wheel
Eyes dart around on the uninterrupted road ahead.
Lips slightly begin to part,
Bullets of rain pound at the roof
Words threatening to spill out.
The car, conspicuous in nature
And its rubescent body
Tires picking up,

Dark green trees and their trunks blur past the spotted window
No hints of stopping are awake.
Legs of the passenger curl tightly into her chest
Her arms wrapping around in self-comfort.
A sigh leaves the lips of the driver beside her,
So, she decides to exchange a word
But this leads to
An irritating, provoking ruckus filling the once tranquil air.
As words thrown at each other speed up,
The window emits a layer of cold,
The opaque sky covered by gray remnants of clouds.
The car hits a bump,
Jolting the two inside,
Eyes no longer on the road,
Now set on her familiar-yet-distant orbs.
He hesitantly searches for the familiarity inside of her
A painful realization,
It isn't there.
A foot slams down on the brake
A moment too late
Both bodies jerk forward
As the metal of the car is met with a *thump*.
Alarms set off in their minds,
Tiptoes make their way out the car doors
Bending over the world, two pairs of eyes lay upon
The still body of a defeathered, wingless creature
Pity and red runs deep through the white,
Silence.

"Is it dead?"
"Yup, I think so."

Surprisingly,
Surprise has no presence in their once-lively-but-now-dull eyes
Mirroring the deformed and lifeless clump of a bird,
They have already known.

THE MOST IMPORTANT THING THAT QUARANTINE TAUGHT ME

AMARI BOULWARE (GIRLS INC. ALAMEDA COUNTY)

The greatest thing that quarantine taught me was that it is okay to take time for yourself and that will help reveal who you are and what you're capable of.

Before quarantining my hairstyles would consist of ponytails, buns, and braids that my mother did. It would constantly make me feel like I wasn't good enough and that I was less than the other black girls in my school. Nobody made fun of me but there were many glances and snickers in my direction. For a long time, my hair would be straightened for most of the month. So, when I wore my natural hair out it would look strange and straight at some points because of the heat and the keratin treatments that I was getting. There were many moments when I wanted to chop it all off and I had many breakdowns where I would burst into tears. I would cry so much sometimes that I thought I was going to drown in my tears.

When quarantine hit and we all had to stay home and do all of our work online it made me lazy and sad because of everything that I couldn't do. One day I had finished washing my hair and had no clue what I was gonna do with it. Put it up, leave it down and hate the way I look or ask my mom to braid it. Those were my only options, and it was like picking the way I die. I didn't like any of my options so I just started parting my hair and braiding each part. It went like that for a few hours before I finished my whole head and while it wasn't the best hairstyle I had ever seen I finally felt like I wasn't a lesser being because I could finally do my hair. I tried many different hairstyles from then on and I just kept progressing. I knew that the hairstyles others would do were going to get more complicated and longer and more colorful and I was just gonna cross that bridge when I got to it. Doing my own hairstyles taught me that you have to be patient if you want something to come out properly, and not everything is going to go your way even if you spend a lot do time on it and you're just gonna have to be okay with that. When I figured out how to do my hair, I felt so relieved because I wasn't gonna be made fun of anymore, and while I would still have a breakdown here and there at least I would know how to do my hair.

[UNTITLED]

HINA YUEN (GIRLS INC. ALAMEDA COUNTY)

I fall in love too easily for someone who doesn't quite like me. With every post I see, and with every word I hear, my regret intensifies. I liked them since elementary school. Or more correctly, I used to like them in elementary school. It was puppy love, small crushes as kids that never happened and never mattered. I was infatuated with how cool they were, and how willingly they accepted me as a friend when I got left out. We had similar interests as kids, and I really doubt I actually liked them. I had far too many crushes for my crush to be true. How aloof and free you were, I admired you. You are unbothered by the world and that's what makes you pristine.

After losing touch in middle school, we only met each other Junior year. When we both transferred to the same school the same year, the perfect chance to be friends again, I didn't approach you. You were in my third-period class, and as a whole semester passed. I regret not talking to you in real life, even though we were not even five feet away from each other at times. I always wondered what kind of person you became. Were you someone who hadn't changed since then? That's impossible considering the years. Were you someone new in the face of a loved one I once knew? We were childhood friends, so how did you stray this far away? People I used to know stayed far away from me, and I regret not talking to them. I remember self-isolating unconsciously and not taking chances to show I wanted to be friends after people lost contact with me or avoided me without reason intentionally because someone didn't like me. I regret not talking to you in real life, but it was always too awkward to take a chance. It's not that I don't love my friends now, but I can't help but miss the idea of you as the person connected to my childhood.

You don't know me anymore either, I've changed as the years passed. But it almost feels like you don't know I exist when I make eye contact with you. You stare into my eyes, and I stare into yours for a brief moment when I walk into the class. A quick glance as I walk past and breeze by. You're always in your seat first, and I wonder where your class before and after the third period is, as I watch you walk away from me again and again. You don't think about me, but every day I think of you and what could've been if I lived another life.

I remember your unchanging account. The Instagram that stayed the same for years and the deleted posts of that empty account I've followed since elementary school. All the lost photos and pictures of memories you might not want people to see, and all the new memories I have seen as you changed without me. My heart yearns for you a little more with every smiling photo of people I don't know and people who make you one hundred times happier than I make you. I remember talking to you. Just two conversations, days apart in November. A whole bunch of small talk, but it was meaningful to me. And with every bit of information you divulged to me, I felt myself feel that familiar safe feeling with you again. I try to pacify my feelings, it might not even be love, just an infatuated obsession of curiosity. Maybe misplaced affection for someone I miss enough to cry. I fall for you a little bit more every time I stare into your eyes, which strikingly reminds me of a fish. Dead and unblinking, your solid eye contact and your dark black eyes that stare at me from a distance like the fish markets my grandparents would bring me to as a kid.

Everything I am is a part of someone else I've met and taken from. And from you, I've taken your kindness. Maybe even your lack of conversation skills, with how dry you were. Or maybe you were just reluctant to talk to me. Someone you know, who's latched on to you for far more than I should've. From a distance away I have admired you through the years, even when I've long forgotten what your face looks

132

like. I remember your features and your actions and all you have done for me and I admire your faults and childishness from a time long gone.

Junior year was supposed to be a fresh start from all the issues I had prior, and all the trauma related to quarantine times. So, it was a real surprise when you sat a few feet away from me one day out of the blue. I forgot about you, and I was shocked at how tall you've grown. Tall and intimidating, far too intimidating for my anxiety to handle. So I never talked to you. I never got to learn what your interests were, and I never got to hear of the people you loved. Yet all my attention in the back of my head revolved around the idea of you. It felt like a cotton candy haze, sweet, unclear, and most of all, sticky. Every time I think of something, I wonder about you and how you would react, and not you who has been warped in my head for years as details about you get lost and fuzzy. I berate myself when I start to hear my voice, in your wondered speeches and scenarios that I make up. I laugh with every story and every post you make, your laugh resonating in my skull as if it were a preacher spreading the words you say to all of my cells. Making me react on high alert every time you pass, and overly conscious of myself as you look at me and I look at you.

All the damage I've retained throughout the years that have weighed on me seems to disappear at the sight of you. You occupy my mind as if you were the very air I breathe. Yet I know I am insane when I haven't spoken to you for more than half an hour for almost a whole year. A whole semester has passed and yet I still know nothing about you. Even if I come across you playing basketball on my way to lacrosse practice, I can't bear to step up and speak to you even as we cross paths and brush shoulders, because I wouldn't want to disturb your fun with your friends with my somber demeanor.

I am insane, maybe for liking you, maybe for remembering everything you do. But I'm more insane for liking someone as boring as you. Not boring, maybe just plain, but you blend into the crowd, and yet I can still spot you clear as day. That might be why I like you because I'm utterly plain myself. I don't attract attention, and I can't talk to you. However, I show my care through the snacks I hand to you, and not even my friends in the same class. You aren't interested in anyone, and I don't know why I like you, I just do. Maybe that's all there is to infatuation.

A CACOPHONY OF ORANGE

NICK BIDDLE (NORTHGATE HIGH SCHOOL GRADUATE)

You lie awake. Soothing darkness swirls and pools in the
corners of the room, pushed there by the harsh light in the palm
of your hand. A light which absorbs your undivided attention,
and in return offers you safety from the darkness. Despite
the salvation offered by your metaphorical Library of Babel,
something's missing, something doesn't feel right—nevertheless,
you continue. The entire culmination of human existence,
millennia of knowledge, slide past your glazed eyes.

"M&M changes their mascot due to recent controversy, 8 dead in
school shooting, 10 tips to help you fall asleep."

All encompassing; all soothing. Your mind falls quiet, filled
with the apathetic consumption of hollow media—all of it real,
none of it can hurt you. You want to stop, you know nothing will
come from this, but you can't. To look away is to allow a thought
to form; a thought which cascades into awareness; awareness
that leads to guilt; guilt for your apathy; apathy for an angry
world; a world which seems to care so much.

"Right-wing cartoonist claims to be a victim of 'cancel culture',
Death toll in Ukraine continues to rise as civilian town is caught
in crossfire, A quick history of soft-shelled tacos."

People argue, a world divided. It's all so loud. A cacophony
of outrage. Bombs fall; somebody was cut off in traffic.

The world is on fire; someone's name was misspelled on their coffee. 216 shootings in five months; someone cuts their hair and changes their name. It's deafening. More connected than ever, but never more divided.

"Monumental case Roe v Wade overturned by Supreme Court, Texas mall shooter's 8 weapons were legally obtained, authorities say, An update on the latest TikTo—"

You sit in shock. The soothing darkness rushes over you, stealing your vision, pulling you back to reality. It all sinks in. Your phone's dead. It's so quiet.

WRITING FROM MT. MCKINLEY HIGH SCHOOL
CONTRA COSTA COUNTY JUVENILE HALL

AUTHORS IDENTIFIED BY INITIALS

Do you hear me? I don't think you hear me
Poetry ain't for me, it ain't in me
But I try, and I'ma try
I ain't gone complain, and I won't change
I want to go home, but the judge actin'
Like she don't know
I ain't into writing songs, but my feelings are going far
As I sit thinking in my room wishing I
Was seeing the stars
I noticed that my actions weren't worth it
All along
After school I'ma go to sleep, when I
Awake I brush my teeth
I read book after book, it's boring and gets boringer
I pray they release me back to my father
I'm sad here, this place makes me mad
Why the police always take me away
When I start gettin' to a bag

D. A. C.

When you close your eyes
You think of great memories
It's like your brain's full of flies
When the door closes on your history

K.

When I was free I could run
When I was bored I could play games
Now I think about doing that in my cell
When I'm not free it feels like hell
When I go to court I always get sent back
to my cell.

S. B.

I'm physically caged but my mind is free
From sins. The evil is not in me
Why satisfy them? I got the key
Why give up hope when I could see

S. T.

I was sitting in a shop, just made. I waited two months on the shelf. One day I saw a larger human and felt like he picked me up. I felt my feet spin to the cash register. After that I went outside where I started rolling down the hill until my feet rolled off and my frame snapped and the human went flying. Long story short, I had a broken tire and frame and my handlebars were gone. I went back to the shop and got fixed one week later. After that I was left in a dark garage until my next ride.

D. R.

When I hear success I think about power
A view where I can see the sun setting on the city
10 car garage filled with beamers and bentlys
My clothes fitted and my hair cut
My family straight
My friends straight
Everybody good

everybody around me got a purpose
everyone feel they worth
but naw let me get back to reality

the smell of metal
one wrong move the guards mad at me
doors closin
my buzzer goin off
dress code in order
they got me in a cage like I'm a dog
restless nights and cold days
jail food on rubber trays
you just wanna go back to sleep
back to my dream where I could fly away

M. C.

Red rose this
Red rose that
I'm the black one out the bunch
And that makes me *that* nigga

I. K.

A Letter to Hope

Dear hope,

Roses are red, violence is blue
My heart is dead; why aren't you?
I weep because I'm a monstrous creep
And when I sweep at you, you stay and don't decay

I must say, why do you stay?
Why don't you come at bay?
I guess you're here to stay

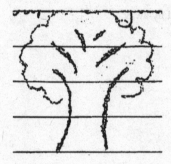

S. T.

You're growing up, you're not a little boy anymore
I feel as if it's time you figure it out some more
Jail is no home for you, stop thinking about others and
Think about you. Going down the right path will never
Go left again, spending more time with my family and my
Set of friends, you're so far away from home it feels
Like you won't make it back, you have support, and
You have goals, achieve them, be brave, be strong

And forever be positive, good things will come for all
My days that were cold, this road I'm stuck on isn't
Forever, but this is getting old. You promise you won't
Make mistakes know more, I know my choices were more
Than poor. Promise you won't make mistakes no more.

D. A. C.

Damns salvation all into segregation—
Redemption hits on like I slept in—

G. O.

When I think about freedom I think decisions,
the freedom to do what you want
When you want
The freedom to go where you want
Eat what you want
And see what you want
Freedom is the power to choose to be who you want to be around
To be who you want to be
To be free when you want to be free

M. C.

TWO NEW LITERARY PROJECT WORKSHOP ALUMS,

ONE SIMPSON FELLOW,

TWO STARN FELLOWS,

& ONE TEACHER

"MY LIFE HAD STOOD—A LOADED GUN...": ON TEACHING AT MT. MCKINLEY

ANDREW DAVID KING (SIMPSON FELLOW)

In the first session of my class at Mt. McKinley, I had my students read aloud, several times, William Stafford's poem "Remembering." What I wanted to prove to them was that a modest chunk of text on a sheet of copier paper could capture, like a photograph, the moment a human mind goes supersonic—the poem's speaker describes the exhilaration of running alongside a mountain range, a memory he says he carries with him in a tiny, cell-like box. We had no shared concept of "poetry," let alone a critical terminology, so I plumbed intuitions. What was the mood here? What was the feeling? You might not understand every sentence, but what's this speaker, speaking across space and time, talking about? A student answered with an offhand remark: "It should be illegal to make us read about freedom."

Paradox runs through McKinley and its parent institution, John A. Davis Juvenile Hall. As others who have taught for New Literary Project at McKinley have noted, it's both a prison and a school, but especially a prison. No one moves freely through any door; every interaction is monitored; the aesthetic is glass, cinderblock, and steel; the administration and the wards are, in an especially American way, racially distinct. Information travels in fits and spurts, clandestinely; only around my sixth class did I learn, from another teacher, that I was in the unit reserved for wards convicted of the most serious offenses. Learning happens, if it does, despite the carceral mood. Poets talk a lot about form, repetition, and formal constraints, but here, in the wards' strict schedules, these things are carried to logical extremes, and the result hardly makes

143

a sonnet. The rehabilitative mandate of the juvenile justice system battles with the shadow pedagogy of prisonership.

If *stanza* means "group of lines" as well as, in Italian, "room," we were inventing rooms inside of rooms, places where it might be possible to think again of freedom. Poetry itself feels like contraband in such a place—Pandora's box, Prometheus's fire. The students had nothing to lose; I had to demonstrate, over and over again in an experience that was somehow refreshing, why any of this mattered. At all. "I don't like books that look like the Bible," said one of my students, meaning books without pictures. "I like sports, I hate school, and I'm having fun right now," said another, when asked to state two truths and a lie in a brainstorming game. Even their disrespect showed wit and insight, the grist of literature. So we read Langston Hughes and Kafka; watched Tupac videos and talked about rhyme; compared Nas's patterns with Dante's *terza rima*; wrote stories in which we became objects and poems in which we borrowed each other's words. We clapped when each piece was recited, even if, as happened once, a student tore up his poem after he'd read its last line. He was afraid someone from court would see it.

His fear wasn't entirely unfounded. At the request of the school's correctional arm, two poems by one of the class's most committed and talented students, have been redacted from the portfolio of student work included here. As I left McKinley one afternoon, I overheard a probation officer remind a ward to make good choices. To enjoin youth to responsibly exercise agency while denying them their own voices is an approach I find puzzling. At the very least, I know it's there, that agency, glimmering inside their poems—and hopefully, too, under the dull sheen of despair that envelops carceral life, a hope that can take the form of anger.

A poet who'd taught at McKinley through a different program told one of my NewLit predecessors about his experience. *I've cried in that parking lot so many times,* he said. When I left my final class, I took a sprig of jasmine from the parking lot's bushes. It was early June, the sky overcast, things late to bloom after a long winter. That sprig, brown now, is still on my dashboard; sometimes I pick it up to see if it holds scent. "Some days I do this again and again," ends the speaker of Stafford's poem. Some days I do this again and again.

HUMAN TRAFFICING AWARENESS BAKE SALE
CARLA BLACKWELL (STARN FELLOW)

"You have to go higher on your side, Naomi." I was already the tallest person here at 5'10", but I still had to stand on the highest rung on the ladder, on my tiptoes to tape the left side of the banner on the building. "Perfect!"

The sign was bolded above the Alpha Kappa Theta building: Human Trafficking Awareness Bake Sale. I thought it was an odd phrasing, and more than that a strange way to fight against human trafficking, but I was just a pledge. I didn't get an opinion. The last part of the initiation was to pull off this bake sale.

I actually didn't want to join a sorority. It was a lot of extra work and time, without any college credit. However, sororities looked good on your resume. There were perks and the housing was cheaper. I could make connections through sororities, and I learned that many of my journalistic role models were Alpha Kappa Thetas. Having a degree was half of the equation of landing a good job, and the other half was making connections. If you were charming enough, qualified, and happened to have an AKT pin on your lapel, that just enhanced your chances.

Many of the other pledges had drunk the Kool-Aid of sisterhood and making a difference in society. It wasn't that they didn't really believe or that I was opposed to the community. I just wasn't a joiner. I felt like I was intruding and didn't really feel included. That could also be because I was one of the only black pledges in the sorority, but at a PWI, I was always one of the only black students around.

Sarah had mentioned that they had been trying hard to recruit WOC to their sorority and be *true allies to the cause*. I was a little weary about being their token black person, but Sarah seemed genuine and at least she was honest. Plus, the school counselor thought that joining a group would be beneficial to my mental health.

"You sure this is okay, but I don't want to do this again if you think it's crooked in twenty minutes," I leaned back slightly to look at the banner.

"It looks good," She assured me.

I looked behind me and saw a handful of students following a faculty member. Judging by his zip-up sweater with the school logo on it as well as his hat, I assumed it was a coach. He looked upset and yelled something at the students that made them cower away slightly. "What's that all about?"

Sarah looked at the scene and scoffed. "It's just an excuse for these student reporters to try to get a story in the newspaper. Four years ago a football player didn't come back after spring break and his body was just found. We all figured he just dropped out cause this guy took off last Christmas break for two months and while everyone was worried about him, he was living it up at some ski lodge in Colorado. I guess he must have gotten into a motorcycle accident or something."

Not surprising. I slowly climbed down the ladder, watching my feet touch each rung. "How are cookies and brownies supposed to raise awareness for trafficking," I questioned. Tina had tried on the right, but it was still askew. I climbed up on her ladder to fix it before she could ask.

Sarah smiled despite my snarky tone. "The proceeds of the bake sale go to charity. People like donating when they get something out of it. Plus, we sometimes raise thousands of dollars at these events. Anything helps."

I got down from the ladder and wanted to point out that it wasn't a donation, but an exchange of goods, but decided against it. I was doing well so far in the tasks they had assigned to us. I designed the sign, with strict instructions from Monica, with all of its colorful glue and confetti. It looked like a unicorn threw up on it, but it grabbed people's attention.

After all of the croquet games, game night, after party cleanups, quizzes about the history of sorority, and essays on what sisterhood means, this was the last step of the initiation. I do this and I'm in. Monica came outside and looked up at the sign. "It's too high. It needs to be brought down eight inches."

Monica was a force to be reckoned with. She stood three inches shorter than me, but her presence filled the area. All of the other pledges ran to her for approval on their tasks. I stuck my tongue out at her behind her back and Sarah smiled. Sarah and Monica were copresidents. Near exact opposites of each other. Monica was assertive, bold, and sometimes controlling. Sarah was just as confident, but kinder and more sympathetic. It made them perfect partners. Sarah was the shoulder to cry on when they had a problem and Monica was the one to fix it.

"Come on, don't make her do it again. I've had her up there for twenty minutes. I think it looks good," Sarah said. She draped an arm over Monica's shoulder. If anyone else had done that, they would probably end up with a broken wrist.

Monica crossed her arms. "It needs to be perfect. All of this. This is an event that goes back to the formation of AKT. Our founding sisters put together this event. We only do this once every four years. Some people might find it stupid." I swear she looked my way when she said this. "But it's important. It's to represent the sisterhood of our sorority and how we have each other's backs. This needs to be a lower, pledge." She had been giving these speeches on and off for the past week. As if they could forget that this was the most important day.

I resisted the urge to reply with a biting remark and simply nodded. I could tell that Monica didn't really like me, but Sarah championed me, so I knew it would come down to a pretty fifty-fifty chance if there was a deciding vote. The best I could do now was not try to screw it up. She swung her head to the other pledges lingering. "Tina, Jackie, you need to come with me. We need to bring up the tables and prepare them for Friday."

Monica strutted away with the two girls following her.

I sighed and climbed back up the ladder. Sarah gave her a cheerful thumbs up with an apologetic smile. "One more event, Nay!"

You would've thought that the president was coming to the bake sale with the way the girls acted. They prepared the cupcake batter days in advance. They taste-tested the different types of frosting and there was some kind of binder that went between the seniors holding some top-secret information. I heard Monica and Sarah discussing it with another girl while I was coming up to the basement with a dusty storage tub.

"Are you kidding me? Not him. His dad is a senator. Like full on DC senator."

"I know but I just thought—"

"No," Monica snapped at the girl and it brought me to a standstill. I was on the last step before they could see me coming up. I couldn't see them but I could hear Monica's circular pacing. "You weren't thinking. This is the one event we need to kill this year. This is a rookie move."

I heard Sarah chime in. "Mon, calm down. Polly didn't know okay? And you caught the mistake. Take a deep breath."

I walked out of the shadows and placed the storage bin on the floor. I felt the tension in the room slowly abate. Polly took this moment to scurry away from Monica's glare and I didn't blame her. "Sorry, it took me so long."

Monica narrowed her eyes at me but said nothing. She gave Sarah a pointed look and just walked off. Sarah looked at me apologetically. "She hasn't had caffeine yet."

PLANTING MOON

GRACE DECKER (NORTHGATE HIGH SCHOOL GRADUATE)

I forgot what clouds without a promise looked like
the size of an earthworm the
veins of your hand

What's a better fantasy than
growth for the sake of growth?

The 'you' in my head is bigger than anyone
could ever be and
it watches as what's left of you now
withers and dies.

So I'll keep losing my head on the bus
and think of clear rivers unmarred
by thousands of years' worth
of skeletons at the bottom
and thank the sun when I remember.

What I mean is that late spring feels
like throwing it all away for the promise of
a seared earth, of rampant expansion–
whether you like it or not.

EX(egesis)ODUS
Exodus/Exegesis

OLIVIA LOSCAVIO (NORTHGATE HIGH SCHOOL, ONCE UPON A TIME)

Do you ever
even just for a minute
wish you could drive your car off a cliff?

I shut up and park my car at sea level. Stuff my anger in a garbage
bag and hurl it at the ocean. It didn't work, so I start the car and burn
some rubber. Split the road in half and spin my wheels till the treads
stick like gum and ride the rims. Sparks on the divider line like a
match strike.

Do you ever just wanna light it all on fire?
To revel in the bone deep delight of watching it burn?
To let the excitement run so hot it singes the marrow?
To char yourself over an open flame?

149

It was always meant to end this way. Transformer lines hum funeral hymns like electric fences along the highway. I always wanted to be a bird on that singeing wire, to straddle life and death at the same time. Screaming toward that point on the horizon where the road meets the sky and explode there.

I gallop along God's curved bow. Tip of the arrow. Hit a bump and feel my wheels release from the pavement–that selfish, sticky tar that's kept me stuck my whole life. I always needed to fly. The pressure on the ground would have killed me. I had to shatter in order to breathe.

My splintered bones form new constellations–vestal flames forever white and burning.
The ocean and her shackles could never hold me. A million ever-exploding eyes watching amongst the sun and stars.

mediodía / shattuck

--camila elizabet aguirre aguilar (Starn Fellow)

the buslady   zigzags
a mascara wand over
her bottom lashes in the rearview
while the man
in ski goggles
screams "FUCK THE POLICE"
for the twenty-ninth time—
& pulls out a sandwich
with the crusts cut off

fat pigeons
people-watch
on telephone lines

150

```
        making wire dip
              up and down
                    like an EKG

        the cop
        speed wobbles
        on his segway
        —but still believes
        he is god—

        at noon, the stars
        count us

        & make up stories
        about how
              we
              got stuck
              like this
```

MONTEREY

ANDREW DAVID KING

Two letters in the morning made a gray day grayer. Breakfast
was included so we took the glass elevator down the atrium's
ribcage, gawked at the fake plants, the bullshit people in the
future would find. A man wobbled back to his table with an
omelet in each hand and a shirt that read *The Founding Fathers
Would Be Shooting By Now*. Smiling, grandkids at his side, white
golf shoes. Juice from concentrate in a dirty glass. Shooting at
who? The night before, my brother took a picture of a waterfront
motel, rundown, trailers from the sixties crowding the lot like
beached whales, wind snoring through the left-open hallways.

Long exposure: its security bulbs bleeding in the fog, some massive mother ship, government secret sliding into the public mouth. We walked the bike path that frozen summer, past a statue of Steinbeck, abandoned catamarans, a McDonald's made to look like an upscale restaurant so property values wouldn't sink. On our way home we stopped by the racetrack, then the mission at Carmel, where you could purchase an army of saints or ceramic Marys who would at least hold their hands out, beggar-like, to prove they were empty. At mass the sermon was about the parable where Jesus tells the rich man to give up all his possessions. Eventually I stopped listening and thought about the stained-glass rose in the churchfront, crooked for centuries from gravity, imprecision, someone's slight. The point was something about the use of figurative language in the Bible. Someone, I thought, had to have stood back and seen how malformed the shape was but judged it not worth fixing, or maybe unfixable. Now when I look at my brother's photograph it leaks the sadness of that year—we're nowhere in it, none of us—though I still think of a great, otherworldly ship leaving or arriving.

A TEACHER'S LAMENT

DAVID WOOD (ENGLISH TEACHER, NORTHGATE HIGH SCHOOL)

The time will come when teens will not delight
And raucous halls will only make me cry.
Youthful antics bring no laughter, simply spite
And venom's ire no matter how I try.
I know I will not miss the tests that turn
Our brains to mush, the calls for Bronco pride,
The purple prose that makes my stomach churn,
And passive voice—a fault I must deride.
That I am here brings many to remark,
Some others think that I have gone insane,
Though fiery youth does still ignite a spark.
Thus far my love has not begun to wane.
But I see the moment when I will sigh,
And slip silently off without goodbye.

JACK HAZARD FELLOWS

Fellows are selected by New Literary Project to receive summer fellowships, financial awards to celebrate and foster promising writers' projects in fiction, creative nonfiction, and memoir. The fellowship recipients are creative writers who are full-time high school educators teaching anywhere in the United States. Application details (eligibility, deadlines, and so on) may be found on the NewLit website.

2023 JACK HAZARD FELLOWS

William Archila
STEAM Virtual Academy
Los Angeles, CA

Ariana D. Kelly
Boston University Academy
Boston, MA

Victoria María Castells
Miami Arts Charter School
Miami, FL

Kate McQuade
Phillips Academy
Andover, MA

Leticia Del Toro
Campolindo High School
Moraga, CA

Tyson Morgan
Crystal Springs Uplands School
Hillsborough, CA

Elizabeth DiNuzzo
The Albany Academies
Albany, NY

Shareen K. Murayama
Henry J. Kaiser High School
Honolulu, HI

t'ai freedom ford
Benjamin Banneker Academy
Brooklyn, NY

Sahar Mustafah
Homewood-Flossmoor High School
Flossmoor, IL

Emily Harnett
The Haverford School
Haverford, PA

Ky-Phong Tran
Long Beach Renaissance High
School for the Arts
Long Beach, CA

Jeff Kass
Pioneer High School
Ann Arbor, MI

Vernon Clifford Wilson
Horace Mann School
Bronx, NY

THE PEACOCK

SAHAR MUSTAFAH

2023 JACK HAZARD FELLOW

West Bank, Palestine
2018

Feryal sits at the hotel bar and sips her sugary cocktail. Annoyed with the cumbersome fresh fruit garnish, she removes the plastic spear of sliced pineapple and strawberry and watches their juices soak into a tiny napkin the bartender gave her. He was much more amiable when he'd mistaken her for a tourist. As soon as she opened her mouth and spoke perfect Arabic, he nodded coldly at her order and set about blending her frozen virgin drink, casting glances over his shoulder.

Feryal swivels around and watches the hotel patrons. A white European couple sits in the lounge area, a private conversation drawing their bodies close, shutting out the rest of the world. A small group of hijabi women in stylish abayas and lavish couture purses, laugh and chatter above each other. They sip from the same tropical drink as Feryal's. She's the only woman sitting alone. Her neck flushes and she swivels back to the bartender.

In her peripheral vision, a man heads to the bar, his silhouette tall and slender. When he doesn't clear his throat or tap her on the shoulder, Feryal casually turns toward him and smiles. He glances at her then leans into the bar, his back to her. He thumbs his mobile and continually checks the entrance to the lounge until his pensive expression breaks. A beautiful woman appears at the man's side and they order champagne. The bartender offers them an expansive smile before pouring two glasses that nearly fizz over. Between sentences, the woman's laugh bubbles up like the champagne she's sipping. Not once does she look over at Feryal.

Feryal is disappointed. The man is handsome and fit—he doesn't have to pay for sex. She hopes, for her first time, her appointment is attractive. She measures every man against Othman, the only one she's been with. She misses his hard, muscled chest and dark features, in spite of his not loving her back. What a fool Feryal had been, believing he would leave his wife—even when Feryal lied about being pregnant.

If you have the baby, it will destroy your family. Don't be stupid, he told her. *I will pay for you to pull it down.* The easy way Othman had said it, like he'd found himself in this situation before, still scalds Feryal's heart. How could he have professed to love her if he was perfectly willing to get rid of his child?

She took his money, told him she'd made an appointment at an Israeli hospital, bought herself a bus ticket, stuffed the leftover bills inside the compartment of her old messenger bag, and never looked back. To the undiscerning passengers seated across the aisle, she was a student attending university.

Feryal taps her sandal against the foot rest of her stool until another man approaches. This time she keeps her gaze fixed straight ahead, fingers her plastic straw. Behind the bartender, she studies the reflection in the mirrored panel. A balding man with hunched shoulders shuffles toward the bar like someone about to deliver somber news. Feryal's stomach sinks.

Don't stray from the lounge. He'll find you, Ani had advised her earlier, standing naked in the kitchen of their flat, rifling through a basket of clean laundry. Her roommate's lack of inhibition shocked and impressed Feryal. Ani found a pair of panties and a loose summer dress, and slipped into them.

They met at a posh outdoor café in Ramallah. Feryal was sitting at a table by herself, newly arrived in town. She was anxiously calculating the cost of her meal before ordering, when she caught a stranger studying her from across the terrace. A woman with short fashionable hair, dark-tinted sunglasses that nearly swallowed her face, and a pair of golden hoops dangling from her earlobes. She flashed an amused grin at Feryal.

A server returned to her table. *The sister wants to treat you to a meal, Miss.* He pointed across the canopied terrace and the woman waved, summoning her over. Feryal's cheeks turned splotchy red: she felt bumpkin in her long tunic and mules.

The stranger removed her sunglasses and two cat eyes peered intently at Feryal. Long bangs swept her forehead and she tucked them behind her ear with manicured fingers until they fell loose again. Ani is half Armenian, half Palestinian, though she doesn't tell Feryal which side belongs to which parent, only that she's a *double-tragedy of history.*

Where are you from, ya hilwa? She drew on a black vape stick and tipped her head to release smoke away from her face.

Ain al-Deeb, Feryal responded, a pang of fear and nostalgia rushing her lungs.

The only thing in al-Deeb is a factory, I believe.

A warehouse, Feryal says, surprised this elegant woman has heard of her village. *For textiles.* She sensed men and other women glancing Ani's way, catching their attention before they resumed their conversations and tea.

You're visiting alone? Her cat eyes roved down her face to her breasts.

I'm never going back, Feryal blurted, cheeks blazing.

You're a pretty girl, ismallah, Ani told her appraisingly, nodding toward a basket of pocket bread cut into neat triangles and a small bowl of hummus. *Please.*

Self-conscious, but ravenous, Feryal dipped the bread, brought it carefully to her lips.

Ani watched her intently. *What will you do here?* Another deep intake of her vape stick, smoke snaking into the air.

An important question to which Feryal had no answer. She was at the head of her class in math and linguistics, earning one of the top tawjeehi scores in her neighborhood. Yet there was no celebration for her matriculation from secondary school. Sitti Rasmeah, her paternal grandmother, prepared a batch of ghraybeh, Feryal's favorite shortbread cookies. When she was a little girl, she had sat across from the old woman, eagerly waiting to offer her small contribution—a single thumbprint in the center of each, forming a tiny mound to be filled with ground pistachios or fresh-made apricot jam.

Now each cookie has your special mark, her grandmother winked at her. She cleaned the batter from her fingers with a dishrag and pull out a piece of hard candy from the breast pocket of her thobe. There seemed to be a wonderful surprise every time Sitti Rasmeah slid her hand inside the chest-panel of her embroidered dress: a silver shekel, a stick of gum, a sky-blue marble. It was a trove of delights. When she nestled in her grandmother's lap, she traced a row of opposite-facing peacocks, sewn in variegated purple and yellow thread, each cross-stich perfectly uniform.

After she sat for her matriculation exams, Feryal's mother announced her schooling was done.

It's a shame. The girl is smart enough to be a lawyer, mashallah, her Sitti Rasmeah had argued. *A doctor, even.*

She can marry a lawyer or a doctor, her mother had scoffed. *Until then she must pull her weight around here.*

Feryal went to work in Othman's warehouse, where a quarter of the villagers earned their wages. She expected to work the floor, pulling boards of fabric for orders, or standing on a wobbly ladder, dusting row upon row of crushed velvet, denim, and lace. She was grateful to be assigned to the office, and away from the prying eyes of the older women. Othman's previous assistant, a sympathetic hijabi woman in thick glasses named Salma, was finally getting married. She trained Feryal on the computer, explaining the application process between enthusiastic interjections about her khateeb. *He's from Nablus,* Salma told her. *He's prohibited from traveling north, but he promises I can see my family whenever I want.* She patted Feryal's shoulder. *Azeem! You pick up very quickly—mashallah!*

At a small desk in the office, Othman drew the blinds after the workers went home and fucked Feryal in his swivel chair. He seemed utterly enamored with her, impressed at how quickly she learned and performed her duties, telling her how clever she was. She opened up to him like a crisp, new textbook, ready to be learned.

I hear you were first in your class, he said, zipping up his pants.

I could have gone to university, she told him, her chest flooding with pride.

But then you wouldn't be here. He pinched her bottom. *Did the invoice for the Husseini order get settled? Those bastards never pay on time.*

At the café in Ramallah, Feryal told Ani, *I wish to enroll at university.*

Ani's gold-speckled eyes glimmered and narrowed. *And how will you pay for it, ya hilwa?*

Feryal bashfully chomped at her expensive shawarma sandwich which Ani insisted she order. It wasn't as flavorful as the ones back home which were for half the price.

If you trust me, I can help you. Ani leaned conspiratorially. *Women like us need to stick together.*

Feryal wasn't sure what kind of women they were—or more importantly who she was—but Ani's easy laughter and the way she tenderly touched Feryal's hand across the small table were disarming. She was already missing her grandmother's kindness.

~

The bald man lingers a few stools down from her. In spite of what she can make of his looks and age, Feryal hopes he's the one so she won't feel obliged to order another drink in case her actual date is running late. Ani has been gracious since she's arrived, paying for Feryal's food and keep, welcoming her to a box of Kotex pads and her expensive shampoo. *You'll pay me back,* Ani smiled at her, *as soon as you get on your feet.*

He appears Arab—foreign-born, confirming what Ani has told her. She has a contact in the Palestinian Authority who arranges these things.

He's some kind of a scholar. A director of a museum in Belgium, Ani offered as she waved her wet glossy nails dry. *He's on a temporary visit. Acquiring something for a special exhibit, I think. I'd take him except Mario has been giving me shit lately.* She paused to admire her nails—the color of slick eggplant skin—then batted her eyelashes at Feryal. *Do this for me, ya hilwa. I've already confirmed.*

The fact that he's affiliated with a museum makes it less egregious for Feryal to accept the proposition. And he certainly looks the part, she observes now.

"Good evening," the man tells the bartender, glancing sidelong at Feryal. "A Scotch, if you please." His Arabic is clipped as if he's not accustomed to speaking it often.

Basheer—another customer had called the bartender by name—heartily greets him, placing a small round coaster in front of the man. "Welcome, ya Ustaz."

Feryal notices a laminated badge on his lapel. Her heart beats wildly. For a moment, she thinks of leaving, hopping off her barstool and exiting as quickly as possible. But she waits, sipping the remainder of her cocktail until she hits ice cubes and is forced to stop slurping.

Wait until he addresses you first, Ani had instructed, zipping up Feryal's long, tight-fitting black dress. It has a high neck with a mesh bodice. It belongs to Ani, is not something Feryal would ever own. Though she's completely covered, the jersey fabric accentuates every part of her body and is uncomfortably tight around her bottom. *You don't want to stand out,* Ani says. *A wink, a smile. Nothing loud or crass. You want to appear as a quiet invitation.*

"Good evening, Miss," he finally says, his eyes darting nervously around the bar.

"Ahlan, ya Ustaz," she says a bit too hastily, swiveling her entire body toward him. "How are you, Professor?" Icy sweat trickles down her back.

He slips her a plastic room key. "Wait ten minutes. Room 405." He gulps the rest of his drink and abruptly stands, giving the bartender an overly jovial goodbye.

Feryal is stupefied. She expects dinner—something to break the ice. The hotel has an acclaimed Japanese fusion restaurant Ani raves about. She's eaten there several times with customers.

Basheer gives her a long look and his lips part as if he wants to say something to her. Feryal quickly settles her bill—which she'd also expected the professor to pick up—and finds a washroom. Her key allows her admission to a hotel toilet off the lobby. The cocktail syrup churns in her stomach and she begins to retch. She clutches both sides of the stall and breathes through her nose. At the sink, she palms cold water and gargles before reapplying gloss to her full lips. She fluffs her hair which Ani had spent a long time straightening. It looks dull, the ends like straw. The mirror reflects her pale face, brown eyes shiny. She checks the time on her mobile and finds a guest elevator. A hotel attendant presses a button and bids her a good evening.

Imagine it's someone you want, Ani had winked before Feryal heads out the flat. *Someone you once loved.*

~

She knocks on the door before waving her plastic key across the handle's electronic pad. "Hello?" she calls, tentatively stepping in.

The professor is already naked except for his undershirt and socks. He's laid a towel in the center of the bed, across crisp, white sheets. The fancy duvet is neatly peeled back to the foot of the bed. There's a pair of folded hand towels on his nightstand and a single condom.

"If you please," he says politely, gesturing to the bed.

She unzips her dress and pauses. He says nothing, studying her coolly, as if she's a new exhibit and he hasn't quite drawn a conclusion about her. She slips out of her panties, unclasps her bra.

He's immediately on top of her, eyes clamped shut, and she stares into his nostrils, the long black hairs like the quills of a porcupine. Perspiration beads his bald head.

As he struggles to enter her, she examines his face, wrinkles deepening in ecstasy and tries to imagine what he's like when giving a serious lecture. Do those same age lines contract in serious contemplation?

Ani chuckles at Feryal's shocked face, that a scholar would requisition sex. *All men have cocks, ya hilwa,* she says. *In the end, the only thing that separates them is which head they think with.*

The professor finally begins to rock back and forth on top of her. After a short time, he grunts and she knows he's close. He emanates a strange combination of menthol, camphor, and lentil soup—not the crisp and spicy fragrance of Othman. Perhaps these are the natural odors of an older man. His body is no longer active, his brain becomes his major organ—besides his cock—until both begin to fail him. Feryal imagines the professor's biceps haven't always been so flabby. His paunch slaps against Feryal's stomach, an embarrassing sound that makes it difficult to think about anything else.

~

Feryal's body has never really belonged to her. Not ever since she was nine years old and her maternal uncle coaxed her into his lap and pressed his erection against her. When her body transforms, the boys in the harra notice, even under her loose clothes, hungry wolf-eyes penetrating through the fabric, imagining her small, hard breasts, her rounded bottom. The store clerk rubs the back of her hand when she exchanges money for groceries until she learns better, spreading the coins across the counter, keeping her eyes down. The opposite sex suddenly lay claims upon her body, one she barely feels in possession of herself. Her existence becomes an affirmation of their desires, their power to ravish her. She no longer belongs to herself.

Her mother grows harsh, as if Feryal's body is a liability, a precarious entity on the brink of catastrophe that will bring down their home. She stares while Feryal does her chores around their flat, sweeping floors, dusting the window frames. Her mother calls her away from the small veranda that overlooks a narrow street. *Do you wish to be on display for all the neighbors?*

Feryal's father is the only man who looked at her with love, not scrutiny. She was thirteen years old the night their building was raided. Israel's occupation forces arrested her father, hauled him away on suspicion of conspiracy to commit acts of terrorism. Three soldiers threw a black sack over his head, so Feryal was unable to see his face for the last time, his pure adoration twinkling in his eyes every time he beheld her.

Sitti Rasmeah attempted to intervene, clawing at one soldier's body until he knocked her down with the butt of his rifle, shouting at her to stay put. Feryal ran to her side and was violently shoved backward by another soldier. Her mother was on the floor, clutching her husband's leg and held on until a swift kick to her head finally released her father.

The next morning Feryal's first period arrived.

Her father languished for four years in prison before Israel ejected him into Jordan. Her mother was inconsolable, snapping at Feryal, their only child, calling her a "habla" and "good for nothing." She wondered what she was supposed to be good for, how in her father's absence she might ease her mother's pain. She moved around their bayt like a ghost, trying not to make a noise or disturb anything that would incite her mother. After her chores, she finished schoolwork and read a book her teacher Miss Basima had loaned her, a translation of *Anne of Green Gables*. Once a year, her mother travelled to a refugee camp on the other side of the border where her father took up shelter. Feryal pretended to be orphaned—not only of her father, but happily of her mother—and in her imagination, she embarked on new adventures like the red-haired, precocious Anne.

Sitti Rasmeah, who has lived with Feryal's family since she was born, gives daily du'aa for her son and the members of her family—

including her daughter-in-law whom Feryal secretly believes unworthy of supplications. In her mother's absence, a calm settles over the flat, a gossamer happiness like the long white strands of her grandmother's hair. Feryal looked forward to two months free from her mother's cruelty, the horrible verbal lashings. Sometimes it was a hard slap across the face, or rough fingers snatching the soft flesh of her upper arm and twisting it awfully, making Feryal's eyes instantly water.

Pray to the Prophet, Sitti Rasmeah would admonish her daughter-in-law. Then she smiled at Feryal. *Come here, my dear,* Sitti Rasmeah smiled. *Help me with this.* And she'd set her to a task that made her feel useful and good for something. Her grandmother, on powerful and sturdy haunches, showed Feryal how to core squash without piercing the skin and how to mince parsley and onion for folding into freshly ground lamb.

You can still be book smart and a good cook for your children one day, Sitti Rasmeah had said with a wink, retying a white mandeela at the base of her neck, a few gray, straggly hairs escaping her temples. Around her black thobe, bright green and yellow smudged her white apron, joining other faded stains.

One day, Feryal pointed to the row of peacocks prancing across her grandmother's bosom. *What kind of birds are those, Sitti?*

Al-tawoos, her grandmother smiled, trailing a craggly finger over one. *You see their feathers? They'll be in jannat illah when we arrive someday, by the Lord's will.*

They are regal creatures to Feryal, evoking respect and veneration. Among a dozen stitched by her grandmother, she loved this thobe best of all.

～

When the professor is finished, he rolls off Feryal's body, wraps the slimy condom in tissue paper and tosses it into a wastebasket. He lights a cigarette from a pack stamped in foreign words, not offering her one though she doesn't smoke. He shuts his eyes as he exhales, murmurs something to himself she can't make out. Then he writes in a tiny notebook on his nightstand, as if he's just worked out the answer to a problem in his head.

Feeling ignored, Feryal props herself up on one elbow. She hasn't properly taken in her surroundings. The hotel room is modern décor, finished in a muted white, black and royal blue palette. The professor's belongings—a single opened suitcase, a few paperback books scattered on a lacquered cherry wood desk, and several prescription bottles—disrupt the tidy space. Directly across from the bed is a television screen hidden behind the doors of an entertainment center. There's an oil painting on the same wall, the silhouette of a woman standing on a sandy shore, one hand clasping her straw hat against the wind. Frothy waves crash at her feet as she watches the last traces of the sun dipping below the horizon.

Feryal wished she could linger alone in the cool sheets of the bed, order room service—Ani told her about the late-night meals she orders on her dates and which Ani consumes naked beside her lover. Eating might help Feryal feel normal again. It's quiet inside this room, unlike the noise of their flat, cars honking below their steel-barred window, loud music pulsating from a barber shop below.

Sadness prickles her skin. She wants the professor to disappear along with all of his odors. She reaches for a water bottle on the nightstand beside her and gulps, trying to wash down her dejection, the same feeling she lugged home after an hour with Othman in his office. He'd kiss her cheek, examine his hair in a mirror hanging behind the door, and lock up.

Her eyes travel across the other side of the room. For the first time, Feryal notices a headless mannequin standing near the washroom. The figure is draped in a white thobe covered in a sheath of plastic.

"Who's that for?" she asks the professor.

His head shoots up from his notebook, his interest suddenly ignited. "It's a very important acquisition," he declares, springing from the bed. He stands beside the mannequin, producing an absurd juxtaposition of real and counterfeit bodies. His penis is deflated in a nest of graying pubic hair. He appears ready to give a lecture on the embroidered dress as he peels off the plastic sheath.

Feryal sits up against the headboard. "You came all the way from Belgium for a thobe?"

"Not any thobe," he says disdainfully before smiling in mock congeniality. "This belonged to a prominent family in Yaffa. My museum is acquiring it from the University. A pre-war relic like this will enjoy a much wider audience."

He delicately holds up one sleeve as if he's taking the arm of a beloved. "You see here," he says, his eyes shining. "There are idiosyncratic touches in the way the cross-stitches are…"

But Feryal has stopped listening. Sitti Rasmeah's face suddenly intrudes and her past tidal-waves into the hotel room. She's swept back to her family bayt, her grandmother brushing her hair when her mother has lost patience. Her grandmother's calloused palm, cradling a small luscious plum she's extracted from the breast pocket of her thobe. *Sweet like you, habibti.*

Feryal finds it hard to breathe, the ceiling suddenly collapsing, the professor blurring into the blue walls, his droning warped and distant. She squeezes her knees together and clutches the bedsheets until the hotel room regains its normal proportions.

The professor is pointing at the chest-panel, unperturbed. "The reflective nature of the peacocks reveals a perfect harmony."

"My grandmother loves peacocks," Feryal blurts out. "They roam in Paradise. That's what she told me when I was a young girl." She bites her lower lip to keep tears from falling.

He gives a mirthless laugh. "It's far more sophisticated than the eye can see." He lingers near the mannequin, brushes off a piece of lint before replacing the plastic sheath over the dress. He wraps a white terrycloth robe around his body and walks to the pair of trousers he was wearing earlier and withdraws a worn leather wallet from a back pocket. He extracts fewer bills than Ani had advised her to accept.

"I was told a thousand shekels," Feryal says.

"Perhaps a misunderstanding, my dear," the professor responds. "Take it or leave it. I'm having a shower. Please see yourself out." He slips his wallet inside the pocket of his bathrobe and locks the washroom door behind him.

The blood in Feryal's body runs white-hot. She can hear Ani's mocking laugh. *Demand what you're owed, ya hilwa. He'll give it to you in the end. No man will want a scene. Remember—you're in control of the situation,* Ani told her as Feryal slipped into a pair of silver strappy heels.

She rises from the bed, dampens a hand towel with her water bottle and wipes between her legs. It's not much different than her first time with Othman. He kissed her gently on her lips and neck before handing her a roll of rough paper towel he'd brought from the employee restroom at the warehouse. *You're still bleeding*, he'd said, and Feryal could hear a kind of pride and it made her feel special and proud, too, that he'd been her first.

She hears the shower running and finally climbs out of the bed, slipping into her bra and panties. Before she reaches for her black dress, she studies the thobe, touches the chest-panel over the plastic. She runs her hand under the protective layer and slips it inside the breast pocket. Once, Feryal had discovered a tiny bouquet of tiny jasmine flowers, the magical source of the delicate perfume that wafted from Sitti Rasmeah's body every time she drew Feryal close.

Unsurprisingly, the pocket of this thobe is empty. Whose grandmother had once worn it? What had she carried inside?

There was nothing technical or ancient about Sitti Rasmeah's thobe. Feryal had never regarded it in any deliberate way. It's how it made her feel—safe, loved—that lingered still. Such associations mean nothing to the professor, pose no real value in his important acquisition.

Feryal's heartbeat quickens. She quickly and carefully lifts the thobe from the mannequin. She pauses, listens for the shower and hears a faint singing coming from the washroom. She pulls the thobe over her head and sinches it at the waist with the professor's belt, which she removes from his trousers. A musty scent emanates from the linen fabric.

She gazes at her reflection in a full-length mirror mounted on a narrow wall between the bathroom and exit door. She touches the sparse, though recognizable plumage of the peacocks, then runs her fingertips along one triangular sleeve where a parade of rosettes are stitched.

Before quickly gathering her purse and sandals, Feryal drapes the naked, headless mannequin in her crumpled black dress—Ani's dress—its high collar drooping down one narrow shoulder without a neck to support it.

She leaves the money on the nightstand.

Foolish girl! Ani might tell her if she decides to ever return to the flat.

For Feryal, it's more than an even trade.

167

BACK FROM THE AFTERLIFE:
MISADVENTURES IN NEAR-DEATH EXPERIENCE

EMILY HARNETT

2023 JACK HAZARD FELLOW

I SAW HEAVEN, OR SOME VERSION OF IT, in the late 1990s. This was on the days I stayed home sick from school, bingeing on Corn Pops and reruns of *Unsolved Mysteries*. Back then, the show was hosted by Robert Stack, a sort of Clinton-era Rod Serling with a raspy old-man voice and scary eyes who broke the fourth wall at the beginning of every episode. The show's narrative staples, then as now, were murdered moms and missing children. Standard true-crime stuff. But occasionally, you'd catch an episode featuring first-person accounts of the afterlife. In the one I recently rewatched, a guy named Dannion—silky little mustache, strong southern accent—gets struck by lightning in his own home. We see it all play out in a (very bad) reenactment. Dannion's shoes melt; his heart stops; his soul drifts skyward. He finds himself in an otherworldly tunnel, awash in blue light and bad computer graphics. The ambience recalls the misty hours before dawn and early Microsoft screensavers. But before Dannion can meet any angels, a mysterious force shunts him back into his body. He jolts to life on a hospital gurney, scaring the shit out of his best friend Tom and shaping, in some subliminal way, my understanding of mortality for the next twenty years.

I'm not saying that I believed these stories then, or ever. But they seemed as believable as anything else on basic cable at the time. Maybe life and the afterlife really were just a bandwidth apart, different channels that you toggled between. If you were to peer into the corners of my subconscious, you'd find lots of this sort of stuff: rerecorded VHS tapes and the standard tropes of death-denial. You'd also find scattered pages from

Life After Life by Raymond Moody, which I discovered on my parents' coffee table a few years after first seeing Dannion on *Unsolved Mysteries*. The book, originally published in 1975, was the first to collect testimonies from people who claimed to have been to Heaven while clinically dead or gravely imperiled. These journeys into the afterlife—what Moody termed near-death experiences, or NDEs—were described in scrupulous detail, and seemed to confirm the sorts of stories I saw on TV.

Since its publication, Moody's book has sold more than thirteen million copies. It established NDEs as both a cultural phenomenon and an area of academic research. Moody was not, as you might imagine, a fringe personality or aspiring mystic but a psychiatrist-in-training. The book drew on interviews that he conducted with over 150 experiencers while a graduate student at the Medical College of Georgia. It piqued the interest of Bruce Greyson, one of Moody's graduate supervisors, who later wrote that he became "immediately intrigued" by the phenomenon after reading letters that Moody received "from experiencers all over the world." Soon, Moody and Greyson formed a sort of supergroup with two other researchers, John Audette and Ken Ring. The organization they founded was called the International Association for Near-Death Studies; Elisabeth Kübler-Ross, famous for her formulation of the five stages of grief, later served on its board of advisers. Greyson and Ring would eventually author their own books on NDEs, while the IANDS would later publish the peer-reviewed *Journal of Near-Death Studies*.

Knocking on Heaven's Door

In recent years, partly out of nostalgia for the entertainments of my youth and partly out of lapsed-Catholic curiosity, I've developed a quasi-fascination with NDEs and their attendant literature. Every few months, I would waste an afternoon by noodling around on the IANDS website, where I could read the newest issues of its journal. That's how I learned, in August 2019, that the group was hosting its annual conference an hour away from my house.

It was scheduled to take place in a tony Philadelphia suburb called King of Prussia, best known for its eponymous luxury mall: a monument to suburban decadence with a Gucci store and charging stations for Teslas. The mall drew people from all over the region, including where

I had grown up. I have pleasant memories of wandering under its glass ceilings as a kid, feeling as enclosed and enchanted as a figure in a snow globe. The local priests did their Christmas shopping there, and I used to imagine them flapping around the food court in their silken vestments, administering Chick-fil-A to each other like the Eucharist.

The conference cost $600 and took place over Labor Day weekend. I applied for press credentials and figured I would go for a few hours each day, record some dispatches from heaven, and reward myself with a trip to Shake Shack. And so, in the dead heat of late summer, I walked into the lobby of a conference center full of ambient lighting and aging bodies. Around me streamed a throng of conference attendees sporting lime-green lanyards, all retirement age or older. As they passed, I took note of their name tags, most of them trimmed with an emerald ribbon bearing the word EXPERIENCER in fine gold font. A delicate older gentleman—his name tag sported an additional ribbon reading VETERAN—scraped by on his walker. There were a few hundred people here, I estimated. All of them, it seemed, had been to Heaven or to war, and all of them seemed happy, moving through the lobby with the cheerful lassitude you see at theme parks and restaurant buffets.

As I waited for my press pass, I downloaded the conference's special app by scanning a QR code on my phone and scrolled through the massive color-coded schedule. There were workshops like Kelvin Chin's "Overcoming the Fear of Death" and a screening of Powell and Pressburger's 1946 film *A Matter of Life and Death*, which happens to be one of my favorites. Dr. Eben Alexander, author of 2012's bestselling *Proof of Heaven: A Neurosurgeon's Journey into the Afterlife*, was one of the marquee speakers at this year's conference. While IANDS positions itself as a scholarly association, the programming seemed mostly therapeutic. Every night there was a performance by Kevin Kern, a self-described Steinway Artist who performed musical "sound paintings" that apparently reminded many experiencers of their NDEs. There was a class on "Kundalini Awakening," and something called a Healing Room in the basement where you could enlist the services of reiki practitioners, numerologists, and other specialists.

I made a quick stop at the coffee station, where I chatted with two friendly redheaded ladies about crop circles. Then I headed to my first session: a presentation by Robert and Suzanne Mays, self-described NDE researchers and frequent contributors to the IANDS journal. I studied them from the back of a high-ceilinged, windowless room. They were a bespectacled couple in their seventies with small, kind faces, as perfectly matched as a pair of doves. I liked them instantly. They radiated the plaintive wholesomeness of Quakers and people who sell jam at farmers' markets.

Robert, in coat and tie, took to the podium. In recent years, he explained, he and Suzanne had turned their attention to the prophetic visions that a number of experiencers have undergone during, and sometimes after, their NDEs. While the visions themselves were invariably apocalyptic, the Mayses spoke of them with an almost clinical detachment. Their work encompassed several methodologies: "an extensive literature review of prior research," surveys they had sent to twenty-two subjects, and analyses of fifteen accounts by "published NDE authors." From this material, they had identified five categories of NDE-related prophetic visions, including "current political conflict and civil strife in the United States"; "economic and social chaos caused by widespread power failures"; "severe tsunamis, earthquakes, and natural disasters." My favorite was the fourth category, described as "reset of the Earth, millions to billions of people die: supervolcano, asteroid hit, or nuclear war." (The fifth was "post-reset world.") It seemed appropriate that the first interesting PowerPoint I had ever seen would augur the end of civilization.

Robert described how some of these scenarios might play out: a woman a lot like Hillary Clinton is foiled by a Trump-like antichrist who presides over a Boschian tumult of unrest. Before the end of December 2020, a wall of shattered glass bursts through the streets of Los Angeles as an earthquake with a magnitude of 9.0 demolishes skyscrapers, collapses power lines, and leaves corpses decaying in the street for days, and a resulting tsunami on the Oregon coast turns Sacramento into a lake. To illustrate this narrative, he did a little flourish with his hand, as though uncorking a genie.

But, Robert emphasized, we could still prevent these disastrous futures. "The visions are real, but the outcome does not have to be," he said, determination in his voice. Beside me, a woman burst into applause.

Until then, I had imagined—stupidly!—that believing in Heaven would shield a person from feelings of apocalyptic foreboding. I had *not* imagined Hillary Clinton as some sort of benighted messiah. But what did I know? I learned nothing of paradise during my eight years of CCD: essentially Catholic night school for kids, in which we'd blearily color in pictures of Jesus to prepare ourselves for the gift of the sacraments. I had watched *The Passion of the Christ* with an audience of preteens in puka-shell necklaces and Blink-182 T-shirts; I had eaten His flesh and drank His blood; I had said the Lord's Prayer as penance for half-assing chores, but I still couldn't tell you what happens to us when we die. The closest I had come to broaching the subject was in conversations with my dad. He was an agoraphobe who spent most of my adolescence parsing Aristotle, listening to Enya, and slowly dying from cancer. When I was in college, he told me his interpretation of Thomas Aquinas's theory of Heaven: it exists, but we lose our memories when we get there. He thought Aquinas was right and hated him for it. I hated him too. After my dad died, I pictured him shuffling around eternity in his bathrobe, trying to remember his address and my name. I didn't believe in an afterlife, but still I hoped for something better than endless forgetting or the end of the world.

Sometimes You Feel Like a Nut

For all the talk of Heaven, the IANDS conference felt less like a tent revival than a taping of *The Dr. Oz Show*. One of Oz's repeat guests, Mark Anthony, the Psychic Lawyer®, was even slated to give a talk. NDEs apparently functioned as a sort of gateway drug for occult practices and New Age beliefs, most of them descended from old American ideas. You could sense the ghosts of Spiritualism and Emersonian shades of "experience," summoned here by the dark id of daytime television. But even if Anthony and the other IANDS celebrities were scammers, I still preferred them to so-called "transhumanists" like Ray Kurzweil or Peter Thiel, Silicon Valley plutocrats who believed that technology would soon fulfill the promise of eternal life for the lucky few. The prospect this conjured—Heaven as a chorus of angel investors, the pearly gates thrown open to anyone with seed money—filled me with despair. And so there was a kind of satisfaction in the idea that New Age grifters had already proven that Heaven was real: an actual place accessible not only to those with mountains of private capital but to any lucky prole who took a tumble down the stairs.

Or, as in the case of Chris Kito, to anyone who ate the wrong nut. I saw Chris speak at a panel discussion between three local experiencers, sitting at a long table with two other men of grandpa age. He appeared to be in his mid-thirties, neatly bearded and radiantly bald, with an air of smoothie-drinking good health. His NDE had begun with a slice of cake at a birthday party. Unbeknownst to Chris, who has a terrible nut allergy, it contained a tiny peanut fragment. (Actually, he later learned, it was a peanut butter *cake*. How, I wondered, does a man not recognize the taste of his own allergy?) His mouth started itching, but he went home, took a couple Benadryl, and went to bed. When he woke up a little over an hour later, his entire body was covered in welts. "Maybe I need to take another Benadryl," he thought, "because if three don't work, I guess maybe four will solve it." We all laughed at the memory of this inner monologue. The story, in his telling, was a lightly comic escapade, a series of pratfalls into the afterlife.

His EpiPen, when he found it, had already expired. It was Sunday night in Los Angeles. He figured, with the clarity of anaphylaxis, that he should simply drive himself to the hospital. By the time he stumbled into the ER forty-five minutes later, he was "half-dead," gasping for breath and barely able to pull out his ID. At this point he had "no concept of time." Nurses were rushing all around. A doctor gazed down at him and said: *I'm sorry, I can't save you.* But by then, Chris already knew he was dying. "It was beyond euphoric and peaceful," Chris said. There was no pain— just a rush of tenderness and love. A sudden epiphany that "material things don't matter." And then he saw them: both his grandfathers. His voice wavered at this point in the narrative; he sounded like he was about to cry. "My mother's father goes, 'You can't die yet, you have work to do.'" So Chris went back to his body and his unfinished life. They gave him those "little blue socks" and sent him on his way. By any account, he said, "I should be dead or severely brain damaged." Instead he's spent the last eight years of his life trying to process the beauty and shattering strangeness of what happened to him.

His NDE was a story of reunion and revelation. It was also, perhaps, a story about the delights of oxygen deprivation. Affiliates of the IANDS often rebut insinuations like mine, refuting the arguments of scientists who dismiss NDEs as deathbed hallucinations. Chris never claimed, as many experiencers do, that his NDE was some kind of medical mystery—just that his recovery was medically *unlikely*. He did not seem to think of himself as an accidental prophet or a spiritual scientist. He was just a guy who ate a peanut and saw the beloved faces of the dead. His experience seemed hapless, wounded, sincere. It made me sad. What would it be like, I wondered, to see the family you lost like this, when regaining your life meant losing them again? It seemed heartbreaking, and yet Chris, like most NDEers, understood what had happened to him as transformatively joyful. It seemed that such joy was worth dying, or almost dying, to achieve.

A Poof of Heaven

The following morning, I crab-walked through rows of snowy-haired seniors to find my chair in the hotel ballroom where Dr. Eben Alexander was giving his keynote lecture. The crowd gave off an energy I had never experienced before: a mix of submerged mortal sorrow and friendly curiosity. It felt like a TED Talk in a hospital chapel. A banner across the stage read One Giant Leap for Mankind—a nod, for some reason, to the recent fiftieth anniversary of the moon landing. Under it was Alexander, a tall, tan man in his sixties with salt-and-pepper hair and gently oversized ears. He looked like a humbler, less taxidermied Mitt Romney.

I was familiar with Alexander from YouTube clips of his appearances on *Fox and Friends* and *Oprah*. A neurosurgeon with a fancy Ivy League pedigree, he briefly rose to celebrity in 2012 after the publication of *Proof of Heaven*, which chronicled his near-death experience. Then a damning profile in *Esquire* revealed that his NDE had been preceded by a series of malpractice scandals. While the article torpedoed his mainstream media career, he remains a regular on the alternative spirituality circuit, putting in more or less yearly appearances at the IANDS conference. On TV he usually wears a bowtie, but even without one there's something of the barbershop quartet about him, a practiced patrician hamminess. He's been singing the same song for years—the story of his fantastic journey from Harvard to Heaven—and even I know it by heart.

After some disparaging remarks about the "faith-based religion of materialist science," Alexander embarked on the familiar narrative of his NDE. In 2008, he contracted a rare form of bacterial meningitis and was placed in a medically induced coma. In his telling—disputed, in *Esquire*'s reporting, by his doctor—he was effectively "a dead man." And yet he found himself conscious, struggling through some dark passage, a cramped, uterine space with the "roots of blood vessels all around" him. He emerged into a vibrant meadow full of dancing people and "children playing, dogs jumping, incredible festivities." Above him were "swooping orbs of light, pure, golden light," each one full of "an individual pure spiritual essence." He rode on the wings of a giant butterfly with a "beautiful guardian angel," who communicated with him telepathically. Later, he writes in *Proof of Heaven*, he would learn that this woman was his biological sister, from whom he had been separated upon his adoption as an infant.

This experience was necessary, Alexander believes, for him to see beyond the "reductive materialism" that had blinkered his perspective as a surgeon. And yet, he said, "I'm more of a scientist now than I've ever been." He predicted that NDEs would transform the scientific establishment as totally as his own near-death experience had transformed him. "By the year 2028," he said, "I don't believe any self-respecting, scientifically minded, well-read person on Earth will doubt the reality not just of the afterlife, but of reincarnation." Society, in his view, was "on the verge of the greatest revolution in human history that will make the Copernican revolution look like child's play." Soon, we would look beyond the "puny little" ideas we had mislearned from Darwin, the ideas of "competition and survival-of-the-fittest [that have] pervaded our economic models." We would come to understand that we are all connected through "the reality of the one mind," an infinitely loving cosmic consciousness.

I'll be honest: a lot of this hippie stuff appealed to me. I loved that little diatribe on Darwin and our, uh, "economic models." And yet I also sensed that there was some overlap between Alexander and those Silicon Valley pseudo-mystics working to upload their consciousness into the Cloud. They operate on the same principle of what Alexander called "nonlocal consciousness": the idea that the mind is a nonmaterial reality. But that reality, as Alexander described it, seemed unforgivably corny. I always thought that, if it existed, Heaven, like God, would be abstract and incomprehensible, like a video installation at the MoMA. It would chasten my mortal mind and wrench open the narrow doors of perception, or whatever. Alexander's Heaven, by contrast, was all platitudes and primary colors, a paradise for preschoolers and people on acid. It was so unsubtle—so *stupid*, honestly—and so at odds with Alexander's paean to the powers of mind. If human consciousness really is a portal to the infinite, then why does the infinite seem like a portal to an episode of *My Little Pony*?

At this point in the conference, the sadness had begun to set in. I wanted to go home; I wanted to go to the mall. I wanted to rifle through polyester halter tops at Forever 21 until I felt like I would never die. In other words, it was as good a time as any to go to the Healing Room.

Back in the basement, a woman with a little purple streak in her hair let me flip through a binder of all the spiritual practitioners on offer. I decided that I wanted a numerology reading, if only because I couldn't fathom what it was. I was led into a room with green carpet and a little tropical-printed welcome mat in front of the door. Low flutey music played in the background. I sat across from a lady in a pink sweater set and fine gold jewelry who appeared to be in her seventies. There was nothing conspicuously New Age-y about her; I imagined a home full of doilies and grandchildren, glass-fronted cabinets full of Hummel figurines. She asked for my birth date, then drew a little chart on a piece of paper, sort of like a sudoku grid. She explained that "there are only nine energies" because "when you come to ten, one and zero make one again." Apparently I had "a six, in the top, in [my] soul position, and here in the challenge position." This meant that I had been "a healer and a teacher many times in the past." The whole experience filled me with a posthumous calm; it was like getting my taxes done while overhearing my own eulogy.

The August heat outside felt welcome after the mortuary chill of the conference center. As I drove home, the suburbs played on loop outside my windshield: church, school, Chipotle; church, school, Chipotle. I was too deflated to go back to my apartment. Instead, I drove to my mom's house some forty-five minutes away. My dad's pickup truck was still rusting out in the driveway; scrappy little plants had started to grow, green and hopeful, in the crannies of the truck bed. Boxes of his papers were waterlogged and rotting on the porch: copies of the weird stories I had written as a kid, his unfinished treatise on Aristotelian aesthetics. His dog had finally died a few months before, but her bed still lay in the kitchen. She had outlived him by eight years. The book died when he did.

My dad believed that there was no good philosophy after Thomas Aquinas and no good poetry after John Keats. Even Keats, in his estimate, only wrote "a few good poems." An avid bird-watcher, he would often recite bits and pieces of "Ode to a Nightingale," in which the young Keats, in good Romantic fashion, listens to birdsong and muses on the pull of oblivion: "Many a time," he confesses, "I have been half in love with easeful Death." Keats was twenty-three when he wrote that. By then, he was already sick with the tuberculosis that would kill him. I learned, in the course of writing this piece, that Keats is sort of the poet laureate of the IANDS. Bruce Greyson uses a phrase from his poem "On First Looking into Chapman's Homer" to describe NDEer's reunions with the recently deceased in Heaven. The website for the University of Toronto Libraries has a little commentary on "Ode to a Nightingale," which likens it to classic "out-of-body and near-death experiences." Indeed, the poem seems to capture the queasiness that I felt at the conference—the worry that these people who didn't believe in death were in fact half in love with it.

Late Awakenings

If I, like Raymond Moody, had learned to my own satisfaction that the soul is real and life is eternal, would I really rush to convene an association of "interested researchers"? I didn't think so. I'd take up skydiving or scripture. I would not submit my divine revelation for peer review. After all, religious experience has never drawn its power from rational discourse but from the fact that rational discourse has always felt insufficient to explain it. The very notion of "proof of Heaven" is inimical to faith, which depends on the absence of certainty, on a leap into the unknown. Even if you *could* reconcile epiphanic experience with science, it wasn't clear to me why you needed to.

So after the conference, I called up the Mayses, who spoke to me for hours from two different phones on the same landline, to try to better understand. They told me about growing up during the endless, apocalyptic upheavals of the 1960s and 1970s: the Cuban Missile Crisis, the assassinations of the Kennedys and Martin Luther King, the Cold War, Vietnam. Like many young people at the time, they spent much of those tumultuous years seeking out spiritual community. Since childhood, Suzanne had yearned for a less punishing form of belief than the one practiced by her grandmother, a Jehovah's Witness; she found it at the Rochester Zen Center, where she also found Robert, as well as a lot of others. (When I asked her what drew them to the Center, she laughed and exclaimed, "They were hippies!") Prior to meeting Suzanne, Robert had been a chemistry student at MIT, depressed by the spiritual hollowness of science, its inability to furnish answers to his most fundamental questions. After a half-hearted suicide attempt, he, too, turned to the Zen Center, which started him and Suzanne on a path of New Age belief systems: transpersonal psychology, the Theosophical ideas of Rudolf Steiner, and eventually the books of Raymond Moody.

One year after Moody published *Life After Life* in 1975, *New York* magazine published Tom Wolfe's "The 'Me' Decade and the Third Great Awakening," about the revitalization of religion across the United States. In Wolfe's assessment, the rise of evangelicalism and New Age spirituality marked the 1970s as the Me Decade: a cultural retreat from the collectivist politics of the 1960s into self-centered, consumerist spirituality. Wolfe makes no mention of the consolidation of the conservative movement, the politicization of the religious right, or the election of Richard Nixon. Instead, he explains the decline of the left as the inevitable result of the postwar prosperity boom, which made a mockery of the dreams of the "old utopian socialists." The comfortable salaries of "truck drivers, mechanics, factory workers, policemen" and the like meant to him "that the word *proletarian* can no longer be used in this country with a straight face." The "common man," Wolfe contended, had taken his money and run to the suburbs and self-improvement scams, while the New Left traded Marxism and Marcuse for parapsychology and Jesus Christ. These new spiritual trends, Wolfe writes, exposed the enfeebled New Left as a "religious episode wrapped in semi military gear and guerrilla talk."

I don't recognize the Mayses in Wolfe's analysis of the 1970s. They might have been New Agers, but they certainly weren't narcissists; Suzanne spent years playing therapeutic music for people in palliative care. I did, however, recognize a familiar brand of cynicism. Permeating Wolfe's assessment of the Me Decade is a contempt for utopian thinking of any kind. He makes no distinction between left utopianism and old-fashioned holy rolling—both, in his mind, are expressions of the same self-obsessed irrationalism. In Wolfe's analysis, class consciousness had become a joke by the 1970s; the New Left always was one. The utopian politics of the previous decade—of the previous century—had just been the comedic setup for the punchline of the New Age. It's not an uncommon view. From the standpoint of secular liberalism, utopian beliefs—whether in a worker's paradise or the Kingdom of God—all flow from the same cracked pot. Religion, despite the supposed Great Awakening of the 1970s, has been in steady decline for sixty years. Marxism strikes many Americans as, at best, an embarrassing anachronism, not much different from believing in spirit mediums or psychics. And yet wages are more or less the same as they were in 1978; income inequality is on the rise; young generations enjoy far worse financial prospects than their parents; the list goes on. Most Americans have discarded the idea of paradise, and yet we've come no closer to achieving it here on Earth.

The NDEers, however, have retained the old utopian dreams of the 1960s, just in a strange, sublimated form. They believe in the possibility of world peace and the power of love; they urgently want to save the world, and think—quite literally, in the Mayses case—that the gospel of NDEs could do so. Dr. Alexander insists that "just knowing" about them could inspire people to conquer hate and heal the planet. It seems that once the idea of paradise took on the tinge of superstition, the International Association of Near-Death Studies came along and simply reinvented it as (pseudo)science. It is a very American turn, given that STEM dorks are supposedly the stewards of our future. It's also a depressing one. When I spoke to Alexander on the phone, he told me that the "golden rule is written into the fabric of the universe," a thesis robustly supported by NDEs and the findings of "modern consciousness studies." A nice thought, I guess. But what do we gain from deciding that the golden rule isn't just *good* but also *true* in some material way? In this view, moral and scientific authority are neither distinct nor opposed; in Alexander's estimation, moral arguments don't seem to have authority at all.

The IANDS may exist to give scientific legitimacy to the claims of near-death experiencers, but I suspect most of its members would believe in Heaven even if it didn't. Their belief isn't predicated on scientific research but on the essential strangeness of life and death; I thought again of Chris Kito in his little blue hospital socks, almost killed by a peanut and flooded with love. To my mind, NDEs aren't proof of Heaven, but they do prove that nearness to death changes you, rearranges your sense of the possible. And so it does. I stopped believing in God in my furtive way after my dad died—some switch was flipped, and that high clear tone, a frequency I could once hear, went dead. God was there and then he wasn't; my dad was alive and then he wasn't. And yet the world seems vaster and stranger than I had fully accounted for. Even now, I sometimes let myself imagine running into my dad at the grocery store—I turn the corner and spot him in the dairy aisle, wearing sweatpants with suspenders and trundling along with his shopping cart. Just plainly *there*, unremarkably alive. To see him resurrected in an Acme would confound my sense of reality, but I'm not sure it would be any more confounding than his death. On any scale, death feels arbitrary and inexplicable. It shouldn't happen, so when it does, you get to thinking that anything might.

Maybe it's true, as the NDEers claim, that physical death unites us in the next life. It's certainly true that it unites us in this one, though largely against our will. At the conference, I was perplexed by Alexander's dazzled insistence that "we are all deeply connected" in the glittering web of the universe. Strip away the woo-woo embellishments, and you have a basic account of life on Earth. We are strange animals on a shared planet, tethered to each other by our social and biological dependence, by the complex networks that govern our lives and deaths. Only in a society deformed by individualism could this fact be repackaged as a mystical insight.

Last March, commentators began to echo the same idea as though it were breaking news. The coronavirus, evidently, had proven once and for all that our lives are contingent and interconnected. Ideally, this recognition would generate more robust political commitments, a stronger opposition to human suffering. I doubt, honestly, that this transformation will take place. But NDEs suggest that more mysterious transformations happen all the time. They might not be evidence of Heaven but of something closer to grace—proof that encounters with death can leave you, against all reason, ennobled and longing for goodness. The hope is that, when this wave of tragedy recedes, we will all be so changed.

While I'm still not persuaded by the NDEers' claims that Heaven is real, I'm moved by their insistence that it's realistic to believe in Heaven. In their view, you don't need a special dispensation or an obscene fortune to go there—just a bacterial infection or a bad allergy; just your fragile, finite human life. Paradise need be posthumous; it can be glimpsed now, before you're really gone. I think this is right. But to my mind, paradise isn't a paranormal possibility; it's a political one, too lovely to cede to the New Age or Evangelicals. In the end, there are common enough explanations of NDEs as the comforting hallucinations of a dying brain, our mind's attempt to soothe us as the lights go out. It would seem that none of us can die without some vision of a perfect world. I'm not sure that we can live without one, either.

HELEN IN TEXARKANA

KATE MCQUADE

2023 JACK HAZARD FELLOW

Claire has been dreaming of crows. Shiny black rumbles in the back of her brain. Dark feathers twitching against her skull. They've been keening every night outside her bedroom window, the same rhythmic caw again and again, and she's beginning to think she almost understands it, their guttural, back-of-the-mouth language. Sometimes she rolls it in her own mouth just to have a say in the matter—quietly, into her pillow, so she doesn't wake the baby. The words feel foreign and sticky. *Caw*. Like toffee on her tongue. She wants to suck on the sounds, hard enough to hurt them.

Dark, winging thoughts. Not the thoughts of a mother, she thinks, then unthinks it.

Meanwhile, the baby is speaking French again. This is the third time in a month. When it first happened, Claire thought it was a fluke—a funny story, one to share with her husband over dinner. "À *demain*," the baby kept calling from her crib. "À *demain, à demain*," pointing her chubby fingers toward the window. Claire remembered the phrase from eighth-grade Intro to French: à demain, see you tomorrow. But in the mouth of her one-year-old, it sounded so close to *animal, animal* that Claire thought the baby was just pointing at the crows. They had already begun to cluster in the neighborhood, though spring was still raw then, had scarcely cracked the ice.

At dinner all her husband said was, "Now you're putting words in her mouth too?"

The baby loved the crows. Back then, even Claire could muster up an appreciation: if nothing else, they carried with them an eerie beauty.

On the power lines, they settled and grew still, folded their wings, spaced themselves evenly in rows like bright black pearls. Claire would hold the baby and they would press their hands together against the window glass, point and echo each other's words. *Crow, animal, yes, fly away, yes.* Their fingerprints left gauzy patterns, pointillist blurs that reminded Claire of the paintings she had made once, before her studio became a nursery. She was often tempted to leave them there, these ghost-hands marking the glass like small, breathy spirits pressing in from the outside. But her husband polished them away, and after a while the crows migrated from the power lines to the roof, where their talons scuttle and tap invisibly: dashes and dots, a code she can't interpret.

The town has sent notices. We are aware of the issue; the crows are attracted to vermin; this street has not adhered to county waste-management protocols; are you sure you haven't brought this on yourself?

Claire is not sure. Most things feel like she has brought them on herself without knowing exactly how. The emptiness in her bed. The craggy scar on her stomach. The baby chips a tooth (a stumble, a chair leg) and she feels the neighbors side-eyeing her at the swing set, looking for bruises, thinking: *What kind of a mother.* The baby's head is scabby with cradle cap, molting dandruff that glows in her dark brown fuzz, and every person Claire meets knows just what she's doing wrong—the nannies at library circle, the grocery bagger, even the crusty grandmother with dementia at the park—all of them full of wisdom and correction. Use this oil, leave it alone, comb it out, rub it in, give it time, don't wait, time is of the essence. She remembers strangers' hands reaching out to touch her round belly: the sudden claim the world had to her body, a body that had become alien to her.

Even the French—this is another fluency she lacks, which embarrasses her, since she was an artist (perhaps, in her finest moments, an intellectual) before she was a mother. Her husband, a professor of ancient Greek, has no such lack. He can translate six languages and has published in all of them. In the hospital he spent most of Claire's labor exchanging French jokes—which went literally over Claire's head—with the obstetrician, who was from Marseilles; if he wanted to, he could speak French to the baby at will, without hesitation, and with a perfect accent.

He may very well have done so in those dark, lost hours before Claire woke from the anesthesia.

Perhaps this is why she finds a secret comfort in this: the baby refuses to speak French to her father, to anyone else. Only to Claire.

The second time it happened was a week ago. The baby was in her high chair eating grapes, whole, chokeable grapes Clare hadn't cut in half because already she could see a certain worn path within the landscape of this new life—always cutting things in half—and it was becoming clear to her that what was at stake was only partially her sanity. It was also about her child becoming a child of the world, a world where any number of dangers lurked around sudden corners (the wall socket's black eye, the hungry mouths of staircases, plastic bags, bottles, boredom, the sudden corners themselves), and how would her daughter survive if she didn't end it somewhere? Didn't stop this trickling down of danger, hidden deaths even in this, a mere grape? Plus her husband had just left her. Plus all the knives were dirty, and who knew if she could wash another knife without cutting something?

So: whole grapes.

It was a fragile morning, spring having recently split Ohio's gray to a tender yellow-green. Sun coming through the window made slippery patterns of light on the kitchen table; the breast milk in the baby's cup would look the same if Claire reached out and spilled it. That's what she was thinking about, light that seemed milky and cruel, when she heard the sound. Guttural, a foreign threat. Like a marble skittering, or a crow. Claire felt something soar into her throat as she looked up (the baby's dark eyes bugging, the clenched fear of her tiny lips), and she was moving before she told herself to move, she was pounding on the baby's back, trying to lift her, all of this without thinking. But the straps were fastened and the buckles were complicated, so Claire lifted the whole thing into her arms instead—the wooden high chair, the baby strapped, the milk flying—and she shook everything upside down until something flew out of the baby's mouth.

Claire expected a grape. It was not a grape. What flew out was a sound: *"Je suis désolé, maman. Je suis désolé."* Claire didn't know the words—she would look them up later—but there was a shape to the sound that was like a shadow, both there and not there, an outlined absence she could recognize.

The baby was crying desperately. Claire put the chair down and unbuckled her, lifted her close. She felt a splintering love. Or maybe, even more deliciously, its aftermath: she felt something coming back together. "It's okay." She said it out loud to the baby, and also to herself. She said it so many times, it lost its meaning. "It's okay, it's okay, it's okay." The baby's breathing slowed, but her wrists stayed clamped around Claire's neck, fingertips cool as pearls. Out the window, Claire could see crows sweeping purple shadows across the yard. Her arm muscles began to shake, a gorgeous ache coming gradually into color as she looked down at the high chair. Antique, a gift from her mother-in-law. Solid wood. Impossible that she had just lifted it, yet alone turned it upside down. Impossible that the baby was fine, was in fact laughing now, tickling Claire's neck as if it had all been a game. And yet this was true: she had known exactly what to do, an instinct let loose from inside the cage of her body. She felt the door still swinging.

Little fingers pecking at her skin. Sweet pink voice still babbling: "Désolé, désolé, désolé."

So Claire is watching for it when it happens for the third time. Almost eager for it, though she dreads it too, an inner jumble that reminds her of the art studio where she met her husband. Back then, she was a tense and wary painter, and she remembers the dark satisfaction of the moment her brush would inevitably slide beyond the borders of the image in her head. A mistake, yes: she understands there is something wrong with a baby who speaks French in Ohio. But also the cool rush of relief. Finally, she could stop anticipating her own failure. Finally, the shapes of her shortcomings would be known.

It happens in the backyard. The baby is playing in the sandbox, poking black feathers into little hills. Claire is walking the perimeter of the house with the exterminator, who is explaining that little can be done. "The thing about crows," he says, nodding at the roof, "is that they're social creatures. Same as people, really. Once you get a group of them together, they're like a family. Hard to disperse."

The exterminator has sinewy brown arms and green eyes that glow in the heat. It's springtime, but the thermometer says ninety, promises higher, and it's been nine days since Claire has spoken to anyone besides the baby. The sun is stretching its golden legs deep into the afternoon. Her mouth feels dry with words, though that may just be last night's whiskey.

"Not all families are hard to disperse," she says.

She watches his eyes skitter down her long brown ponytail, her breasts, her pink blouse. Silk. Unbreathable. Much too hot for this weather. The air is throbbing with the distant calls of crows.

Claire is waiting for him to ask the question she needs to hear out loud: *Where's your husband?* To which she could acknowledge, finally, to someone other than the uncomprehending baby: *On sabbatical in the Berkshires, fucking Gladys, who teaches romance languages and has tremendous, perky, unsuckled breasts.* She wants him to ask. She wants to shock someone.

But the exterminator only looks away. "True," he says, clearing his throat. "In any case, this isn't like getting rid of an anthill. We don't have any chemical remedies. Nothing, really, beyond the traditional. Which means your main options involve fear."

"Fear?" This approach sounds so simple to Claire, so breezy, and at the same time, comically impossible. "You mean scarecrows?"

"Sure, or even just movement. Garden pinwheels on the roof. Strings of fishing line. Any movement will do. You've got to make sure they don't *want* to return."

"I suppose that's always the best way." A crow peeks down at them from the roof with one shiny, unblinking eye. "Passive aggression."

"Exactly. They're animals. But they're smart animals."

"Animals." She stares at the crow, who stares back, a challenge. À demain, bitch.

"Noise can work," says the exterminator. "If you're desperate. I've heard you can record the crows' distress calls. Play the tape on a loop, full volume, to keep them away. But that fix might be worse than the problem."

"Phantom crows," she says.

He laughs. She doesn't. She's lingering on the possibility of harnessing distress. Packing it into a cassette, an object no larger than her hand, and making it useful.

"Will a gun work?" she says.

"Like a shotgun?" He laughs again. "You live in town."

"Well. The neighbors got a gun."

This is mostly true. The gun is Claire's, a snub-nosed Ruger she bought last week after a dream about intruders. But the question stands: she's not clear how effective it would be.

The exterminator looks at her for a long time. His green eyes are a forest. The fairy-tale kind, full of haunting things and plunder. Then he looks at the baby, who waves at him with a gritty hand. "A gun is probably not the best plan," he says slowly. "See, you can't just scatter them. They'll find their way back. They always find their way back to each other."

Claire's throat grows tight with something that wants out. She feels tears brimming and he looks quickly away. The exterminator is polite like that—thoughtful, considerate. He would be a generous lover. When he crouches down next to the baby, who babbles nonsensically at him, he's smiling again. "She's sweet, huh?"

"She likes you. She only throws sand at people she likes."

"I get that a lot." He holds out a hand. The baby touches his finger with her own—two tips connecting, God and Adam—and continues to babble. "I have no idea what she's saying."

"Same," says Claire. "It's all French to me."

"You mean Greek."

"No. French."

The exterminator rises. His body unfolds to a length that twangs deep in her stomach. She can practically feel it in her palms, the heat of his back, his spine stacked against her fists like knobby puzzle pieces— the logic of bones, of their bodies, each chiseled part clicking into place. "Like that Frenchman on the news," he says. "You hear about that? Guy wakes up with amnesia in New Orleans and it turns out he's some French tourist with head trauma. And now he can't speak French anymore, only English. And the thing is, he didn't even *speak* English before."

Had she read this in the paper? It sounds vaguely familiar but only in the way a dream is vaguely familiar. All the separate parts recognizable, but not the story they add up to. "That's incredible," she says.

"Right? Total blank. Can you imagine?"

"I can," she says, and it's true: as he turns to leave, she can feel an old panic reaching across time. The inscrutable, silent canvas in front of her, white as hospital sheets. Brush in her hand and the edgeless possibility of any mark to be made. She presses her palm to the exterminator's shoulder and feels him freeze, feels it all funnel down to a single red point. "Can you?" she says, and together they look down at the baby, who throws her hands high into the air.

"*Oui, allons-y!*" she shouts, scattering sand at their feet. "*Oui, allons-y!*"

Claire met her husband at Kansas State, where her father was an adjunct in agricultural sciences and her future husband a professor in the Atelier program. The Atelier was a graduate seminar, a multidisciplinary course deconstructing Greek myths through collaborative art. But somehow, on the strength or misreading of one of her paintings, she had been accepted into it—she, a full-ride undergraduate (need-based, not merit), a painting major who still lived at home and worked nights at the saltine factory where her older brother worked days. Her future husband was a classics PhD candidate with round tortoiseshell glasses and the sort of carefully arranged messiness—sandy scruff and tousle, ageless tweed pilfered from another time period—that she knew by then only money could buy.

His glasses were fake. She could tell from across the studio on the first day of class, as he lectured on and on about the differences between Homer's Helen, Virgil's Helen, Ovid's Helen. "The lie of Helen," he said, waving his pencil with abandon, "is that there was ever one Helen of Troy. There are innumerable Helens, *unresolvable* Helens—the whore, the faithful. The traitor, the loyalist. The feminist, the pawn. The object, who was stolen. The subject, who wanted it. And this, of course, is the gift of Helen to the artist: the ability to make her *yours*." With every turn of his head she watched his glasses, the way the light was never distorted, the edge of his face never broken into separate planes: fake glass. She was sure of it. For reasons she couldn't articulate, the glasses infuriated her, rumbled up in her stomach the fact of her scholarship, the vague haze of her post-graduation plans, the imposter feeling she had every time she showed up for his class. The glasses made her think of the smell of crackers and their neat, unbroken, parallel lines when they came down the plane of the belt, a queasy feeling, though she interpreted the lurch as mere desire. He was exceptionally attractive. And she was exceptionally tired, as a college senior, of living at home.

So when he approached her after class one day, all the other paint-flecked artists and tortoiseshell translators filing out of the studio, she was hungry for it: a word, a criticism, anything. Even from him. Especially from him. She had always been an A-minus student, eager to please, effortful and not quite magnificent, but full of the sort of floral promise that made her feel constantly on the verge of being recognized. *A budding talent,* her teachers had said over the years. *A developing eye, a late bloomer, tremendous potential.* She'd been a full-ride kid at boarding school too, and after graduation, when she moved back home for college—the only girl in her class to do so—that feeling hadn't gone away, the sense that everyone was off to their real lives while she remained, eternally, on the cusp of hers. So yes, she was hungry. She wanted her work to be seen through his empty glasses, witnessed with unmitigated clarity. She wanted him to say out loud what was in front of him so she might finally know it herself.

But all he said was, "You're overthinking it."

Claire continued to dig into her palette with the knife, blending, blending, until the ocean blues tamped down to a steely gray. He was standing so close behind her. She could smell his aftershave, a crisp, wooden smell like cedar, and the human tang of his breath that was not entirely unappealing. "Overthinking what?"

"The whole scene. Helen, the ramparts. Your Trojan horse is a *horse,* for God's sake. Remember, the goal of translation, both linguistic and visual, is to get past the literal to the *sense* of a text. Which is to say: your issue here is rationality. Too much head, not enough pulse."

She turned around and held the wet palette knife between them. It was perilously close to the soft brown weft of his tweed jacket, as overt a defense as she could muster with years of midwestern passive-aggression behind her. What she wanted to say was that his words meant nothing to her and she suspected they meant just as little to him. Instead, she said, "You haven't even asked me what it's about."

"What is it about?"

"Imposters. Fakes." She watched his eyes as she said it, but they didn't blink. "The sack of Troy isn't really about Helen. It's about deception. Troy

189

falls because a fraud gets through the gates, a horse that is not really a horse. That's the artistic problem I'm exploring. How do you represent something that everyone knows is a misrepresentation from the start?"

He was starting to smile. His eyes, which were a blackened toffee gold, a burnt palette she couldn't break down into its components, glinted with a joke she didn't understand, and she felt the rumble in her stomach again, but clearer this time: anger.

"Don't laugh at me," she said, and the thrust of her voice surprised her.

"I'm not laughing," he said, laughing. "I'm just…pleased. You're starting to think like a translator."

"But I'm not a translator. I'm one of the artists."

"We're all translators. Translating is just moving things from A to B. You're still at point A, which is literal. You're paralyzed by the first image of Helen that comes to your mind because it comes to everyone's mind. That's why your painting looks like every other painting we've discussed, even before you've finished Helen. You aren't considering B."

Claire turned to her canvas. A gray swirl of smoke, the burning city, the muscular bulk of a wooden horse. In the middle a white space yawned, vaguely sketched, an emptiness she was saving for some iteration of Helen's body. She hated to admit it, but it did, in fact, already look familiar, even with nothing there.

"Okay," she said. "What's B?"

He took her hand gently and guided the palette knife toward the canvas, pointing. "We already know this story," he said. "The Trojan horse arrives at the gates. A war gambit, a con job we misread as goodwill. The Greeks are the imposters. We invite them inside and Troy falls. Right?"

"Right."

"But *that's* the misreading. The real fraudulence belongs to Helen. This woman no one has been able to read consistently, that no poet can pin down, this beautiful mystery."

Claire could feel his breath on her neck. Hot ghost on glass, fogging the edges of her attention. She was still technically a virgin, and she had never studied a man's hand so closely in the light: the golden landscape of the skin that covered hers, the fine hairs that quivered like filaments as he scraped her palette knife gently, then not so gently, against the canvas.

The friction of metal against gesso jazzed up her spine, and a burning building disappeared beneath a smear of gray. She didn't stop him. She wasn't sure why.

"In Stesichorus," he said, still pressing the knife in her hand to the painting, "Helen never went to Troy at all. The gods split her in half and made two Helens, one real and one an eidolon. A phantom. It was the phantom who went to Troy with Paris, the ghost they all burned for. The Helen we *think* we know, the Helen that has obsessed us for millennia, was never even real. The real Helen was in Egypt the whole time, at home with her husband."

"Doing what?"

"Who cares? No one writes that story. And it's not the point. The point is, as you said, fraudulence. Because Helen of Troy is an empty space, a floating signifier, she can be whatever we want to make her. She can be, for instance, a ghost." He flipped the palette knife over and slid the caked gray paint through the white space of Helen's absent body. "But she might also be a lover, a conspirator." He took Claire's empty hand and pressed it hard against the wet canvas until their prints slid together through the horizon; near and far began to blur, the world shallowing to a flat plane. "And she might also be dangerous. As creative as she is destructive." He wrapped their fingers together around the hilt of the knife. The gray layer of paint between their hands slipped and warmed. "The imposter was always Helen," he said, and he pressed the knife into the canvas and pulled down—they pulled together—until a long slash exposed the pale wooden frame beneath. "This is why we love her and hate her, why we can never resolve her. Because there is no *her* underneath it all."

The room was silent, but Claire could still hear, in its aftermath, the sound of splitting fabric. The laceration gaped like a wound. Later that night, alone in the vague dark of her childhood bedroom, these were the things she thought of as her hands crept down and the memory spiraled to a hot white point, focused and sharp.

The next day Claire's other professor—the one who was actually an artist—was waiting in front of her split canvas, rapt. Brilliant, he said. Visionary. Had she considered next steps, an MFA, perhaps an installation? Across the room, the man who would someday be her husband was watching through his distortionless glasses, silent. When she slept with him a week later, she pretended to know exactly what she was doing, though they both knew the truth.

Ten years later, it's the eidolon that Claire remembers as she watches the exterminator drive away in his white van. The way a body can seem substantial one moment, incorporeal the next. How swiftly and efficiently she could make a ghost of the green-eyed man: the warm heft of his back a clear promise beneath her palm, a solidity there for the taking,. and just as suddenly—vanished. *Excuse me, ma'am, but I think you might have the wrong idea.* Even adultery a language she can't speak.

It takes some digging, but she finds the Frenchman in an old newspaper from last week. A fortunate consequence of neglecting the recycling: here he is, the man she is looking for, waiting in a dusty corner of the garage. The Frenchman's photograph is made of many tiny gray dots that come together to form a wry, clever face. A familiar face, the face of her husband from long ago, back when he was wry and clever instead of gone. When she touches his mouth, the dots smear against her fingers and blend. When she pulls her hand away, tiny parts of his face stay stuck to her skin. Smudged, the resemblance is even more striking.

Pascal Duval, says the newspaper. Concussion, amnesia, linguistic dissociation due to damage in the frontal lobe. Transferred to University Hospital in Houston, where a doctor specializing in speech and language disorders has been quoted: "Imagine waking up into a life that isn't yours, a fluency to which you have no claim. He is recovering well, given the traumatic circumstances."

This is when the crows start to crash into the windows.

At first, just one thump. Claire hears it from the garage and finds herself running, heart hammering, thump resonating—a thump the same tenor as a baby's head against furniture. But no, here is the baby, stacking blocks and knocking them over again and again, and it takes Claire some time before she sees the body of the crow lying just outside the sliding glass door.

She unlatches it and kneels on the patio. The crow is still twitching, neck wrenched to a startling angle, bluish-black wings heaving. The beak, which is dark but unpolished, a less expensive glisten than the feathers, is long and slightly pointed, and Claire can see a tiny black tongue inside. She feels a strange urge to pull on it. To plumb it with her fingers, follow its path deeper, yank open the glossy throat and discover what callousness resides at the root, what ugly, thunderous heart has been forming the noise that follows her each night to sleep. (She could just as easily slice open from the stomach, she knows. The way her father used to do with Kansas pheasants in the garage before handing her the pretty tail feathers. The way the doctors must have done to her while she was fast asleep. She imagines the drag of the scalpel through flesh, remembers the sound of the palette knife splitting canvas and how as a child she used the pheasant feathers as paintbrushes, all of this coming without any sort of connected logic, like a string of babble from the baby.) But the neighbors might be watching. So she presses her hands against the wings, a gentle touch, one that would appear, from a distance, to be motherly. She waits until the crow's breath slows to match her own breath, the way she waits sometimes for the baby to fall asleep in her arms even though all the books say not to.

She sits there until she is sure. She sits and thinks of the baby stacking blocks behind the glass, an endless piling up just to knock them down and start again. She thinks of Pascal Duval, a face of dots coming together in patterns, and the miniscule gray layer of him that exists between the crow and her fingertips. She thinks, as she stands and looks at the baby through the glass, of her husband. Of floating signifiers. Of nine days. Of the exterminator's iridescent green eyes: *Any movement will do.*

Without thinking—instinctively, like any bird drawn to its own reflection—she begins to pack for Houston.

The town of Troy, Ohio, was a joke at first. Something they laughed about during those perfect, glittery years of early marriage—first the elopement from Kansas to Boston, and then the beautiful city unfolding like a fairy tale, its golden dome, its silver buildings and boats made of swans. His postdoc at Harvard. Her first show in Cambridge and that rave review in the *Globe*, the eager call from a South End gallery. Perhaps, in her previous life, she would have noticed them sooner, all the dark doubts winging at the edges. How the reviewer, her husband's Harvard colleague, had flirted with her shamelessly at a department mixer; how the gallery owner, an old family friend of her husband's father, asked to speak with him first. The way their lovely Back Bay apartment, penthouse loft his trust fund could afford, always made her feel like a very important guest. But for a while, all she could see was the golden skyline, the future that rolled before them like one long, open horizon.

New York next, they agreed. In New York, there was Columbia, SoHo, a city they would plunder together, two stars rising in tandem. And after he got tenure, perhaps some time abroad in London, Paris, Vienna.

"Of course, there's always Ohio," he would joke. A colleague had sent him a posting: tenure-track Greek at a women's college in Dayton, with affordable housing in nearby Troy. He dismissed it immediately (the real job offers would come, of course, from the research institutions) but laughed about it with her in bed. "You have to admit, there's a certain romance. Troy, the place we began. Troy, the place we could end, looking down at the ramparts of academia. The charred remains of the dreams of better scholars."

"Stop it. You sound like an asshole."

"And you?" He kissed her neck.

"And me?"

"Painting all day in the Midwest. The lush, fertile, verdant Midwest. Helen all night, burning."

"You mean Northeast. Isn't Ohio Northeast?"

"Unequivocally Midwest." His mouth, going southbound, sounded sure of everything. She smiled into the dark, found his hands beneath the sheets.

It was only when the job offers didn't pour in, when the trust fund proved shallower than expected, when the bills began piling up in slippery stacks, that Troy became something other than a joke. A pit stop, he said now. A chance for him to finish his book, to publish and make his name, remap his scholarly path.

"And me?" she asked.

"And you? Think of it like one long artist's colony. A house amid nature. Woods and birds, peace and quiet—people kill for that. And what a place to raise a family. Don't you think?"

"Don't I think what?"

"About family." His eyes flicked just past her shoulder, and she understood in that moment that he was afraid. That perhaps the skyline was big enough for only one of them.

Of course, the college in Dayton loved her husband. A big tweed fish in a tiny pond. And he loved them back for what they offered—time to write, adoration, tenure. The art market of Ohio was precisely what she expected it to be, which is to say: by the time her husband suggested her studio might also become a nursery, she didn't argue, because what was the point.

They bought a lawn mower. A sectional. A multiyear insurance plan as square and safe as Kansas. In the mirror, her pregnant body Picassoed to pieces, rounding here, darkening there, until she couldn't recognize the whole. Until her husband refused to touch her with anything but exquisite, art-object delicacy; refused to slap her, even when she asked.

("Honestly, Claire," he'd say, more surprised than repelled. But still. "You need to start thinking like a mother.")

What he'd never explained—and she told him this one morning in Troy, staring out the kitchen window—is who the eidolon thought she was. Did she know she was a ghost? Or did she think she was real?

"You're being dramatic again," he said.

Perhaps she was. But it seemed a fine moment for drama, her belly a globe by then, a world that shuddered with invisible will, limbs pressing upward in grotesque peaks. At any moment she could be earthquaked right open. He sighed and wrapped his arms around her stomach, and they looked out together at the blank green lawn. "The point is not how she felt," he said, "but how *you* feel about *her*. Romance or tragedy—it's your story to shape, Claire. That's the beauty of translation. Bend it this way and it's a love story. Bend it that way, the whole city burns."

Southbound. In her lap, a map to Houston and a hospital room number (1001, a leering palindrome, eye-like), which a cheerful receptionist gave her over the phone. *Oh, Pascal! Such a charmer. Don't tell him I said it, but we're all a bit in love.* Behind Claire, the baby jabbers long soliloquies from her car seat. On either side of the road stretches an indecipherable horizon. Here it is scribbly with overpasses. Here it is dog-eared with cornstalks. The cornstalks bend down and become cotton; the cotton darkens to a field pocked with buzzards. How much time has passed, how many miles? The only certainty is the freeway, cracked gray spine holding the country together.

Sometimes, in the rearview mirror, a feathery fleck of calligraphed black—but gone before she can catch it in focus.

They stop occasionally to stretch and nurse. The baby seems to like road trips. She waves from the backseat and shouts, *"Bonjour, maman!"* at random intervals. She points out the window and yells, *"Avion! Dans le ciel, avion!"* Claire lets her eyes float upward to the vast, empty blue and finds it: a ropy, smoky slash from an airplane so small, she can't even see the thing itself, only the ghost of its passing.

"Ghost," Claire says out loud.

"Fantôme," says the baby.

"Phantom," says Claire.

"Eidolon," says the baby.

She feels the memory unclasp. "That's Greek," she says, eyeing the baby in the rearview. "What are you saying? Did your father tell you to say that?" But the baby just smiles, reaching toward the window for the plane, her sticky hands splayed wide as stars.

(In the gauzy dark of a years-from-now bedroom, when Claire tells her daughter the story of Pascal Duval, this will be the vision that cleaves to it: the baby's hands, so far away from that distant silver body. Her unapologetic, open-fisted way of wanting. It's a small moment in a long journey, certainly less dramatic than the broken glass that happens later, the yard full of dead crows, the thrust of the man who will cry her name over and over as if in pain, all these shatterings still to come. And yet the bit of grit this story will someday pearl itself around will be those tiny hands, straining to hold the pretty smoke that is nothing more than aftermath. The proof of an invisible presence sliding its shell across the sky.)

When the car breaks down, they're on the outskirts of Texarkana. First a guttural moan from deep beneath the hood, and then a slow roll, a stop. The engine death-rattles steam into the air, which is black and soulless with rural midnight. And lonely. The highway she's stalled on is sparsely traveled, and Claire knows the smart thing now would be to stay in the car, wait for morning, a country traveler, a police cruiser, help. Never leave the vehicle: that's the rule. Of course she knows that. Certainly the smart thing is not to walk along the side of the road, baby sleeping against her shoulder, toward the glints in the distance that look like farmhouse lights but turn out, once she gets closer, to be nothing but streetlamps. The smart thing is not to stand there, weighing the options on the shoulder of the highway, until headlights bloom behind her— headlights that could be anyone, with any kind of intention. Headlights that ogle, lustrous, seize her body with glare and press its outline against the dark sky, headlights that wake the baby. The smart thing, of course, is not to wave them down.

And yet—who is this woman stepping into the road? Claire watches her walk toward the light. Hopes she might know what the hell she's doing.

It turns out the headlights belong to a trucker—an old man, stern and gray and headed for San Antonio, who leans out of his cab with a leering smile. *"Houston?"* he repeats, hawking the word like tobacco. "Right far 'way this time of night. And you all alone out here. Where's your husband?"

There on the shoulder of the road, the image of Gladys hovers like a country ghost. Her long, thin hands. Her skin like cream in tea, and her husband's apology-that-was-not-an-apology, standing in the door before the screen slapped him away: *I just need to see where this goes, Claire.*

"We're meeting my husband in Houston," Claire says. "He's in the hospital. Doesn't speak the language."

"A foreigner, huh?"

The trucker has a walleye that unnerves her in the moonlight. It makes her feel hazy, as if she's standing just off-center from herself. "He's…from Paris. That's where we met."

"Oh, Toto. I don't think we're in Paris anymore." The trucker chuckles, or maybe coughs, an imprecise sound crackling with phlegm. Then he opens the door and holds out a hand. The baby squeezes Claire's blouse into fists of curdled silk. *"Fais de beaux rêves,"* she whispers.

As the trucker drives the last stretch to Houston, the baby murmurs French lullabies in her sleep, and Claire's dreams plunge her home. Her house is empty. Her husband returns. He walks from room to room,

197

taking note of the abandoned mess—scattered blocks, tipsy towers of food-scabbed dishes, dust thick in the crotch of every chair. He is apoplectic. Where has his family gone? He raises his hands to his face, which is made of burlap. He tries to speak, but the shiny black thread on his lips holds tight, his mouth a gash stitched up to silence. And so when the caw of a ringing telephone spirals through the air, loops its music through the long wire hitching the house to faraway Arkansas—or is it Texas by now?—he tries to answer but can't. His hands are made of hay, his throat is filled with sawdust. *Pick up*, she tries to tell him. *Hello? Are you there?* His back is to her and she can't see his face, just the scarecrow slump of his body on the pole, and when he finally turns around, his face is not his face, his face is Pascal Duval's, and she wakes. The sun on the horizon is a single bloodshot eye. "Houston," says the trucker, and the baby wails, hungry for milk.

Claire has been to Texas only once before, to stay with a boarding school friend as her mother was dying. The girl, Evie, had asked her to visit during spring break of their senior year. By then, Claire barely knew Evie. They'd been close as first-formers but had drifted so far apart that Claire couldn't fathom why, of all their Briarfield dormmates, she was the one Evie called from Texas. But how could she say no?

And so she'd used her last airline credit to fly to a Houston hospital and watch Evie watch her mother die. That must be the reason, Claire figures, that *this* Houston hospital—which is not the same but feels the same—incites such a strong sense of déjà vu. Perhaps all Houston hospitals use the same interior decorators, she thinks. Or the same generic cleansers: that disinfectant pucker, a smell like turpentine, and beneath it, the tang of bodies unbecoming themselves. Doctors and nurses stare as she walks down the white halls, baby on her hip. As if they know—how do they know?—that she is an imposter. And this, too, reminds her of spring break with Evie, a trip she realized almost immediately was a mistake. Evie's mother slept the entire week. Evie perched at the end of her hospital bed, braiding and unbraiding her own long hair, and Claire felt hopelessly out of place, never knowing what to say or where to look—anywhere but the newborn baldness of the mother's head. She mostly said nothing. On the last day, when the complications worsened, Claire took a taxi alone to the airport. "I'm so glad you were here," Evie told her in the hall, but her gaze went right through Claire, arms folded in a stance that made clear a hug was unwelcome. Claire didn't attempt one. She said goodbye and flew back to Briarfield and regretted that not-hug the whole way home.

Claire hasn't thought of Evie in years. And what comes back now is less the specific memory of Evie than what Claire felt like in that hospital room, somehow both invisible and conspicuously fraudulent. Like the exterminator flinching away from her hand—how he looked at her then, a wary squint, as if he could no longer see her clearly. Like the doctors who gawk at the baby in her arms, then shift their eyes through her when she catches them staring. Even the trucker, when he left Claire at the sliding glass doors, seemed suspicious of her capabilities. "You *sure* you don't need help?" he asked, and it was a point of pride to say no, a choice she refuses to regret now, though the halls are endless and the baby's weight (when did she become this strange, heavy person?) makes Claire's biceps tremble. She thinks of the high chair's heft in her kitchen, the muscular shake of putting it down and holding the baby and watching the crows dive toward their shadows on the grass. A natural instinct, she thought then. Something primitive guiding them to their own dark outlines, a shape that must have looked, from up above, like another self.

(*Push, Claire.* Sudden memory of a knife in her back, a knife pushing straight into her spine from the inside. Pain so articulate it felt poetic. *Back labor,* said the maternity doctor. *The baby's head is pressing on your spinal column. As she descends and turns, it will resolve itself.* But what if resolution meant Claire were split in half by the end? Already, she could feel the separation, one part of her in the grunting world of beasts, the other ghosting airily beside the bed. Her husband's hands pressed hard against her face, her salt-raw cheeks. *Push, Claire.* As if by sheer force he could hold her together.)

Claire blinks the thought away and steps onto an elevator. Her sleeplessness throbs, memories jangling incoherently. The walls inside the elevator are silver and sterile, and when the doors slide shut, she feels an odd comfort: everything contained. There is a teenage girl beside her, the type of girl so plain and familiar, she looks like déjà vu too. Auburn hair, as long as Claire's but untied and wild, frizzing broadly in the Texas heat, and irises the color of mud. (Raw umber: the name of the color coming to Claire's mind unbidden, the image of a rolled-up tube of acrylic.) The girl looks exhausted. She stares at the baby with red-rimmed eyes.

"What floor?" she asks Claire.

Claire isn't sure. "The speech clinic?" she guesses.

The girl pushes 10 without comment. As the numbers tick upward, she watches the baby snuggled against Claire's chest with a strange look on her face. Desire or revulsion. A naked, intimate look. The girl doesn't necessarily look like Evie. But she reminds Claire of Evie. Something about the eyes, that horror-struck hunger—how Evie looked when she looked at her bald mother, sleeping. Claire feels the elevator lurch, a sudden tippiness, as if time has unhitched itself from the world and is sliding them together along a rope much too thin for the weight it carries. The girl seems about to cry. She stares at the baby nestled sweet and tight against Claire's chest, and Claire feels the urge to reach out, to comfort her. To mother. She reaches.

"What the fuck?" the girl yells, jumping away from Claire's hand. "What are you doing?"

Claire winces back. "I'm just—I'm sorry, I didn't mean—"

"What are you, a fucking pedophile?" The girl moves farther away from her, eyes skittish. She no longer resembles Evie, a girl (this forgotten part suddenly returns) who was twice put on probation at Briarfield for dishonesty. "Stay the fuck away from me," not-Evie hisses, pressed hard against the silver wall, and the baby leans closer to Claire's ear.

"*Arrêtes,*" she whispers. "*Laisses-la tomber.*"

It's only once the girl leaves the elevator that Claire looks down and realizes her breast is exposed. It's just hanging there, outside the border of her shirt: naked, foreign, a bald white globe with its blood-dark pole, her pink blouse still unbuttoned from the baby's nursing session in the restroom. Claire remembers the redhead's flinching disgust. Imagines how she must have appeared to the girl, all these seams of her body coming undone without her noticing. And yet the feeling that floods her as the elevator continues its rise is not the shame she expects—the humiliation of exposure, the sense that even this, a basic shirt, is too much for her to hold together. Instead, she feels oddly elated. She can sense something about to slip, but it's less herself and more like a costume falling off, a sticky pink husk sloughing at last. She feels a dark laugh rumbling deep in her belly, the kind of laugh the baby has sometimes. Nonsensical delight at the same thing happening over and over—a peekaboo game, a hiccup—a thing that gets funnier each time it returns until the baby is helpless with joy, with wet-eyed, gut-splitting caws of laughter at the same thing happening again, again.

Room 1001 is empty when she arrives. There is only a single bed, slightly rumpled, pale green covers thrown hastily over the pillow. Beside it, on the bedside table, a half glass of water, a pair of glasses, and a paperback book, spine unbroken: *The 7 Habits of Highly Effective People*. (Is she disappointed? She has to admit, if she had her choice, it would be Baudelaire, Rimbaud, at minimum a novel—though who is she to fault Pascal for seeking self-improvement?)

Claire sits on the blanket and runs her fingers lightly over the wrinkles on the pillow. She touches the dent where his head would be. The baby crawls to the end of the bed and pokes at a machine whose buttons make satisfying beeps. She squeals with delight and messes with mechanical programming that is probably important, that Claire should probably protect and doesn't.

They wait there, together on the bed, for a long time. No one comes.

The glasses on the bedside table are tortoiseshell. They remind Claire of her husband's, but square instead of round. After they were married, Claire discovered his glasses were real. The prescription was so weak that he barely needed one, though of course the years worsened his eyes until he did. By the time he left her, eleven days ago now, he always wore them, the glass thicker, the distortion noticeable from any distance. The thought of her husband having sex with Gladys in glasses that he needs makes her feel inexplicably tender. She picks up Pascal's frames and puts them on, and the room goes impressionist—fuzzy slurs when she turns her head, the edges of objects feathering. Even the baby, laughing at the end of the bed, looks bizarre through Pascal's eyes, her pupils bulbous and dark, the scaly cradle cap magnified to the point of monstrosity. Claire takes off the glasses so quickly it dizzies her. She closes her eyes, feels the center of her body return. And when she opens them again, Pascal Duval is standing in the doorway.

He is tall and thin. Features as sharp as something whittled. Glossy black hair combed stiff with gel. He is carrying a newspaper in one hand, a manila file folder in the other, and he watches as she scrambles to get up from the bed, his expression so mild—curious, half-smiling—that she can't help but feel he's been expecting her. That she is somehow late to a meeting of her own design.

"*Bonjour, Pascal,*" she says, and the baby looks up, startled by her French.

"*Bonjour,*" says Pascal. His accent is decidedly American. He stands there in the doorway and stares at Claire for a long, held-breath moment. "And you are?" His English, too, sounds American. Something seems off about this, the same way something seems off about the dark suit he's wearing, and Claire doesn't know what to say. The plan in her head always ended at this moment, which was simply the moment of finding him and opening her mouth and hearing what came out. Being surprised by it, even. The way Pascal must feel all the time, listening to the wrong language emerge from his lips; the way the baby must feel, even if the baby never seems bothered by it.

How did it happen? she might ask him. *What is wrong with you?*

Or perhaps: *What is wrong with the baby?*

What is wrong with me?

But to ask these questions seems suddenly impossible. Even to answer his—*And you are?*—feels impossible. Maybe dangerous. The edges of Claire's vision are flickering with dark, sleepless spots. Impressionist again, even without the glasses, and pulsing to the rhythm of her heartbeat. The way the man is staring at her quickens the flicker, and she suddenly recognizes, with a lurch in her stomach, how little the curve of his mouth looks like the newspaper photo, no longer that wry, clever specificity. More generically threatening. The baby raises her arms, reaching urgently for Claire. She curls up tight when lifted and stares at the man with skeptical eyes.

"You're not Pascal," says Claire.

"No," says the man. "I'm not."

"Do you know Pascal?"

The man laughs. "Do any of us *really* know Pascal?" Then he stops laughing, so abruptly that Claire knows it was never really laughter. "Tell me who you are," he says finally. "And what you are doing here." He stares at her down his aquiline nose, and she has that déjà vu feeling again— the sense she's been here before, that this man has followed her from somewhere else. But the feeling is gone before she can bring it into focus.

"My name is…Helen," Claire says. "I'm his wife." The words startle her, arriving without thought or warning, as if steering themselves. She thinks of her husband in the doorframe: *I just need to see where this goes.* "Please. Can you tell me where he is?"

But the man only blinks. "*Pascal's* wife?"

"He may not have mentioned me. Because of, you know. The amnesia."

"Right," he says slowly. "Right. And this is…?" He gestures to the baby.

"My daughter. And Pascal's, of course."

The baby starts to cry. She lays her head against Claire's neck and whispers, *"J'ai fini, maman. Je suis fini."*

"Shh," says Claire, rubbing the baby's back. "It's okay. We are almost done. We are almost there."

"Nous y sommes," says the baby, weeping.

"You'll notice the resemblance, of course," says Claire.

The man doesn't reply. He just starts walking slowly toward her. Something about his face is changing, little by little—the eye sockets darkening, the angles sharpening. Beneath his jacket, a brief flash of silver at the waistband, and she thinks of the snub-nosed Ruger in her bedside table, thousands of miles away. But of course that would be crazy. For him to have a gun.

"Perhaps we should sit down," the man says, and inside his mouth, his tongue looks black. Though of course that's crazy too—a shadow. A trick of the eye.

"They say babies look more like the father when they're born," says Claire. "An evolutionary trait, so the male knows not to leave. Not to abandon their offspring. Have you heard that?" She knows she is babbling. But she's pressed against the bed, caged by machines on both sides, nowhere left to go. Besides, she can't seem to still her mind on the dark outline it keeps circling, the shadowy reason all of this feels like a memory. The black spots in her periphery are pulsing harder, taking shape: a flock of black spots, a fleet. "The apple and the tree," she says. "That's the phrase."

"I need you to calm down."

"*Le pomme de arbor.* That's how they say it in French."

"We could sit right here. I could hold the baby for you, and we could talk, nice and calm."

"Please," she says, and only when her voice meets her ears does she realize she's crying. "Just tell me where he is."

"You know I can't do that."

"Oh." She squeezes the baby tighter, but she's already squeezing the baby tighter, and the baby begins to yell. "Okay. Okay."

"Helen," says the man. "Give me the baby."

"It's okay, it's okay, it's okay."

And then it's not okay. Then the man is reaching for her arms, yelling for security. The feathers pushing out of his cheeks are glossy and sharp and growing longer by the second, and his eyes are all pupil, hair fluttering now with a hidden wind. He's trying to tell her something, she knows this, he's saying it over and over. But all she understands are the hands on her arms, hands on the baby, and the fury is a primal roar inside her, a roar without language—flash of fur, a savage yowl. Their jostling knocks the bedside table, and the water glass shards itself to pieces on the floor. Its fangs gnash open a memory: "I am doing this for your own safety," the man is telling her. "I am doing this for the safety of the baby." But with her arms pinned down, her body pressed hard against the bed, the safety hurts—and that dark outline looms, the thing she won't let her mind land on, that she can forestall as long as she holds her breath—

And then she's running. Aimless down the long hallways, a maze of fluorescent hospital corridors, baby tight in her arms, skin to skin. She doesn't look back but knows they're still there, the hands reaching for her, waiting to seize. She remembers just how it felt when they closed in on her: safe and then not, gentle and then not, until she could hold her breath no longer, until the darkness swooped, the sweet and silent release.

"The apple doesn't fall far," her husband said, looking down at the blankets in his arms. "She looks just like you, Claire. She's beautiful. She's the most beautiful girl in the world."

Claire was still rising up from the anesthesia. Her body was a cloud, blood a numb fog without borders. She hovered somewhere between the hospital mattress and the stiff white sheets. Later she would feel that same bone-deep knife stabbing her shoulder over and over, and the nurses would tell her this was merely the referred pain of gas, which they had pumped into her body during the c-section. It would astound her that trapped air could feel so much like dying. But right now, in the quiet enclosure of their private room, she felt nothing. She looked at the baby her husband was holding, and it looked like all babies, anonymous and pink. Impossible to know if it had come from inside her or if it was just any old baby, picked up from the nursery as he walked by.

This was the part where she was supposed to feel love. She knew that. She was supposed to hold the baby like the books said, skin to skin right after labor, and everything would click into place, that primitive connection. But what she felt was terrifyingly unintelligible. It was the feeling of reading and reading and suddenly realizing her eyes were just skimming over the words. It was the feeling of an empty canvas that everyone called hers when she knew the truth.

She said, "That's what you used to call me." Her words were hoarse, the first words she had spoken from this cloudy new body. Her previous words had been to ask the doctors for more time to push. Please, she had said as the beeping machines drowned out her words. Please, stop, I can do this by myself. But they had said no, and then they'd strapped her down, and then they'd put her under.

Her husband looked at Claire, lying in the bed, as if he were only now realizing she was there. "What did you say?"

"You used to say that to me."

"I don't remember."

"Helen. The most beautiful girl in the world. You used to call me that."

"Well, you still are. There are two of you now."

Claire closed her eyes and waited for the things she knew were coming. Mythic, magical things, all the things she had read about. The golden milk that would snake invisibly into her breasts. The tingling

205

that would come back to her toes and sparkle slowly upward, like a million invisible fingers fluttering beneath her skin. The love that would gather a little bit at a time in her brain, at first just a collection of dissociated impressions—the scent of the baby's scalp, the iron-tight grip of her tiny hand—and then a sudden wholeness that would flood her with understanding. *A mother tongue,* they called it. Didn't they? Not something learned, not something she might be missing. It was inside her already, this love. Innate, pulsing firmly in the places she couldn't yet feel but would. For all she knew, it might be pressing itself right now against all her numb walls, running down her corridors and tunnels, the tangled networks of her body, thumping against each locked door, finding its own impossible way out.

"And what happened next?" the little girl will say. "Did we get away?" Though of course she already knows. She will tilt her dark, tousled head on the pillow, curl her feet into eager parentheses and grab them with her hands, rocking back and forth. This is a bedtime story she loves. Romantic epic of birds and mystery, of secret corridors and flight, and the Crow Man with his wide wings—her favorite part—chasing them breathlessly down the halls. She knows the ending, but happy endings never fail to please, even when you know they're coming.

Claire will turn out the lamp and tuck up the covers. She will touch her daughter's hair, her chipped pink smile, and continue to find stray pieces of her phantom husband, the husband who will return and leave and return and leave for years to come, never able to decide A or B. Here, though, are his eyes: a burnt brown, shrewd and skeptical, and darker with every passing year. Here are his hands, delicate, golden in the night-light's cast, reaching for her. Here is his faith in the power of a story told with conviction.

"Of course we got away," Claire will tell her, smoothing her hair, her princess nightgown of palaces and horses. "I saved you, all by myself. Don't you remember?"

"But tell me. Tell the Crow Man part again."

"The Crow Man wanted to take you. He reached out with his shiny black wings. He opened his dark, dark mouth. And we ran and we ran, down every long hallway. I said to you, should we go this way? Should we go that way? Will we ever make it out? And you said, *Oui, maman! Oui!*"

"We!" The girl will laugh. "Tell me!"

"And we gathered speed. We were airplanes stuck inside, we were birds in a cage, we were ready for takeoff—"

"Tell me! Tell me who we were!"

"We were smoke, so fast they couldn't see us. We were superheroes, so fast they couldn't catch us. And we flew around and around those hallways, faster and faster—"

"Yes!" the girl will cry. "We! We!"

"Until we turned the corner and there they were, the doors to the outside, to the sky—and then finally—"

"Lift-off!" The girl will leap on the bed. She will come back down and wrap herself close, believing it will always be this way, that it has always been this way. "We, we, we!"

"That's right, my love. You and me. All the way home."

What really happens is they end up in a bar on Underwood Street, ten blocks from the hospital. Claire has lost the dark-suited man somewhere around a corner. She's lost her purse too, a realization that fills her with electric dread, her body a bright charge waiting to trip. The bartender takes one look and hands her a glass of water.

"Whiskey too," she says.

He glances at the baby. "Really?"

"Any kind. Straight."

A man sitting at the end of the bar, a thick-muscled trucker type with a wild mane of chestnut hair, looks up from his beer and stares. Then looks away, flushing, when Claire stares back.

The baby seems unfazed.

She sits on a pleather-covered stool, baby on her lap. The bartender brings the whiskey. Claire waits for the sound of a door opening, for someone to come in after her, but no one does. A wall-mounted television behind the bar scrolls local news; the world, impossibly, is continuing as normal. On the screen, a plain woman with dyed-red hair and flat cheekbones is talking cheerfully about a voter registration controversy. A two-alarm fire on Lincoln Street. A fungus in the lake water that continues to cause concern. Even on low volume, the news anchor's voice is garishly chirpy, but her eyes are as flat and empty as her face. She reminds Claire of the girl on the elevator, the girl who reminded her of Evie, all these girls pearled together into one long string of reminding, reminding.

The men at the bar aren't looking at the news anchor. No one else is paying attention when Pascal's face suddenly appears on the screen. It's the newspaper photo again. From this distance, his face is a smooth, flat gray, though Claire knows if she moved closer to the screen, it would dissolve into dots again, into pixels of dots. She asks the bartender to turn up the volume. By the time she can hear better, the photo on the screen is not Pascal anymore. It's a detective behind a microphone: pointy nose, chiseled features, glossy black hair Claire remembers for its texture as it brushed against her cheek by the hospital bed. Same manila folder in his hands; same crisp dark suit and Ruger at his waist. The Houston police, the anchor's voice explains brightly, are looking for Pascal Duval, who is not Pascal Duval but an American felon wanted for conspiracy and murder. His attempt at a new life—this amnesia business, this fictional blank slate—was nothing more than an old-fashioned scam. He is sought for questioning after leaving the hospital on foot last night, just as his story began to fall apart. He has not been seen since.

Channel Seven News will not be releasing his real name, as investigations are pending.

The words wash through Claire, and she knows she should understand more of them. But her ears catch only the shapes of the sounds, not the meaning. She waits for the flat-eyed news anchor to go on. To describe, with a condemning look into the camera, an unstable woman also wanted for questioning. A dangerous woman, a woman with a baby, a flight risk, a risk to others. A person of interest.

But the anchor's flat eyes look right through her, and her face is nothing but pixels dissolving into a smile that could be anyone's smile, and why don't we head over to weather with Gary—Hello, Gary!—and suddenly the story is finished.

(*No, the story can't be finished*, the little girl will pout. *Please tell me more.*)

208

The weatherman explains that a storm may be coming but also may not be coming.

(*Tell me who we were.*)

The lake fungus will continue to be a point of concern, related to runoff from the rains. Either that or pesticides; have we brought this on ourselves? The waters will continue to be tested.

(*Tell me who you are,* said the crow. *And what you are doing here.*)

As if it were ever so simple.

And yet what is translation without the attempt? Bend it this way, it's a tragedy. Bend it that way, it's a love story. So here it is, my love: the story of who I am. I'll put it down in a language you believe, I'll tell you the story as long as it takes, I'll tell it again and again, I'll tell it until you sleep.

Imagine, once upon a time, a woman. On a stool in a bar in Texas, holding her baby close. Imagine the ache: her biceps and back, the breasts heavy and hard with milk, the two-days-damp bra and the rancid blouse, feral and pink. The greasy forehead, greasy hair. The itch of unbrushed teeth. Imagine how it feels to be inside that body. To have no car, no answers, no way to move forward, no easy road back, just the cash in her pocket—not enough—and the exhaustion of mapping a safe route home.

Dark, winging thoughts. Headed darker, and nothing to stop them.

Until the baby looks up. She sees the panic on the woman's face. She reaches out her splayed, sticky fingers, presses her hands against the woman's closed eyes, her oily cheeks. "Mama," she says. "My mama." Imagine the chubby arms outstretched, wrapping tight around her mother's neck like the rope they've always been, a rope any mother would choose—the woman realizes this suddenly, with a certainty that stills her—again and again.

What would you have her do?

Perhaps she walks to the pay phone in the back of the bar. She lets the baby press the buttons (the simple joy of those beeps!) and holds her breath (a small hope, but at least in this moment there is still hope). She listens to the thump of the ringing line, a heartbeat looping its steady rhythm through hundreds of miles of wires across America, miles and miles to a ringing phone in an empty house. House of doors locked tight as mouths. House of crows on the roof and crows on the lawn. House of shiny windows the crows won't stop flinging themselves into all summer until somehow, finally, one day for no reason, they will.

The pulse of the line cuts to silence.

"Hello?" says a voice. "Is someone there?"

And maybe for a moment I'll let you believe what the woman in the bar wants to believe: that her husband has returned. That he is holding one end of that phone cord and waiting for her, a phantom on the other side of the country, to come home.

"Are you there?"

Maybe I won't tell you this: that when the line cuts out, it's not a man picking up but the phone company ending the call. That the hoarse, smoky voice she hears in the receiver is just her own voice, exhausted and unfamiliar, echoing. *Are you there? Are you there?* Maybe I'll let you listen for it with her, the happy ending I know you want, the kind of happy ending she's waiting for too—the answer to her own question, the sound of the words flying out of her mouth, their bright and shocking arrival.

Certainly, it's not this kind of happy ending:

She walks home. Slowly, along the shoulder of the Texas highway, the baby on her hip and the sky a flat ocean blue. The pavement ripples with waves of watercolor heat, and she steps over roadkill that looks strangely foreign—armadillos, she thinks, but flattened to gray leather husks. They remind her of suitcases emptied of their belongings. Which doesn't sound beautiful. But it strikes her as beautiful, as something she could paint with a cool-toned palette once she gets back to Troy.

When the first man stops, or at least the first to accept her conditions— only while the baby is sleeping, and only as far as Texarkana—it's the chestnut-haired trucker from the bar. He drives an unmarked silver rig that could be filled with anything. His face is pink and bucktoothed, eyes evasive in a way that suggests a lifetime of loneliness. But he is kind. He offers her water, fashions a makeshift car seat out of blankets with the ease of someone who should have been a father, although he says no when she asks about family. He might be lying. She can't decide if the lie would make him more or less attractive. When she holds him close, finally—in the grass of an empty lot in Texarkana, skyline smoldering with dusk and the baby asleep behind the windshield's glare—she is not thinking of her husband. She is not thinking of Pascal and whatever road he's on, somewhere out there on the borderless horizon. She is not thinking of the husk of her car on a nearby highway, of the calls she will make, the auto shop, the repairs and reparations, the missing purse mailed by some sidewalk Samaritan, the blank canvases stacked in a quiet, empty nursery in Troy. She is thinking, as he brings his body inside hers, of how two states can exist in a single city. She can feel the serrated edges of the thing always at her back, that dark, winging doubt, coming to rest inside her stomach and curling inward, a shape as round and smooth as her love for the baby, every part of her gathering tight around the exact contours of this comforting certainty: She is doing what she needs to do for both of them to survive. She is doing what mothers do.

ACKNOWLEDGMENTS

Grateful thanks for generous counsel & kind assistance, editorial & otherwise, to:

Diane Del Signore

Laura Cogan

David Means

John Murray

David Wood

Danielle Matta

Victoria Fox

Stuart Bernstein

Kate McQuade

Hailie Johnson

Tyson Cornell

CONTRIBUTORS

Camila Elizabet Aguirre Aguilar, Iris Starn Fellow, is a Xicana warrior, educator, student, and poet. Born in Sacramento, and raised in San Diego, she has performed and workshopped spoken word poetry and storytelling with underserved youth for over fifteen years. After graduating with a degree in Sociology from UC Berkeley, Camila taught poetry throughout the Bay area for Bay Area Creative, a local nonprofit organization. In her own work, she explores power, politics, family incarceration, addiction, mental illness, intergenerational trauma, sexism, settler colonialism, and racism. Camila is currently a first-year graduate student and fellow in the MFA Creative Writing program at St. Mary's College of California.

Josiaha Baltrip, also known as JOJO, is a Black student who attends Emery High School. JOJO loves music.

Nick Biddle is a graduated senior from Northgate High School, and is headed to study Film and Television Production at Chapman University. He got into writing through his high school English classes, and through his interest in screenwriting. He loves filmmaking, writing, and art, and hopes to tell stories that will one day make a difference.

Born in San Diego and raised in Florida, Iris Starn Fellow **Carly Blackwell** is a second-year Creative Writing MFA student at Saint Mary's College of California where she specializes in fiction. For her first year and a half, she served as a teaching fellow, creating her own freshman English course in the fall of 2022. Some of her work has appeared in the online literary journal *Write Now Lit*—most recently, her short story "I Shouldn't Have Smiled at Him." She is currently working on a young adult novel and short story horror collection.

Amari Boulware is a seventeen-year-old rising senior at Oakland High School. She loves reading and has recently picked up crocheting as a hobby. In the future she plans to go to college and pursue a degree in Biotechnology. She participated in Uttara Chaudhuri's Simpson Workshop at Girls Inc. Alameda County.

Aquetzalli Popocatl Cahuantzi is a student at CAL Prep. She immersed herself in the literature class at her school, which allowed her to love writing. Her favorite forms of writing are poems and short stories.

Emily Chao is a rising senior at Northgate High School, where she is involved with student government, writes for the *Northgate Sentinel*, and took part in a Simpson Workshop. She has a passion for writing poetry and prefers drinking sparkling water over plain water. When she is not writing, she can be found playing beach volleyball with friends, listening to music, or taking a nap.

Mark Danner is a writer, reporter, and educator who for more than three decades has written on war, politics, and conflict. He has covered Central America, Haiti, the Balkans, Iraq and the Middle East, and written extensively on American politics, from Reagan to Trump. Danner holds the Class of 1961 Distinguished Chair in Undergraduate Education at the University of California, Berkeley and is James Clarke Chace Professor of Foreign Affairs and the Humanities at Bard College. Among his books are *The Massacre at El Mozote, Torture and Truth, The Secret Way to War, Stripping Bare the Body: Politics Violence War,* and *Spiral: Trapped in the Forever War.* Danner was a longtime staff writer at *The New Yorker* and is a frequent contributor to *The New York Review of Books.* His work has appeared in *Harper's, The New York Times, Aperture,* and many other newspapers and magazines. He cowrote and helped produce two hour-long documentaries for the *ABC News* program *Peter Jennings Reporting* and has written a series on US foreign policy and genocide, *Corridors of Power,* that will be aired on Showtime and the BBC in the spring of 2021. Danner's work has received, among other honors, a National Magazine Award, three Overseas Press Awards, an Andrew Carnegie Fellowship, the Carey McWilliams Award, a Guggenheim, and an Emmy. In 1999 Danner was named a MacArthur Fellow. He is a member of the Council on Foreign Relations and the Century Association, and a resident curator at the Telluride Film Festival. He speaks and lectures widely on foreign policy and America's role in the world. Professor Danner served on the jury for the 2023 Joyce Carol Oates Prize.

Grace Decker is a student at the University of Vermont. She was a student in the Simpson Workshop at Northgate. Her work has previously been published in Volumes 1, 2, and 3 of *Simpsonistas*; the *Vermont Cynic*; and *The Gist.*

Joseph Di Prisco is Founder and Chair of New Literary Project and Series Editor of *Simpsonistas*. He is the author of fiction, prize-winning poetry, memoir, and nonfiction. His most recent books include *Sightlines from the Cheap Seats* (poems), *The Pope of Brooklyn* (memoir), and *The Good Family Fitzgerald* (a novel). Forthcoming are his *New & Collected Poems* and a vinyl LP recording from *Sightlines from the Cheap Seats*. He grew up in Brooklyn and then in Berkeley, where he received his PhD from the University of California, Berkeley. For a long time he taught English and creative writing—middle school, high school, college, and beyond—and he has served as Trustee or Chair of nonprofit boards devoted to education, the arts, theater, and children's mental health. jdp@newliteraryproject.org

Charlotte Feehan is a Northgate High School student.

Alexia Flores is a student at Aspire Richmond California College Preparatory Academy, where she enjoys learning and spending time with friends. She explored her writing abilities by participating in a writing workshop at school for two years. Her teacher, Ryan Lackey, helped her to deliver messages in her writing with clarity and creativity.

Emily Harnett, 2023 Jack Hazard Fellow, is a dedicated teacher, and currently spends her working hours as a teacher of tenth- and eleventh-grade students at an all-boys school in the Philadelphia area. Over the course of her six years as a teacher, she has also written literary criticism and reported essays for a number of publications, including *The Atlantic, The New Yorker, The Baffler,* and *Lapham's Quarterly.* Her most recent essay for *The Baffler* was noted in *Best American Essays 2022,* edited by

Alexander Chee. Her current focus is (and has always been) curiosity—her writing and reportage have been an endless pursuit of what sparks her fascination.

Andrew (andy) David King, Simpson Fellow, is a poet and artist from Hayward, CA. Currently a PhD student in English and Critical Theory at Berkeley, their work spans poetry and poetics, essay, photography, philosophy, design, and the concerns of disability studies and the health humanities. They hold an MA in Philosophy from Central European University and an MFA from the Iowa Writers' Workshop, and currently serve as a sub-editor for the *International Journal of Disability and Social Justice*, an open-access journal based at the University of Leeds, and run the access-oriented micropress Clepsydra Press, founded at the University of Iowa Center for the Book in 2018. A 2019–2020 Provost's Visiting Writer and Visiting Assistant Professor at the University of Iowa, they were previously an NYU Shanghai Global Academic Fellow and Research Assistant at the Walt Whitman Archive. Since 2022 they have served as the Director of the Disabled Students Advocacy Project at Berkeley's Graduate Assembly. Creative and critical publications can be found in *ZYZZYVA*, *The Routledge Handbook of Ecofeminism and Literature* (2022), *A Field Guide to the Poetry of Theodore Roethke* (2020), *Objects of Study: Teaching Book History and Bibliography Among the Disciplines* (forthcoming), *Best New Poets 2018* and *2020*, and more. Their research is currently supported by the University of California Humanities Research Institute.

Olivia Loscavio is a poet and short fiction writer from San Francisco, California. She was a student in the Simpson Workshop at Northgate and is finishing her last year of undergrad at Occidental College in Los Angeles. Her writing is a collection box of all the things you're not supposed to say out loud, and she likes it that way. When she's not arranging words on the page, you can find her reading, picking flowers, and spending time with her loved ones.

Raised in Los Angeles, **Carla Malden** graduated magna cum laude and Phi Beta Kappa from UCLA and began her career working in motion picture development before becoming a screenwriter. Along with her father, Academy Award-winning actor Karl Malden, she coauthored his critically acclaimed memoir, *When Do I Start?* After losing her first husband to cancer, Malden published *Afterimage: A Brokenhearted Memoir of A Charmed Life*, her own fiercely personal account of his death and her survival. In the last five years, Carla has published three well-received novels: *Search Heartache* (2019), *Shine Until Tomorrow* (2021) and *My Two and Only* (2023).

Ian S. Maloney is Director of the Jack Hazard Fellowships. He is Professor of Literature, Writing, and Publishing at St. Francis College in Brooklyn, NY; writes reviews for *Vol. 1 Brooklyn*; and serves on the Literary Council for the Brooklyn Book Festival and as Community Outreach Director for the Walt Whitman Initiative. He recently completed his first novel, *South Brooklyn Exterminating*, forthcoming from Spuyten Duyvil Press.

Kate McQuade, 2023 Jack Hazard Fellow, is the author of the story collection *Tell Me Who We Were* (William Morrow, 2019) and the novel *Two Harbors* (Harcourt, 2005). Her fiction, poetry, and essays have appeared in numerous publications and have been supported by the Sustainable Arts Foundation, the Mass Cultural Council, *Best American Short Stories* (2020 Distinguished Story), and fellowships and scholarships from MacDowell, the Sewanee Writers' Conference, and Yaddo. She teaches English at Phillips Academy, a boarding school in Andover, MA, where she lives on campus with her husband and three children.

David Means, Joyce Carol Oates Prize Finalist, was born and raised in Michigan. He is the author of six short-story collections, including *Instructions for a Funeral*, *The Spot* (*A New York Times* notable book of the year), *Assorted Fire Events* (winner of the Los Angeles Times Book Prize for Fiction), *The Secret Goldfish*, and of the novel *Hystopia* (long-listed for the Man Booker Prize). His stories have appeared in *The New Yorker*, *Harper's*, *Zoetrope*, *The Best American Short Stories*, *The Best American Mystery Stories*, *The O. Henry Prize Stories*, *The Pushcart Prize Stories*, and other publications. The recipient of a Guggenheim Fellowship in 2013, Means lives in Nyack, New York, and teaches at Vassar College.

Mia Montifar is a Northgate High School student.

Daniel Morgan is a dark-skinned Dreadhead and Black man. Born in Oakland California, Daniel is currently a junior at Emery High School. Daniel's passions include spending time with his woman and working with kids at his newly acquired recreation job.

Manuel Muñoz, 2023 Joyce Carol Oates Prize Recipient, is the author of a novel, *What You See in the Dark*, and the short-story collections *Zigzagger* and *The Faith Healer of Olive Avenue*, which was shortlisted for the Frank O'Connor International Short Story Award. He is the recipient of fellowships from the National Endowment for the Arts and the New York Foundation for the Arts. He has been recognized with a Whiting Writer's Award, three O. Henry Awards, and two selections in *Best American Short Stories*. His most recent collection, *The Consequences*, was published by Graywolf Press and in the UK by The Indigo Press in October 2022. It was a finalist for the Aspen Words Literary Prize and longlisted for the Story Prize. It will be published in Italian by Edizioni Black Coffee and in Turkish by Livera Yayinevi. His frequently anthologized work has appeared in *The New York Times*, *Epoch*, and *Glimmer Train*. His most recent work has appeared in *Virginia Quarterly Review, American Short Fiction*, *Electric Literature, ZYZZYVA*, and *Freeman's*. A native of Dinuba, California, and a first-generation college student, Manuel graduated from Harvard University and received his MFA in creative writing at Cornell University. He currently lives and works in Tucson, Arizona.

2023 Jack Hazard Fellow **Sahar Mustafah**'s first novel *The Beauty of Your Face* (W.W. Norton, 2020) was named a 2020 Notable Book and Editor's Choice by *New York Times Book Review*, a *Los Angeles Times* United We Read selection, and one of *Marie Claire Magazine*'s 2020 Best Fiction by Women. It was longlisted for the Center for Fiction 2020 First Novel Prize, and was a finalist for the Palestine Book Awards. Her recent publications include "Star of Bethlehem," a short story featured in a special-themed issue of *Prairie Schooner* on home and displacement; and her story "Tree of Life" recently won the Robert J. DeMott Short Prose Contest, selected by Kirstin Valdez Quade. She writes and teaches outside of Chicago.

Joyce Carol Oates is Joyce Carol Oates. She is an Honorary member of the Board of Directors of New Literary Project, a recipient of the National

Humanities Medal, the National Book Critics Circle Ivan Sandrof Lifetime Achievement Award, the National Book Award, and the 2019 Jerusalem Prize for Lifetime Achievement, and has been nominated several times for the Pulitzer Prize. She has written some of the most enduring fiction of our time, including the national best sellers *We Were the Mulvaneys; Blonde;* and the *New York Times* best seller *The Falls*, which won the 2005 Prix Femina. In 2020 she was awarded the Cino Del Duca World Prize for Literature. She is the Roger S. Berlind '52 Distinguished Professor of the Humanities emerita at Princeton University and has been a member of the American Academy of Arts and Letters since 1978. Her most recent books include *48 Clues into the Disappearance of My Sister*, a novel, and *Zero-sum*, stories.

Kayla Paul is a Black girl. Born in Oakland, Kayla is currently a junior at Emery High School. Kayla is passionate about rapping, because that's what makes her happy.

Jazmin Roberts, also known as Jay, is a half-Jamaican American artist. Born in Oakland, Jay is currently a junior at Emery High School. Jay's passions include painting, pencil and pen drawing, looking at cigar boxes that have been made into purses, hating on The Doodlebops, and cooking.

Mona Shariff is currently a sophomore at Emery High School in Emeryville, California. She enjoys exploring her creative side in numerous ways like writing, photography, filmmaking, etc. Something that makes Mona happy is dressing her cat, Asta, in different outfits for all sorts of occasions. She was inspired to write her short story *Underground* because of the issue that the world still faces today, climate change. She enjoys using her love for writing to voice this worldwide issue.

Born in Oakland, California, **Zach Smith** is a Black male and senior at Emery High School. He is a young man who has a deep love for God and music. On his off time, he finds joy in baking, music, eating, and being alone.

Sterling Stymans is a white and Samoan man. Born in Fremont, Sterling is currently a Freshman at Emery High School. Sterling's passions include running track, playing games, and being late on assignments.

Vincent Tanforan is a Northgate High School graduate and incoming freshman at Reed College, where he plans to study history. Apart from writing, he enjoys reading, drawing, and listening to music. In his words, the writing workshop provided an inspiration and a place to feel welcome. "Whenever I'm there I want to write, even if actually getting around to it is a struggle. The important part is that I am not afraid to write, or ignoring it anymore."

Aristotle Webber is a sophomore at Emery High School. He is an athlete at Emery High School who also is a first year in creative writing. When he isn't jumping into the sand or running down the track, he is traveling around the Bay area for places to eat. He also enjoys looking for clothing and loves to sit down and listen to music and type away on his computer at lightning speed. He is currently working on his short story for his creative writing class and also getting ready for a championship track meet.

David Wood has taught English at Northgate High School since 1984 and is a member of the New Literary Project Board; he also served on the jury for the Joyce Carol Oates Prize. He was a board member and board president of the celebrated Aurora Theatre Company, and now serves on the Advisory Board for the Kalmanovitz School of Education at Saint Mary's College of California. A Yale graduate and University of Chicago M.A., he estimates he is coming up on his hundredth year of teaching. "So it goes."

Hina Yuen is a senior at Skyline High School who is set to graduate in 2024. When not writing, they like to enjoy their time becoming a jack of all trades by engineering elaborate daydreams and tinkering with their clumsy hands. While learning to be more adept with their digits, Hina pursues their future by riding the wave, being carried along by every opportunity they can jump at. They took Uttara Chaudhuri's workshop at Girls Inc. Alameda County.

NEW LITERARY PROJECT

Drive social change, unleash artistic power, lift up a literate, democratic society. Thank you for supporting NewLit.

To donate to our 501(c)3 nonprofit, please visit our website
https://www.newliteraryproject.org/

Or mail your donation:
New Literary Project
4100 Redwood Road, Suite 20A/424
Oakland, CA 94619
EIN: 84-3898853

Or contact Diane Del Signore, Executive Director
diane@newliteraryproject.org

Thank you. Your generosity makes all the difference.

Write and read your heart out.

9 781644 284117